Surrendering to temptation . . .

She plunged her fingers into his hair, drew his head down to hers and lifted her face. His fingers tightened on her waist as he stared down at her.

"Are you certain about this?" he asked, his gaze on her mouth.

No. "Yes," she replied, craning her neck up even more to reach him.

His lips were warm and firm, and his hand slid to the small of her back, tugging her up so she found herself half on his lap, one hand holding onto his hair, the other sliding up and down his arm.

His very strong, muscular arm, she couldn't help but notice.

She clutched onto that arm, onto his bicep in particular, her eyes closed, her head tilted back against his other arm. He kissed her, yes, but what was most enthralling to her was that she was kissing him back.

By Megan Frampton

Duke's Daughters
LADY BE BAD

Dukes Behaving Badly
MY FAIR DUCHESS
WHY DO DUKES FALL IN LOVE?
ONE-EYED DUKES ARE WILD
NO GROOM AT THE INN (novella)
PUT UP YOUR DUKE
WHEN GOOD EARLS GO BAD (novella)
THE DUKE'S GUIDE TO CORRECT BEHAVIOR

LADY
BE BAD

MEGAN
FRAMPTON

AVONBOOKS

An Imprint of HarperCollinsPublishers

Excerpt from *Lady Be Reckless* copyright © 2018 by Megan Frampton.

LADY BE BAD. Copyright © 2017 by Megan Frampton. All rights reserved. Printed in the United States of America. No part of this book may be used or reproduced in any manner whatsoever without written permission except in the case of brief quotations embodied in critical articles and reviews. For information, address HarperCollins Publishers, 195 Broadway, New York, NY 10007.

First Avon Books mass market printing: August 2017

Print Edition ISBN: 978-0-06-266662-8
Digital Edition ISBN: 978-0-06-266663-5

Avon, Avon & logo, and Avon Books & logo are registered trademarks of HarperCollins Publishers in the United States of America and other countries.

HarperCollins is a registered trademark of HarperCollins Publishers in the United States of America and other countries.

FIRST EDITION

17 18 19 20 21 QGM 10 9 8 7 6 5 4 3 2 1

For Scott and Rhys. I love you.

Acknowledgments

Thanks to Myretta Robens, Louise Fury, Lucia Macro, and Liz Maverick, all of whom made this book better.

Thanks to Myretta Robens, Louise Fury, Lucia Macro, and Liz Maverick, all of whom made this book better.

*Lady Eleanor's Good
List for Being Bad:*

---

*Be alone in a room
when not sleeping.*

Chapter 1

$\mathcal{N}$ot there, my lady," the bookseller said, unhelpfully. Because obviously what Eleanor was looking for wasn't there since she didn't have it in her immaculately gloved hand.

She turned to regard him, raising her nose and her eyebrow simultaneously. It was a talent she'd learned from her father, the Duke of Marymount, who had taught her little else. Not that she needed to know much from a gentleman such as her father. All that was required of the duke's eldest daughter was to behave properly, marry well, and then give birth to more little children whose only talents might also be in the raising of facial attributes. *They take after their mother*, her husband might say, fondly.

At the moment, her imagined husband looked like Lord Carson, eldest son and heir to the Marquis of Wheatley. At least according to her parents.

It wasn't a future Lady Eleanor Howlett was necessarily looking forward to, but then again, it was what was expected of her. What was, since the unfortunate elopement of her younger sister Della (with the dancing instructor hired to teach the Howlett girls), *required* of her so her remaining three sisters could escape the scandalous stigma Della had brought on the family.

She just wished she had more time before having to go ahead with repairing the family's reputation on the basis of two words—*I will*—spoken to a gentleman she hadn't chosen for herself. Just time to do some things that were not entirely expected. She'd even begun making a list—though the things she wished to do were hardly shocking, it was unlikely she would be able to do any of them. A sad statement on her life, if she were being honest with herself.

But none of these thoughts had anything to do with the book she did want. As opposed to the husband she did not.

"Where is it, then?" she asked. Her maid, Cotswold, glanced in her direction, clearly keen to raise a ruckus should the bookseller not oblige her mistress. Cotswold didn't share her interest in ancient mythology, but Cotswold was always determined that her lady get whatever it was she wanted.

Unfortunately her maid did not have a say in what husband she got. Or the things she would never get to do.

The man pointed past her shoulder. "Over in that second room. It's where I keep the rarer books, you see."

"No, I do not see," Eleanor murmured, making her way through the narrow aisles toward where the man had pointed. She did not see because her mother would not allow her to wear her spectacles in public, and this bookshop—even though it was not a place anyone of her acquaintance would patronize—was a public place.

"My lady?" Cotswold said in a clearly questioning tone.

"Just stay there. I will be out in a moment," Eleanor replied in a terse tone. A young lady was never allowed to be alone except when sleeping, and Eleanor seldom got to truly relish those times. Being asleep and all. It was on her list, in fact.

But now, for just a few moments, she was alone. Granted, she was in a dusty bookshop heading toward what was likely an even-dustier room, but she was almost technically alone.

Until she wasn't.

The room she was heading for was even darker than the rest of the shop, and her gaze was transfixed by the shelves crammed with books, the titles just blurry enough for her not to be able to make out.

She reached into her reticule and withdrew her spectacles when she felt something smash into her side, making her fall against one of the bookshelves, which began to teeter alarmingly.

She yelped and thrust her hand out, the one holding the spectacles, and then began to fall, feeling as though her movements were arrested in time, each moment—*I can't right myself, I'm halfway down, I hope the floor isn't too hard, I hope my spectacles don't crack*—seeming as though it lasted an eternity until she came to rest. Not on a hard floor as she'd anticipated, but on a human body, one with an arm that had reached around her waist to do . . . something. Steady her fall? Make her crash harder? She had no idea.

"What—what?" she sputtered, trying to wriggle off the person, torn between wanting to yell for making her fall or be grateful for making sure she hadn't fallen on the hard ground. Though the body she was on was certainly firm enough.

"Get off me, woman," a voice growled. A man's voice. Definitely a man. A rude man, for that matter. No "Are you all right? Here, let me help you rise." Just a curt command spoken in a low male voice.

Why did it have to be a man? Eleanor thought to herself.

She did manage to get onto her hands and knees, her face low to the ground, low enough that, even without her spectacles, which she was still clutching in her hand, she could see the picture engraved on the book that the man had presumably dropped when he'd also felled her.

And then she forgot about everything, about falling, about the man, about the book she had come in the room for in the first place—everything but the picture she was close enough to see, practically brushing her nose against the paper. It was of a man and a woman doing something that Eleanor knew about only vaguely, but was now emblazoned forever in her memory.

"See something of interest?" the man said, his tone much less abrupt than before. Eleanor was vaguely aware of him moving beside her, a long, elegant finger pointing to one of the places where the man and the woman were joined. "I have to admire the man's strength, to hold his lady up like that," he continued, his finger sliding down the page in excruciating slowness.

Eleanor swallowed. She didn't dare look over at him, for fear he would see everything she was feeling reflected on her face. She wasn't certain she could identify everything she was feeling herself, but she knew that young, unmarried ladies did not usually feel this way. Especially not the eldest daughter of the Duke of Marymount, who was only supposed to be making a respectable, non-eyebrow-raising match. She couldn't imagine an eyebrow would remain static if anyone were to see her. Him. *Them.*

"It's Hercules," she said, pointing underneath the picture to where the words were written. There were other words too, in Italian, but she couldn't concentrate enough to read them. "Hercules and Dejanire. He's Hercules—of course he can hold her up." Hold her up while also connecting with her in a very carnal way, Eleanor couldn't help but notice. And wonder what those other words might possibly say, given what was happening above.

"Dejanire," he said slowly, stumbling over the name. "I know who Hercules is, but I don't know who she is." A pause, then a chuckle. "Then again, it looks as though he does, and that's all that is important."

Eleanor cleared her throat. "She is Hercules's wife, only she accidentally kills him even though she was only trying to help."

"This was them in happier times, then," he said in a wry tone of voice.

She dared to glance over at him. Curious to see this man upon whom she'd fallen and was now, inexplicably, exchanging comments over a particularly salacious picture. And then immediately regretted that decision. He was close, so close she could see him clearly, and what she saw was just—well, *overwhelming* would be one word. Another word would be *gorgeous*. Overwhelmingly gorgeous would be how she could best sum him up.

He sprawled on the floor beside her, leaning casually on one elbow, a lock of long, tawny-gold hair falling forward onto the clean, strong lines of his face. He traced the lines of the engraving with his other hand. *I should get up*, Eleanor thought, not moving.

"You know a lot about these two. Though probably not as much about what they're doing, judging by the color of your face," he said matter-of-factly.

She felt herself blush even harder at his words. At the knowing expression on his face. At the knowledge he'd just pronounced she did not have.

But that he, presumably, did. How did he do that? Look so casually at home, so assuredly confident even when sprawled out on the floor of a dusty bookshop?

"How did she kill him?" he continued. He didn't make a move to get up, and neither did she. She knew she should, likely Cotswold was about to burst in and start exclaiming, but she found she couldn't move. Like moments before when she'd fallen, it felt as though this movement was encased in honey, a sweet, languorous feeling imbuing her whole self. Her whole self that could not move.

"It's complicated," she said, giving in to this moment, whatever this moment was. She tilted her head back and looked at him straight on. Yes, definitely overwhelmingly gorgeous. It was too dark to discern what color his eyes were, but she'd have to imagine they were some sort of beguiling color. If colors beguiled.

She could say with certainty that they did. If they belonged to him.

"I believe Hercules was supposed to marry someone who was in love with someone else, and his wife tried to win him back, only he wasn't in love with her, so she decided to make the best of it and gave the new wife something to ensure constancy, only it had poison on it and he died." And that was why she was not trusted with explaining anything. She just made it sound like a muddle.

He shrugged. "Remind me never to get married."

Married. What was she still doing on the floor?

She did scramble up then, grasping his shoulder without realizing she had to help her upright. He made a noise of protest, but then leaned back, long, long legs—how tall was he, anyway?—stretched out on the floor in front of him.

"I must go," she said in a hurried voice, pushing her hair away from her face, tucking her spectacles back in her bag, then rubbing her hands together to rid her palms of the dust. Or perhaps wipe off how it felt to touch the paper, put her finger on that picture, that scene that was so—well, so whatever it was, just that it wasn't proper for her to have seen, nor was he proper for her to have seen, what with her feeling breathless and tight in her clothing and awkward and melting and hot all at the same time.

Because of him. Or the fall, more likely, she assured herself. Even though he had braced the impact with his body so she'd felt not much more than a sharp bounce. It had to be the fall. It couldn't be him and that picture and the way he'd asked if she'd seen anything of interest, as though she were selecting a piece of cake or something.

It couldn't. Even though it absolutely was.

"But we were just getting acquainted," he said, his tone faintly amused.

"Yours is not an acquaintance I wish to pursue," Eleanor replied. She felt uncomfortable with how cold she sounded. At least until he laughed. Then she just felt embarrassed.

"Unfortunate. It seems we share a passion"—
and he paused, letting the impact of the word roll
through her—"for Greek mythology."

That couldn't be why he was looking at that picture. Nor could she accuse him of being interested
for any other reason, because she had already done
what no young lady in her position—whether literally on the floor or as a duke's daughter—would
do, given that she hadn't immediately raised herself up and given him a haughty set-down.

Instead she'd stayed because she was intrigued.

By him, by the picture, by being alone in a dark
room with a man who was overwhelmingly gorgeous.

And she definitely hadn't even thought to put
that on the list.

She was Lady Eleanor Howlett, she wasn't supposed to be intrigued by anything. She was supposed to be proper, correct, respectable, and every
other word that meant she was supposed to do
precisely what she was supposed to and rescue
her family's reputation at the same time.

Not be intrigued by anything. Or anyone.

LORD ALEXANDER RAYBOURN stayed on the floor
for a few moments after the lady had left, his
gaze idling on the spot where she'd been. Feeling the impact of her body on his as they fell,
hearing the curiosity in her voice, even though
he doubted she'd recognize it herself. But she'd
been interested, despite what she'd presumably

been told her entire life. He could recognize she was a lady, not just because of her appearance, which was exceedingly ladylike, but also because she spoke in the cultured tones of only the best females in society. He wished it weren't his society, but it was.

He'd come to frequent Avery and Sons Booksellers because he'd discovered the shop sold items of a less respectable nature than most booksellers. The collection in the back room had books from a variety of traditions, from texts created by frustrated monks in ancient times to more recent books detailing just what types of positions people could get themselves into in pursuit of the height of ecstasy. He and the owner of the shop (not named Avery, oddly enough, but Woodson) had come to an agreement where Mr. Woodson would set aside any books that might hold particular interest to Alex.

Alex glanced down at the picture that had made the lady's breath quicken and her words emerge equally breathlessly. It really was quite impressive how Hercules was holding his lady—his wife, she'd said—up pinioned on his cock, his arms her only support.

His mind immediately went, of course, to what it would look like if he were to try such a thing. With the lady who'd just been here. Unlike Hercules's wife, the lady was wearing a voluminous amount of clothing, so the fabric would drape over the inappropriate parts. If anyone were to chance across them, it might appear that they were just standing together. Awfully close, to be sure, but just standing.

Of course when they started moving—or rather, when *he* started moving, thrusting into her—well, then everybody would be able to tell.

She had landed forcefully on him, but most of her parts were soft. Warm. And very womanly.

It was unfortunate she was a lady; if she had been a woman not of his class, perhaps he could have pursued the conversation into even more intriguing depths. Inquired as to her desire to attempt Hercules's pose.

He shook his head regretfully, knowing he was already late to meet his brother and the rest of his far-too-respectable family. The family that barely tolerated him, but had to because if they didn't, the scandal would be far worse than anything he had done. And he had done some scandalous things.

Some of which were pictured in this book.

He closed the book with a smile. He'd buy it to join the rest of his collection, a hidden part of him and his interests that made him chuckle whenever he thought of it—the Raybourn family unknowingly having a collection of erotic literature at their town house. His tiny rebellion against all that he was and was supposed to be.

He strode out to the main area of the bookshop, noting that the lady had already made her escape. No doubt too horrified by what she'd seen to linger where she might encounter him again.

"Wrap this up, please, and send it to my address." He reached into his pocket and withdrew some coins, more than enough to pay for the book. He tossed them onto the counter, and they were swiftly picked up by Mr. Woodson. "No need to write up a bill of sale, and please ensure the book is properly covered up. I don't want to shock anyone with its contents," he said with a wink, which Mr. Woodson returned.

At least, not shock anyone more than he just had. What the lady had seen was just one of the pictures in the book, but it would doubtless be more than enough to keep her awake at night, either in prurient interest or shock. Or both, Alex didn't doubt.

"This is quite rare, my lord," Mr. Woodson said in a low voice, touching the book's cover. "I have had many gentlemen inquire about a possible translation for it. I don't suppose you?"—and he glanced up at Alex, a questioning look in his eyes.

"I can't speak Italian," Alex said.

Mr. Woodson began wrapping the book. "That is unfortunate. I am not in the position myself, you understand, of locating a suitable translator. It would be altogether too precarious a position for me to be in." He looked up again with a hopeful glance. "I don't suppose you know anybody who speaks Italian?"

Alex shook his head. "Not anybody who could translate this for me with any kind of discretion." His brother Bennett didn't speak the language, and Bennett was the only person with whom Alex felt close enough to ask such a thing.

Although he would have enjoyed the conversation, his brother being the height of discretion while Alex was—was not.

"Well, thank you, my lord," Mr. Woodson said, placing the book underneath the counter. "And I will send word 'round if I come across anything else. As you will, I assume?"

He and Mr. Woodson had a mutual agreement to let one another know about certain books that might have crossed their paths. Alex kept very few of them for his own collection, while Mr. Woodson relied on the sales of the books to keep the rest of his shop afloat.

It was Alex's own peculiar brand of philanthropy, albeit of an obscene nature.

And he'd found he enjoyed having that purpose, odd and clandestine though it might be. Mr. Woodson was inordinately grateful, as well, which made Alexander feel . . . useful.

Alex left the shop and leapt into his brother's curricle, feeling immediately stifled at the constraints. Of his position, of the curricle itself, of why he was here, and being tolerated by the rest of his family. Wishing he could just escape his responsibilities, but knowing he couldn't leave Bennett on his own.

"You look unexceptionable," Cotswold said, adjusting one of the ringlets that hung around Eleanor's face.

I am sure I do, Eleanor thought. And that was the problem. She stared back at herself in the mirror.

She was not overwhelmingly gorgeous. Not even whelmingly gorgeous. She was of average looks, heightened only because she was the eldest of the Duke of Marymount's five daughters.

Four that were spoken of.

"I know that look," her maid said. "It's the look that means that you are grumbling about something in your head. You might as well share it. You know you can't say anything in public, not without possibly causing a scandal."

"If only I could cause a scandal," Eleanor retorted. "Nobody expects me to do anything but what I am supposed to." Even her list was remarkably staid.

Cotswold shrugged as she tugged on one of Eleanor's sleeves. "I think you might want to consider causing a scandal. If only to get people's minds off your sister."

"You mean swap one scandalous daughter for another?" Eleanor chuckled. "Can you imagine Mother's face if I did something like that? And what would I do anyway?" She grinned at Cotswold. "What if I decided to write lurid poetry and somehow people figured out it was me? Or if I stepped out onto the terrace with a handsome gentleman and kissed him?" She should definitely put some of those on her list. She smiled more broadly at the thought.

"Maybe you could run off with someone even more scandalous than a dancing instructor," Cotswold said, her eyes twinkling. "Like your father's second groom, the one with the"—and then she gestured to the sides of her head to indicate the man's very large ears, giving him the distinctive nickname of "Pitcher."

"Do you think Shakespeare's *Julius Caesar* is his favorite play?" Cotswold shook her head to indicate she didn't understand. "'Friends, Romans, countrymen, lend me your ears.'" She emphasized the last part with a waggle of her eyebrows. Her father would not approve of this use of eyebrow movement, certainly.

Cotswold groaned at the joke.

"Do you suppose I could *have a word in someone's ear* about this whole scandal thing?" Eleanor said with a wink.

Cotswold snorted and shook her head. "I can't keep up with you, my lady." She gestured at Eleanor. "You're done for now."

Eleanor rose, her mood growing somber again. "Curse Della," she muttered. Cotswold didn't reply; there was nothing more to say on the subject. If her sister hadn't been so foolish as to run off with someone so unsuitable, she wouldn't have had to be shoring up the family's reputation on her own seemingly average shoulders.

And even before Della had run off, the girls had all known they would have to be settled in marriage, since they were all only girls. When their father died, the title and all the holdings would go to their cousin Reginald, who was pleasant enough, but already had a wife and a brood of children. The only thing the Howlett ladies had in their favor were their substantial dowries.

It had been a distant prospect, back when they were all together. They'd each talked about finding a gentleman to marry, one who was kind, and handsome, and cared for them.

Not that Lord Carson was not a pleasant enough gentleman; he was very courteous, and had a respectable fortune, and was of moderate good looks.

It was only—well, he was *average*, like she. And she wasn't being given a choice, not now when Della had made their reputations so precarious.

They would marry, and likely they would not argue. But neither would they spark together in passion, all outsized emotions, and she'd never feel what it would be like to practically vibrate with feelings, and wants, and pleasure.

For a moment, her mind drifted back to the gentleman from the bookshop. He certainly seemed outsized—literally, he'd been quite tall, as far as she could tell from his lounging position on the floor. And he had been passionate enough to find that book with those pictures and be looking at it in a bookshop. He was a gentleman—she'd been able to tell that from his clothing and manner of speaking. But he was an overwhelming gentleman. The kind that unmarried young ladies were not supposed to pay attention to, but did nonetheless. The kind that would ignite all sorts of feelings in a young woman's breast.

The kind that was not even close to average.

If only she could have a few moments of sparking passion and outsizedness and overwhelmingness—then, perhaps, she could enter this average marriage with more than average expectations.

*Lady Eleanor's Good
List for Being Bad:*

Expect more.

Chapter 2

*M*other?" Alexander waited at the doorway to his mother's room, its gloominess echoing her usual state of mind.

"Come in, dear," her soft voice said, and he walked forward, squinting to avoid the clutter that littered the way to her bedside.

He reached the chair next to her bed and sat down, taking her hand which lay on the covers. "How do you feel today?" he asked, stroking the paper-thin skin.

She grimaced, her fingers fluttering in his grasp. "The same. It is just—if I could only get enough strength to get up, I am certain I would feel better."

"The doctors will have you up in no time, Mother," Alexander replied, almost by rote. It was a conversation they'd had numerous times, and each time, it hurt. Hurt to see his once-vibrant mother felled by whatever it was that made her so listless, made her need to dose herself with laudanum in order to sleep.

When he had been younger, she had spent all of her free time with him and his older brother, Bennett, playing with them, reading to them, and filling the gap left by their often-absent father. And then she had discovered why her husband was absent so often, and Alexander had lost one of the Raybourn houses through his own foolishness, and she had spiraled into this miasma of sadness and lethargy that nothing seemed to be able to get her out of.

She wasn't the only reason Alex stayed living with the family, but he knew that if he left Bennett would be fine. She, however, would not. He rubbed her skin with his fingers, a soothing gesture that seemed to comfort her. She offered him a wan smile. "You are too good to visit your mother, dear." Her eyelids flickered before he could respond, and he stood and pecked her on the forehead.

"You are too good in general, Mother," he replied in a soft voice. Wishing that she would have some sort of miracle cure, where she was fully alive and engaged, and not this sometimes-sentient person in a large bed placed in a dark room.

"Thank you, dear," she said, her slowed breathing indicating she was falling asleep.

Alexander glanced over at one of his mother's nurses, who regarded his mother calmly, her only task to administer more laudanum and quiet her when her nerves got too much for her. He didn't envy the nurses their duties; his mother was likely a difficult patient, either because it was so dull to watch her sleep in this gloomy space, or because she was frantic, but lacked any energy to do anything about it.

"I'll check in on her tomorrow," he promised as he walked out.

"ALEX!" HIS BROTHER, Bennett, spoke his name from down the hallway, emerging from his bedroom looking perfectly immaculate, as always. Bennett had likely been up at dawn, dealing with things nobody else could even think of. Not their father, who spent time with his mistress and their children, nor Alex, who had been forbidden to deal with anything any longer.

"Bennett," Alexander replied, nodding to his brother. "I've just come from seeing Mother."

"I spoke with her this morning," Bennett said in a low voice. "She seemed . . . better." But judging from Bennett's tone, he was just trying to make it sound that way. "I told her about Lady Eleanor Howlett. The lady that Father has arranged for me to marry."

"And you are just telling me about now?" Alex said, his tone clipped. He grabbed Bennett's arm and began walking him downstairs, shoving him into the room where Bennett conducted most of his business.

He pushed Bennett into a chair, then took one opposite, dragging it forward so the brothers were nearly knee to knee. "What is this about?"

Bennett's expression was neutral, belying what Alex hoped his brother was feeling. "We are in financial trouble again, Alex," he said after a long pause. "And the Duke of Marymount has reason to wish to have his eldest daughter married, so he and our father have come to an agreement. I am to propose before the end of the season."

"But how do you feel about her?" Alex spoke as fiercely as he felt, causing his brother to start.

"It is a business proposition," Bennett replied. "One where she gets the security and solidity of our family name and I get her money." Which made it seem like it was just another transaction, Bennett's emotions permanently put away because they weren't needed.

"You mean the family gets the money," Alex said in a growl. "When you marry yourself off for it."

Bennett shrugged. Not for the first time, Alex wished his older brother would show a speck of anger about the situation their father's feckless-ness had placed them in. But that had always been the case; as soon as Alex had arrived, it seemed that all the emotions had devolved onto him, whereas Bennett had shouldered all of the family burdens.

Until that moment twelve years ago, a moment that made Alex wince whenever he thought about it. He'd tried to assist Bennett; he'd taken funds out from the bank to gamble on what seemed to be a sure thing, only to lose all of their ready money, plus a house that wasn't entailed, and Alex to for-ever lose his father's trust.

It had taken his father begging other family members for loans to rescue them. And Alex would never beg his father to forgive him. Not that his father would forgive him even if he did ask.

"But how do you feel about it?" Alex asked, running his hand through his hair in frustration. "Do you like the lady? Do you even know her?"

Bennett gave him a sharp look. "Of course I know her." He paused. "That is, I have seen her. We have conversed a few times. I am too busy now with business to spend any time working on a foregone conclusion."

"That is all she is to you? A foregone conclusion?" How could his brother be so removed from what this all meant? Or perhaps it meant nothing to him. Maybe it was only Alex who cared that his brother was on the verge of changing his life irrevocably. Maybe it wouldn't be an irrevocable change, after all.

"She is a fine enough young woman," Bennett replied, sounding defensive. "I expect her to support me as my hostess, and other than that, she will be busy raising our children and doing whatever it is that wives do." As though he had barely thought about it.

So it did mean nothing to him. It would be like adding another member to the household, and not even one who did something useful, like polish the silver or lay the fires in the morning.

If only Bennett didn't have to sacrifice himself like this. If only Alex could do something to ease his brother's burden.

"Well, let's go to this polite event, then," Alex said. "And I will have the chance to meet your fine-enough young woman myself." And if she wasn't worthy of his brother, he would have to do his damnedest to prevent the entire thing from taking place. No matter what it might mean.

"I suppose you will have to introduce me," Alexander said to his brother, Bennett, glancing across the ballroom to where Bennett had pointed. From this distance, Alex couldn't figure out which one she was, just that she was one of the ladies in white or off-white standing in a cluster of virginity. "If she is to be your wife and all."

Bennett nodded and began to walk across the floor, the crowd parting as though he was Moses and they were the Red Sea. Or he was the heir to their father's title and holdings and they were . . . not. It was Bennett's job, according to their father, to ensure the Family Name continue as it Ought. Capitals inferred, if not stated outright. Alex had never been happier to be the second son. Even if he wasn't happy to be here at this moment. And even if his father was determinedly and continually angry with Alex, who had given up years ago trying to please the man.

"Remind me—how long have you been acquainted with this Lady Eleanor?" Alex inquired as they marched down the path Bennett's presence was creating.

"A month or so. Her father and ours are known to one another in the House of Lords." Once again,

Bennett's tone was neutral. Mild, lacking any indication of what he might be feeling.

Unlike Alex's usual tone; Alex was renowned among the gentlemen of London's society for his blunt speaking and indifference to anyone's response to it.

He was anything but blunt to the ladies of London society, but they always believed he spoke the unvarnished truth, especially when he extolled their glorious hair, or excellent figure, or anything that might gain him entrance to their bedchambers.

Alex squinted as they approached the ladies, one of whom had turned to them and had a hesitant smile on her face, matching her vague expression. Was it?

Oh no. It couldn't be. Could it?

It could be. It was.

The lady from the bookshop, the one who'd fallen on him, the one whom he'd asked very inappropriate questions of, the one with the passion for mythology—that was Lady Eleanor.

Dear God.

Not just that. Damn. Blast. *Fuck.*

He felt his chest tighten as Bennett nodded to the young lady, who regarded his brother with a pleasant expression. Not as though she'd seen something entirely shocking just that afternoon, not as though she'd even recognized him.

How could she not recognize him? He wasn't vain, but he did know he was striking. *Godlike,* some of his more fanciful ladies had told him. He had a better appreciation for the compliment, given what some gods got up to, according to his newly purchased book.

But never mind that, he was substantially taller than his brother, so even if she had just been looking at Bennett's face, she would have seen his as well.

Was she just remarkably unobservant?

Bennett, meanwhile, was bowing, which meant Alex was even more in view.

No recognition whatsoever. Was it possible she was just not intelligent? Could he allow Bennett to marry a stupid woman?

Although perhaps Bennett didn't care, since it seemed he just—didn't care.

"Lady Eleanor, it is a pleasure to see you," Bennett said as he straightened. Alex drew alongside of him. Her expression still hadn't changed.

"May I introduce my brother, Lord Alexander Raybourn?" Bennett gestured toward Alex.

For a moment, their eyes met. Her eyes were blue; he hadn't been able to tell in the darkness of the bookshop. Plus, to be honest, he wasn't focusing on her eyes, but other parts of her.

They were very pretty eyes, nearly as pretty as her other parts, even if her vaguely pleasant expression made her look rather—well, not very intelligent.

And then he did get the reaction he'd been both hoping for and dreading, those blue eyes widening, her eyebrows rising up her face, her mouth opening into an O of surprise.

Then snapping shut again. Even as her cheeks were currently the color of his mother's chaise longue, a particularly bright cherry-red color that always hurt his eyes.

She opened and closed her mouth a few more times, long enough for Alex to wonder whether she was ever going to speak. And if she was going to denounce him when she did. Now was the time he hoped she was stupid, but he strongly suspected he was wrong.

"It is a pleasure to meet you as well, my lord," Eleanor said, trying to catch her breath. She had to calm her whirling brain. She'd seen two figures approaching, one much taller than the other, and she'd eventually figured out that one of two was Lord Carson, while the other was, apparently, a tree Lord Carson had befriended along the way. At least that was what it looked like in her admittedly terrible vision.

Not for the first time she wished her parents would allow her to wear her spectacles. Being without them made everything so unclear. In so many ways.

Once they'd arrived, and she'd been able to focus properly, she'd realized the tree was, in fact, a human. And not just any human; it was the human she'd toppled onto only that afternoon. She couldn't help but recognize him, bad eyesight or not. He was tall—she could confirm that—he stood at least six inches taller than Lord Carson.

His tawny-colored hair looked much like a maple tree's leaves in the fall—sun-streaked. And his eyes were a verdant green.

So perhaps he was a tree in disguise, what with all the leaves and greenery comparisons she was making. Or she was just panicked at seeing him, the male who'd so discomfited and intrigued her all at once.

Who was currently regarding her with a look that managed to combine insolent awareness with a haughty disdain.

As though he was judging her for how she had reacted that afternoon and was disappointed, somehow, in her reaction.

He was the brother of her presumed betrothed. And he was speaking to her. She gave herself a mental shake and focused on keeping her expression as neutral as possible. This, at least, she was an expert in; if you couldn't see anything around you, it was crucial that you keep your expression from showing anything untoward, in the event that there was something you should be horrified or delighted at that you couldn't see.

"Since we have just met, I will cut my brother and ask you to dance before he gets the chance." He glanced over at Bennett, who shrugged as though it didn't matter, which made her angry, even though he was correct. It didn't matter; none of it mattered except that their parents had dictated the rest of their lives.

Their average lives of averageness. Even though

she knew she was overreacting, which was not an average reaction.

She'd laugh if she weren't so mortified.

"Do you have the next dance free, my lady?" He was regarding her, one brow raised—her father would applaud his skills—with a look that practically dared her to decline. Or accept, she wasn't sure which.

Why didn't she know what he wanted? More importantly, why did she care?

"Thank you, that would be delightful," she said, keeping her gaze on his face.

His mouth curled up on one side into an appreciative—she hoped—smirk, and she felt the impact of that smile shudder throughout her entire body. As though she'd passed a test she didn't know she was taking.

"Lady Eleanor." It was Lord Carson speaking. Yes, of course. He was the brother who—at least to her knowledge—didn't spend time in bookshops buying reprehensible material. They'd only had time to spend a few minutes in conversation, but it was enough for her to know he was not the person who engaged in such extreme behavior.

Unlike his brother.

This Lord Alexander was altogether too much, both literally and in personality. There was no possibility that the knowing, smirking tree wasn't completely nefarious. She would have to maintain her distance, no matter how alluring and compelling he appeared.

"Yes, my lord?" She blinked to clear her thoughts of the troublesome brother.

"I would claim the dance after my brother's, if that would be acceptable."

She forced herself to smile, wishing Lord Alexander didn't know how she'd reacted seeing that picture, wishing she hadn't reacted that way seeing the picture herself, wishing her enthusiasm for mythology hadn't led her to that bookshop in the first place.

Wishing, while she was wishing, that Della hadn't run off. That she wasn't the eldest daughter, the one who had to do her duty to the family so the four unscandalous duke's daughters could have lives suitable to their position.

"That would be lovely, my lord," she said, lowering her gaze to the floor. She couldn't quite see the floor, but at least it was clear of any dangerously overwhelming sights.

Until she did something stupid like fall onto it, accidentally looking at some very inappropriate pictures when she did.

Had she been begrudging her average life? Making a list, even, of what she wished she could do?

What if Lord Alexander told his brother what she'd seen? What if he found her distinctly not average in a scandalous way, and decided not to go through with the family's plans?

Oh dear. She hadn't even mentioned seeing shocking pictures as one of the scandalous things she could do when in conversation with Cotswold, and yet she'd gone and done it.

Perhaps she was secretly scandalous, secretly even to herself? Did she even need a list?

"This is my dance, my lady," that dangerous sibling said, holding his arm out for her to grasp. She took it, steeling herself not to react. Not to look up at him, at all of his tree-ness, to gaze into those dark green eyes to discover just what he thought of her.

ALEX COULDN'T KEEP from looking at her, hoping—and yet not hoping—to see a glimpse of the woman who'd so intrigued him that afternoon. This pale, vaguely feminine person whom he wasn't sure he could pick out in a crowd was someone entirely different, and it gave him an odd feeling to know he had seen another version of her. A version that Bennett didn't appear to have seen. Or want to have seen, for that matter.

Her arm was looped in his walking onto the dance floor. The top of her head only came up to his shoulder, although that wasn't unusual. It was difficult to find any woman he could look in the eye.

Except for when they were lying down, that is. Perhaps that was why he so often wanted to achieve that situation?

And then he wanted to laugh at the ludicrousness of that thought. As though sexual relations were only a conduit to looking into another person's eyes.

He glanced down at her as they made their way into the set. Thank goodness there was not much opportunity for conversation. He didn't want to have to ask her anything, find out more about her that meant either that she didn't deserve Bennett or that she was actually intriguing enough so he'd envy his brother.

Neither possibility was good.

"The Countess of Estabrook is renowned for her taste in music," the lady said. In nearly as bland a tone of voice as her appearance warranted.

She was pleasant-looking enough. Her eyes were large and a pretty color, but their expression was . . . vague. Not snapping with life as her voice had been. He smothered a chuckle as he thought about what she might say if he asked if she could explain more of the stories behind some of the other pictures. Bacchus and Ariadne's picture, for example, had quite intrigued him. The lady mimicking Ariadne's position would have to be extraordinarily flexible.

They bowed to one another in the first movement of the dance. He wondered if she was extraordinarily flexible. And then wondered why he wondered.

"It was certainly unexpected to meet you again," he said, then cursed his blunt speaking. He hadn't meant to say anything about it, to reference their first encounter at all. And here he was, practically the first thing he'd said to her was about it.

"It was," she replied in a suitably demure tone of voice, one that irritated him, even though he didn't know why.

"Were you looking for that same book yourself?"

he asked, knowing he was being shocking, but somehow—as usual—not particularly caring.

The dance separated them before she could reply. And when they did return to one another she was that cherry-red color again. Would she blend into the chaise longue if she were to lie down on it?

And why was he even considering her lying down at all?

"I was not," she said in a terse tone. He felt his interest getting piqued all over again at her obvious irritation. Well, as obvious as an unmarried lady at a public social event could be. Which just meant she did not smile as she spoke.

"I purchased the book," he continued. What was he doing? Why couldn't he stop?

"Did you."

Her tone left no opening for further conversation.

And yet—"I did." And wasn't that the most ridiculous response he could make?

"I was hoping to forget this afternoon, my lord," she said, her eyes lit with the same challenging stare she'd had when they first met. As though she dared him to continue. He was delighted—and horrified—to recognize the woman he'd first met.

"Whereas I find it is impossible to forget, my lady," he replied, deliberately lowering his tone.

They finished the dance in silence, her glaring at him—subtly, of course, since it wouldn't do to cause any kind of notice—and him wondering just what the hell he was doing.

Likely what she was asking as well, only without the cursing bits. She was a lady, after all.

"Thank you for the dance, Lord Alexander," she said, dipping into a perfect curtsey.

"Permit me to escort you to my brother," Alex said, not allowing himself to say anything more.

"I can find my own way back, thank you," she replied, raising her chin to look him in the eyes. She still had that vague expression on her face, but now her voice was sharp, as it was in the shop. Damn it. He didn't want to discover she was more than she appeared, but yet he did. He wanted to know more about her, and not just so he could be assured Bennett would have a suitable wife.

This was going to be his own labor of Hercules, and far less pleasant than the one he'd seen the fellow do in that picture this afternoon.

*Lady Eleanor's Good
List for Being Bad:*

Dare to be rude.

Chapter 3

$\mathcal{A}$h, there you are," Lord Carson said as Eleanor made her way back to where he stood. She smiled as she walked toward him, relieved at how her breath stayed the same, her heart didn't race, and she wasn't all flustered by his mere presence. She wasn't likely to have indelicate thoughts regarding him, not with how pleasant and kind and altogether . . . well, average he was.

It was a good match, her mother assured her. Her father didn't bother assuring her of anything; he just assumed she'd do what he said.

And she would.

That was the problem.

Unless she wouldn't? But she couldn't even think something like that. Could she? And what did it mean that she was posing questions to herself for which she had no answer?

"This is our dance, I believe," Lord Carson was saying. He drew nearer, and she was able to make out his features. Pleasant. Handsome, even. She could see the resemblance between the brothers now that she'd met the other one. Both had hair in the brownish-gold family, both had strong features and firm noses. But this brother didn't have the height, nor the commanding presence. His eyes were hazel, not green. It was as though someone had made a draft of Lord Alexander before making the real thing.

She wished she hadn't seen the final version before having to accept the draft.

The music struck up as they walked onto the dance floor, and Lord Carson turned to her with a smile. "A waltz! Perfect." He held his arms out and she stepped into them, positioning her hand just so on his shoulder, holding his hand with her other one. He nodded, and they began to dance, Eleanor allowing the music—it was excellent, the countess did have good taste in musicians—to flow through her, allowing her mind to drift off and forget everything for just a moment; her duty, her sisters, the details of that picture. How it had felt to land so squarely on top of another human.

"I am so pleased you and Alexander got to meet," Lord Carson said, interrupting her non-thoughts about anything. Forcing her back to the present.

"Yes. He is—" What could she possibly say? Remarkably compelling? Incredibly naughty? Overwhelmingly gorgeous?

Apparently fond of looking at inappropriate pictures?

"Nice," she said at last.

Lord Carson uttered what sounded like a snort. The most emotion she'd heard him display thus far. That did not bode well for an interesting future together. "He must have been trying to charm you. I don't think anyone has said Alexander was nice since he was about six years old. Not that he isn't the best of brothers, or anything," he continued hastily. "Just that he has a reputation for"— and then he paused, and Eleanor felt as though she were leaning over a precipice, waiting for him to finish his sentence—"blunt speaking."

"Ah," Eleanor replied. *Blunt speaking.* That would explain his very direct words at the bookshop. And while they were dancing. *I purchased the book.* He would probably laugh at the thought of a list. "Well, we didn't actually converse that much." She felt something spark within her, nearly holding her breath as she felt the words emerge from her mouth. Practically daring him to respond in some intriguing way. "Perhaps later on he will inform me how dumb-witted I am, or that my gown is in an unattractive shade unbecoming to my complexion." And that was the most herself she'd ever allowed herself to be. At least with a respectable gentleman. Certain person's brothers not included.

Between not being able to wear her spectacles and not being able to say anything, it felt as though she were just a mere shadow of herself in public.

Lord Carson smiled in response, squeezing her hand. She wished she thought he was anything more than pleasant. It would make what she had to do much more tolerable.

Although—was it possible there was more to Lord Carson as well? What would they all do if they were allowed or even encouraged to be who they truly were?

There had been a moment, when their families had first introduced them to one another, where Lord Carson seemed more than average. They'd all met for tea, and he had discussed his favorite horse, and she had gotten the feeling that he cherished his rides because they allowed him to escape. Only when she had tried to ask more questions, he'd retreated into average replies, leaving her disappointed.

"I am certain Alex will appreciate you as I do," Lord Carson said at last. Eleanor swallowed. This was the closest he had come to saying aloud what their families had agreed upon. Did he appreciate her? She couldn't tell.

But did it matter? And why wasn't she delighted to be moving one step closer to married respectability? Fulfilling her destiny as the Duke of Marymount's eldest daughter?

Why did she want more?

And why did *more* look suspiciously like a very handsome tree?

"You have to tell us everything."

Eleanor opened one eye to find her sisters Olivia and Pearl perched on her bed. It was Olivia's voice she'd heard; Pearl was usually the quiet accompaniment to her twin's mischief. Their younger sister Ida must have been off burying her nose in yet another book.

She debated whether or not to open the other

eye, but knew her sisters wouldn't stop until they did know everything. Neither of them had made their official debut into society, nor would they until Eleanor was safely betrothed, which made her having to accept Lord Carson more than just something her parents wanted; she had two sisters who were desperate for company other than their parents and Ida.

Not that she could blame them; their mother was The! Most! Excitable! Lady! and her conversation was mostly filled with exclamations of wonder. Their father was more likely to grunt than to say anything, and Ida was prone to looking down her nose at everyone who wasn't actively engaged in scholarly pursuit.

In short, their parents were silly or non-verbal and their sister was a pedant.

She opened her other eye.

She wasn't going to tell them everything, but she could share some of it. She'd just leave out the viewing illicit pictures while resting her body on a male person. "It was lovely. I wore the gown that was delivered yesterday—"

"Allow me to guess which one that was," Olivia interrupted. "The white one or the off-white one?" She wrinkled her nose. "When I am allowed to go to parties, I will never wear white." She accompanied her words with a sniff.

Pearl nodded her head in agreement. "Never," she echoed.

Eleanor chuckled. "Well, yes, it was the off-white gown. 'Pale blush' the dressmaker called it."

Olivia waved her hand in dismissal. "Forget all that. Tell us about who you saw. Was Lord Carson there?"

Both girls sighed dreamily. Lord Carson had visited their father one afternoon—the afternoon Eleanor's fate had been sealed—and Olivia and Pearl had spied on him from the upstairs hallway. They, at least, thought he looked far better than average.

"He was." A pause as both girls looked at her expectantly. "We danced together, a waltz." More sighing. "And I met his brother," she continued, hearing how her voice got more strained. *Please don't ask me what he's like.*

"What's he like?" Olivia said, shifting on the bed so she was directly in front of Eleanor.

"Um . . ."

"You don't like him," Pearl said in a knowing tone. "If you liked him, you'd say that right away. Because you are so polite, you always are, but you don't like to lie." It was the longest Pearl had spoken without being interrupted by Olivia in nearly a month.

"Tell us what he's like," Olivia said in a pleading tone, edging even closer to Eleanor.

He's—what could she say? He resembles a tree, only more handsome? Her sisters would think her insane. For goodness' sake, *she* would think herself insane. He is a direct, some might say, rude person? Only then they'd want to know what he'd said, and she couldn't tell them about Hercules and Dejanire.

She could barely think of them herself without blushing.

"He's nice," she said, repeating what she'd said to Lord Carson. "He asked me to dance," *and let me fall on him, even though he seemed quite grouchy afterward,* "and he is taller than his brother."

"That's all?" Olivia said.

"That is all," Eleanor replied, lying through her teeth.

"Oh," Olivia said, sounding disappointed.

"Oh," Pearl echoed.

"Yes. Oh." Eleanor made a shooing motion. "Now get out of here and let me get up and get clothed. The sooner I am presentable, the sooner I can go get myself engaged, and then the sooner you two can have your moment in not-white clothing." Both girls leapt off the bed at those words, making Eleanor acutely aware of their eagerness to see her married off. As though she didn't know that already.

It seemed everyone but she was hoping for it.

And what did her wishes matter anyway? They didn't.

But if they did, she'd wish she could just run away.

"FLOWERS HAVE ARRIVED for you, my lady," Cotswold said, bustling into Eleanor's bedroom with a cup of a tea and a smirk.

"Mmph." Eleanor glanced up from her book. She was rereading the story of Hercules and Dejanire, just to refresh her memory of the tale, of course.

"From Lord Carson, naturally." Cotswold was

an enthusiastic supporter of Lord Carson's suit. For one thing, she and the duke's valet did not get along, and Cotswold would just as soon leave the duke's household with Eleanor. And for another, Eleanor's younger sisters always had an opinion about what Eleanor was wearing, and Cotswold took any criticism as a personal insult.

"Yes, thank you." Eleanor closed the book, marking her place with a spare ribbon Cotswold had provided. She ran her palm over the cover, as always relishing the feel of the leather and the faint imprint where the title was stamped.

"More myths?" Cotswold said, glancing over at the book. "Those gods and goddesses are a saucy lot."

If only you knew, Eleanor thought to herself. *The things they got up to in private.*

"What would you do if you were a goddess, Cotswold?"

Her maid, who had been pulling Eleanor's covers up the bed, stilled her motion. Her expression drew together, as though she were considering it.

"I suppose I would find the most handsome man in the world and make him my . . . my . . ." She waved her hand to indicate the word she shouldn't be saying.

"Cotswold!" Eleanor exclaimed, delightedly. "That sounds scandalous!"

"Wouldn't it be what you did?"

Eleanor shrugged. "I was thinking more along the lines of being able to have and read all the books I wanted to."

Cotswold returned to her task. "Choosing a book over a handsome man." She shook her head, mock ruefully. "And here you were wanting to do something scandalous."

The honest part was, it would be scandalous.

If it were possible to not be a duke's daughter and be someone else, she would choose to work in a bookshop. Not one that sold the material it seemed Lord Alexander wanted to purchase; one with fairy tales and mythological books and any kind of literature where it was just as likely a dragon would drag you off somewhere as a viscount.

"I just might," Eleanor said in a defiant tone, making her maid snort.

Ida turned her nose up at Eleanor's reading material, but it allowed Eleanor to escape who she was, so she didn't pay attention to her sister's derision. Plus Ida's derision didn't just stop at Eleanor's choice of reading material; it seemed her sister had an opinion, usually a derisive one, on everything.

"What do you wish to wear today?" Cotswold asked, walking to the wardrobe.

Eleanor smiled. "As though you'll pay attention to what I suggest," she replied. She waved her hand. "It's all variations on the same gown, isn't it?" Olivia and Pearl had been dismissive, but nonetheless correct. The only clothing she was allowed to wear as an unmarried lady was made in white or off-white shades.

It probably wasn't the best reason to wish to get

married, but wanting to infuse some color into her wardrobe was a good incentive to say "yes."

"Lord Carson is certain to call this afternoon," Cotswold continued. "Just to make sure you received the flowers. Roses, a mix of white and red. Lady Ida would be able to tell you what that means."

Eleanor snorted. "I highly doubt Lord Carson has imbued his gift with a secret meaning, no matter what might be read into it. He is far too busy with handling things for his family," *and courting me*, "to worry about if the flowers he gives are sending the right message."

Cotswold folded her arms over her chest and sniffed. Her usual way of indicating without actually saying it that she thought Eleanor was being far too practical. Like when she would choose books over handsome men. Not that she had been given the choice, not in real life.

But, Eleanor wished she could retort to her argumentative maid, she had to be practical since she wasn't allowed to be impractical. Not in her real life, no matter how much she and Cotswold might talk about scandalous things Eleanor could do. Because she couldn't. That's why she escaped through stories. Not that the stories offered much encouragement for choice; usually the lady in the stories had to make some sort of horrible choice between a dragon and the loss of an entire village. She'd take the viscount, if that was her option.

"You'll wear this one, then," Cotswold said, taking one of the many white gowns from the wardrobe. Eleanor nodded to indicate her agreement, then glanced out the window as Cotswold bustled around the room, laying everything out in preparation for the day.

Lord Carson had danced with her last night and sent her flowers today. He would be paying a call on her this afternoon, and might even propose.

It was what she had expected. And yet—and yet something inside her was chafing against all the expectations.

Now she wished there'd be a delay in the form of a dragon or something. Anything to potentially alter the course of her life.

"OF COURSE I'LL accompany you," Alex said. Bennett was uncharacteristically fussing, his hands moving from his cravat to his waistcoat to his hair, repeating as he paced in their father's study.

Their father wasn't present, of course; he spent most of his time with his mistress, although the ruse was that he was off attending to business.

"It's not that I don't want to get married," Bennett continued, pausing in his pacing to gaze at Alex accusingly. As though Alex had repeated his question of the day before. "It is just that a wife deserves a husband who can give her proper attention." He shrugged, his expression partially guilty, but also seeming annoyed at the marital interruption. "I cannot provide her with that. Not at this time. Likely not ever."

"Does she understand that?" Alex spoke more

sharply than he meant to. The combination, perhaps, of having met the lady in question and found her more than the sum of her warm, soft parts.

Bennett shook his head. "I don't know. We haven't spoken enough for me to ascertain. I assume so. It is the way things are normally done."

That wouldn't be enough for Alex, when his time came. If it came at all—he was the second son of a financially struggling family whose normal pursuits were confined to women and erotic literature. But would likely not accommodate a wife, since he did not see the point of entering the state unless he absolutely had to. Such as falling in love or some other improbable situation.

Thankfully, he saw no reason to ever have to give up his pursuits, since neither was expensive. His last big expenditure was a specially built carriage, one that could accommodate his height, and he had paid for that out of a bequest left to him by a distant aunt.

"Father said you are to propose today," Alex said, wincing as he realized how baldly he'd put it. *Our father is commanding you to change the rest of your life because of his whims.*

Thankfully, Bennett was too accustomed to Alex's bluntness to take offense. "Yes, today. And so we are off, and I am grateful you will be with me." He placed his hand on Alex's shoulder, gripping it hard. "I know you wish you could do more, but you do well, brother. Thank you."

Alex had long ago made his peace with the fact that there were times Bennett could make him feel

like the lowest kind of worm, just by complimenting him. It didn't make him feel any better when it
happened, but at least he knew to expect it.

"You're welcome," he said, reaching to cover his
brother's hand with his.

Lady Eleanor's Good
List for Being Bad:

Purchase and be able to read all
the books you've ever wanted.

Chapter 4

$\mathcal{V}$iscount Carson and his brother, Lord Alexander, to see you, Your Grace."

Eleanor's mother jerked upright as though someone had yanked on her hair. "Oh! Do send them in, Joffrey." Their butler, knowing his ladyship's pattern, paused at the door, waiting for the lady to continue speaking.

She did not disappoint. "And ask Cook to send up those tiny little biscuits, and make a fresh pot of tea, and do find His Grace and see if he might stop in, and you girls need to leave, the gentlemen won't want to be visiting with children, not when they have my Eleanor to speak with." And at this the duchess beamed approvingly at Eleanor, who had earned more of her mother's love when it was known the Viscount Carson wished to make her his wife.

Olivia pouted. "I don't want to leave. I want to watch Lord Carson"—and here the twins sighed in unison—"ask Eleanor to marry him."

Eleanor glanced toward her sisters. "It is not as though you would be allowed to stay even if you were out in society. These things do not usually have an audience."

Olivia scowled, while Pearl just looked downcast.

"Come on, you two," Ida said, closing her book. Eleanor had forgotten she was even in the room, she had been so quiet. She rose, her expression revealing she was at the edge of her tolerance for her flighty sisters.

Eleanor dearly hoped Ida would soften eventually, but for the moment, she was glad for her sister's stern insistence. It made removing Olivia and Pearl much easier.

The girls had just barely left when the door opened again, allowing Viscount Carson and Lord Alexander to step inside.

There was something to be said for Lord Alexander's height; even vision-impaired, Eleanor could distinguish between the two men, making it easier for her to look in Lord Carson's direction and offer a smile. She was not interested in staring at Lord Alexander.

She was *not*. But the atmosphere of the room changed when he entered; her skin felt tingly, and she felt like opening her mouth and making some sort of comment that might reveal who she was. Not who she was supposed to be.

She wished she could actually do something, not just be something: The duke's eldest daughter. A marriageable woman. A lady who did what she was supposed to.

What if she could make a difference? Perhaps she

could through marriage? In which case maybe she wouldn't have to dread this moment after all.

Even though her skin tingled and she was keenly aware of the tall gentleman at her about-to-be betrothed's side.

"Good afternoon, Your Grace," Lord Carson said, walking across the room to greet Eleanor's mother. "And Lady Eleanor," he said, turning to her. Now she could see him better. He looked not quite as he usually did; he was turning his neck as though his cravat was tied too snugly, and his hair appeared to be more windswept than usual. Perhaps it was a new style in gentlemen's hair.

"Good afternoon, my lord," Eleanor's mother replied. "It is afternoon, isn't it? And a lovely one. I was just saying to my dear daughter"—and then she nodded toward Eleanor, as though Lord Carson couldn't possibly tell on his own which daughter she was referring to, given that there was only one daughter in the room—"that today is a lovely day."

"Quite," Lord Carson replied. "May I introduce my brother, Lord Alexander? He's just arrived in town."

The handsome tree stepped forward to take the duchess's hand. "Delighted to meet you, Your Grace. I had the pleasure of meeting your dear daughter just yesterday," and Eleanor didn't need her spectacles to catch the look of amusement he sent her way, "and may I say she greatly resembles you."

Eleanor felt a frown start to crease her features, but reined herself in before it could reveal itself on her face. Was that a compliment? On the surface, it was, but there was a thread of mockery in Lord Alexander's voice that made her wonder.

Her mother, however, did not appear to notice the thread. "What a delightful person you are, Lord Alexander. I wonder that we have not met before. Eleanor, don't you think Lord Alexander is delightful?"

Wonderfully sly and altogether far too mischievous, she wanted to say. But she was a lady, and what was more, a duke's daughter, and what was more than *that* was that she wasn't allowed to reveal anything of herself, as though that would give everyone a dislike of her. She smiled as she recalled her conversation with Cotswold, where they'd dreamt up scandals. If only she could share her love of puns, at the very least.

"Absolutely delightful," she replied, suddenly aware that everyone in the room was waiting for her reply. And not her latest witticism.

She felt, rather than saw, Lord Alexander's reaction, an odd shiver running through her as it happened. Just yesterday around this time she'd been on top of him, looking at a picture that had seared into her consciousness.

The door opened to admit her father, who entered with his habitual cacophony of noises—grunts, inarticulate mutterings, and very loud breathing.

"My lord, look who has arrived," her mother began, "it is Viscount Carson and his brother, Lord Alexander," she continued, since she couldn't leave her husband in suspense about who was standing directly in front of him. "And I haven't yet asked them to sit. I am so sorry—please do sit, gentlemen. Viscount, go sit next to my dear Eleanor, and Lord Alexander, you can sit wherever you like."

The gentlemen sat, Lord Alexander taking the place next to Eleanor's mother, while Lord Carson settled beside Eleanor.

"Thank you for the flowers, my lord," Eleanor said.

"You are welcome," Lord Carson said. "I know ladies generally like flowers, or so my father's gardener tells me."

"Do you like flowers, Lady Eleanor?"

It was him speaking. Lord Blunt. Asking her opinion on something, of all things.

It was unexpected.

And everyone was waiting for her answer. Or so it seemed.

"I do, thank you." Why did his simple question make her want to shout, or scream, or say something in Italian?

A language that she'd learned that seemed to hold all the emotion she wasn't allowed to have. So she loved it all the more.

"They are . . . *bellisimi fiori*," she said, feeling daring as she spoke.

"Speak so that everyone can understand, Eleanor," her mother said reprovingly.

"Of course, Mother," Eleanor replied, lowering

her eyes so nobody would see the spark of defiance she knew was there.

"Well, Lady Eleanor," Lord Carson began. Eleanor lifted her gaze to his face. He glanced in her father's direction and continued. "I wonder if you would grant me the honor of a private interview?"

Eleanor swallowed. Here it was. The moment she'd known would happen since her father had informed her of his discussion with Lord Carson's father, the Marquis of Wheatley. Two old men deciding the fates of their two oldest children.

"Of course she would," the duchess replied. Apparently Eleanor was not allowed to speak for herself in any language.

"Yes, thank you, my lord." Eleanor rose, and the viscount did as well.

"Go into your father's study," Eleanor's mother commanded. "We will remain here. Joffrey is bringing biscuits and fresh tea." She looked around, nodding and smiling, as she always did at the prospect of fresh tea. Or fresh sons-in-law, provided they were respectable.

Eleanor offered a curtsey, then stepped to the door, feeling the viscount at her back as she headed to her doom.

"PLEASE BE SEATED, Lady Eleanor," Lord Carson said as he closed the door behind them.

She glanced at it, the whole room suddenly feeling as though it were enclosing her. Encasing her like a stifling cloak.

And then wished she could laugh at her own

ridiculousness. But she couldn't laugh. Not only because he was beginning to speak, but because this wasn't just a cloak she could remove at will.

She sat and kept her gaze somewhere near his face, so he'd know she was paying attention. From here, his features were blurred pleasantly together. Perhaps it wouldn't be so bad, being married to him.

"Lady Eleanor," he began, "you are a lovely person with whom it has been my pleasure to become acquainted with these past few weeks."

Well, that was an adequate start, she supposed.

"And it is our parents' fondest wish to see us united in marriage," he continued.

It's not. My parents' fondest wish is to remove the taint of scandal from Della's elopement. Your parents' fondest wish is to gain control of my dowry.

"And so I would ask you if you would do me the honor of becoming my wife?" As he spoke, she saw him glance over her shoulder, looking at the clock that stood in the corner. As though he had another appointment after this one. The one where he decided her fate.

Unless she decided it for herself. The emotion she'd felt on recognizing Lord Alexander in that ballroom rushed over her, the unfamiliar feelings of want and dissatisfaction and wishing she could just be herself, just do something that wasn't related to who she was—she wanted to stand up and demand that Lord Carson, that anyone, see her as Eleanor, the pun-loving, adventurous woman who adored Italian.

Not a female to be bartered from one family to another.

I can say yes, she thought to herself. *I can try to find myself within this marriage. He seems perfectly pleasant. He* is *perfectly pleasant. Yes, it would be average, but it wouldn't be miserable.*

But she didn't know. What if he was secretly wonderful? But then again, what if he was secretly horrible?

What if he didn't matter, what if it was her who had to figure it all out? Figure out who she was before she said yes to becoming who they would be? Her ridiculous list taunted her with all of its unattainability.

"I—" she began, not sure what she was going to say. Images of that book, the feel of her body on his, the way he spoke making her feel trembly and wondrous and confused, all at the same time. "I cannot. I need more time," she said in as firm a voice as she could manage.

"More time?" he echoed, sounding bewildered. "But our parents—"

"Yes, I understand," she replied, sounding more sure of herself. "I haven't said no, you understand"— though even she could see he didn't understand— "just that I need more time. To get to know you"—*to get to know myself*—"and to enjoy the rest of my time in London."

"Oh."

A silence as awkward as anything she'd ever experienced settled over them.

"More time," he said.

"Yes. More time," she repeated. She felt as though she could breathe just a little bit better now, now that she'd actually said what she wanted.

"Well. Thank you, Lady Eleanor," he replied with a bow. She nodded.

At least he wasn't going to argue with her, it seemed. Or should she take that as an affront? No, he was likely as realistic about this situation as she was. Or thought she was, until she opened her mouth to say no.

And now she had more time. To do what with, she didn't know. Just that perhaps she could find something to do, not just something to be.

"She said what?" Alex asked, blinking at his brother. They had left the Duke of Marymount's home fifteen minutes ago, Bennett telling the coachman to go home without them because he wanted to walk.

For once, Alex was speechless. It had been . . . awkward, to say the least, when Bennett and Lady Eleanor had returned from their private conversation.

The duchess had had no such problem, keeping up a string of sentences that probably made sense at one point, but damned if Alex could figure them out. The duke just glowered and made a few noises, while Lady Eleanor was once again that terrible bright red color. Nor would she meet Alex's gaze. Or anyone's, for that matter. She stared at the carpet as though it was the most fascinating thing she'd ever seen.

Bennett shook his head in confusion. "She said she needed time. She said she wasn't refusing my offer, but that she just—needed time.

"You should speak to her," Bennett continued in an urgent tone of voice, making Alex's mouth drop open. "I can't, not now, not when things are so delicate." He nodded, a resolute expression on his face. "It shouldn't be too hard. She is a lady, and you can convince ladies of anything."

"That's—" Not appropriate, he wanted to say, given how he and the young lady had met one another. And what he usually persuaded ladies to do. He didn't think Bennett wished his brother to lure Lady Eleanor to bed. Not that Alex ever dallied with virgins. "Unusual," he said at last.

"It is. I wouldn't ask unless I needed it. Unless the family needed it." Bennett shook his head. "I wouldn't ask if it weren't necessary." He glanced up at Alex. "You know that."

He did. Just as he was certain that Bennett was keeping the family held together through sheer strength of will, and Lady Eleanor's dowry would go a long way to restoring his family's fortune.

Just as he knew their father would refuse to even discuss any of this with his second son, and if Alex could achieve this, it would go a long way toward making him feel as though he could right the wrong he'd done so long ago. To Bennett, at least. His father would never forgive him.

He took a deep breath, then offered a tight-lipped smile to his brother. "It will be a difficult task, persuading the young lady to marry my older brother"—at which point Bennett punched him in the arm—"but I vow to have her promised to you within a month. Less if you lend me your new curricle."

Bennett snorted. "You just want an excuse to drive it. I don't know why you purchased a carriage when a curricle suits you much better." Then Bennett clamped his hand on Alex's arm. "Thank you. Thank you for doing this." He sounded truly grateful, and once again, Alex wished he were a better man so there was more he could do. More than persuade a young lady to marry his responsible, far-too-busy eldest brother.

*Lady Eleanor's Good
List for Being Bad:*

---

*Take tea in a different
way than usual.*

(Yes, that is a sad comment on my very dull life.)

Chapter 5

*Y*ou will not stay home tonight." Eleanor's mother stood in the doorway to Eleanor's bedroom, her arms folded over her impressive chest. "I will not have anyone say you have not managed to gain Lord Carson's attention and are hiding at home."

Even though I just wish to be at home? Eleanor thought. It wasn't that she wanted to hide; she just wanted to be more by herself. To read, or sit, or just think. Not stand, shortsightedly, in the corner of a ballroom as people carried on conversations and laughed and did whatever it was that normal people did.

She didn't feel normal. She didn't know how she felt, not after this afternoon. But it wasn't normal.

But she couldn't tell her mother any of that.

"Get her ready in half an hour," her mother said to Cotswold. Her gaze returned to Eleanor. "And you will accompany us and you will present yourself as you always have so no one knows the ridiculous decision you made. A decision that will be rectified soon, I assure you." She punctuated her words with firm nods of her head and left without waiting for a reply.

As though it were her mother's place to accept Lord Carson. If that were true, Eleanor would already be married, and likely breeding as well.

She could delay the inevitable, but it felt . . . inevitable. That she would be averagely married to Lord Carson, and she would never be able to just *be*, to choose who she wished to be. Even if she chose to be average. It would never be her choice.

"THE DUKE AND Duchess of Marymount. Lady Eleanor Howlett," the majordomo intoned as the three of them stood at the entrance to the ballroom.

Eleanor wasn't even certain whose house they stood in; it looked just like all the other ballrooms she'd been in since making her debut. Chandeliers hung overhead, dozens of wax candles alight, casting a warm, yellow glow in the room. Flowers that belied the season sat in enormous cut-glass vases on tables set at discreet intervals. The floor was polished to a brilliant sheen, while ladies in embellished and embroidered slippers slid across it holding on to their darkly hued dance partners.

Everything in the room swirled together in Eleanor's vision, a miasma of color and movement. Perhaps she should be grateful for her eyesight, since it meant she couldn't distinguish anything about her surroundings beyond a general impression.

"This way, Eleanor," her mother said in a sharp tone, walking to the edge of the room where her acquaintances presumably sat. Eleanor followed dutifully, keeping her eyes on the outline of the feathers waving from her mother's headpiece.

"Good evening, Your Grace," one of the ladies said. "And Lady Eleanor, how delightful." The woman's tone held a sharp, curious note. Unless that was just Eleanor's imagination? "Lord Carson has not appeared yet this evening," she continued. So not Eleanor's imagination after all. "Perhaps he is not quite as intrigued by the evening's entertainment as one might have hoped."

Oh, dear. The increased sharpness of the woman's tone made Eleanor wince, knowing her mother couldn't resist responding.

"Lord Carson is quite intrigued, I assure you," her mother replied, the feathers in her hair shaking vehemently. "He is likely at home this evening making arrangements for things."

"Ah," the woman replied. "And he is not put off by any . . . unfortunate circumstances? It can be so difficult to keep one's children in line, particularly when there are so many of them."

There it was. The nearly overt reference to Della's running off, a circumstance Eleanor's parents had tried to keep quiet, but of course people would notice that there were only four Howlett daughters promenading in the park.

"The Marquis of Wheatley is a brave man, to allow his eldest son to be . . . intrigued by a female coming from such an errant family."

Her mother's sharply indrawn breath alerted Eleanor to the firestorm that was about to come.

"My family, Lady Vale, is not errant, despite what you might have heard. My daughter Lady Della is visiting family in the north, and since she has not yet made her debut, we did not think it would be remarked upon. Apparently we were wrong, since some people"—and she paused, emphasizing the *some* with a suitably dismissive tone—"seem to find it worth their time to speculate as to any number of things."

Which didn't really answer the lady's implied accusations and misrepresented Della's whereabouts, but judging from her mother's *hmph* of satisfaction, it appeared she felt she had presented herself well.

"Of course, Your Grace. I did not realize Lady Della was in the north," Lady Vale replied, her voice indicating her doubt of what "in the north" really meant, "and of course Lord Carson can make up his own mind as to what is intriguing to him."

"Of course," Eleanor's mother echoed.

Eleanor wished she could just slink away and hide behind one of the potted plants she thought she saw in the corner. Unless it was just a very large woman wearing green, but she thought it was most likely a plant.

"When Lady Eleanor is settled we will have the pleasure of seeing Lady Della here next year, then?" Lady Vale continued.

Perhaps Eleanor should just pick Lady Vale up and shove *her* behind a potted plant. It would certainly make things a lot less awkward. But that presumed that only this woman was discussing Della's absence, which Eleanor knew full well was not the case. If Lady Vale felt comfortable enough to mention it in Eleanor's mother's hearing, then she knew that talk had spread all over the finest chandelier-and-flower-decorated ballrooms. She was surprised, honestly, she hadn't heard more of the talk, but perhaps the gossips didn't bother addressing the family themselves, just discussed it between dances and over card tables.

And tonight would just mean that her mother would be even more adamant that Eleanor accept Lord Carson's proposal, if only to salvage the family's reputation. As though one respectable marriage would cancel out wherever Della had gone. Was she even married? The only word they'd had from Eleanor's sister was that she was safe, and that they shouldn't come looking for her. That had been six months ago. Eleanor had kept sending letters, taking comfort in the fact that at least they weren't returned as undeliverable.

Their father had refused to go hunt for her: *"If she wants to run off and ruin herself, that is now entirely her problem. I certainly won't help her, not since she has jeopardized the family name."* But it was up to Eleanor to save the family name with the judicious joining of her average self to Lord Carson's average self, a truth that was hitting harder at this particular moment.

No doubt Eleanor would get an earful on the carriage ride home. She wished she could hear as poorly as she could see.

But she still had the entire evening to get through before the carriage ride.

"Excuse me, Mother, Lady Vale. I will return in just a moment."

The ladies' dressing area was nearly as good a place to hide as behind a plant. She made her way through the crowd, hoping she was headed in the right direction.

"Pardon me?" she said to a passing footman.

He nodded and pointed in the general direction she was headed, thank goodness.

"Thank you." Hopefully she could find the room without needing to draw more attention to herself. *Oh look, there goes Lady Eleanor, running away just as her sister Lady Della did. The family says Lady Della is visiting relatives up north, but their dancing instructor left at the same time, and one wonders. Is Lady Eleanor running away to find the Howlett ladies' language instructor perhaps? She has an inordinate fondness for the Italian language, we've heard. One does wonder.*

She reached the room and slipped inside. There were only a few other ladies there, all of whom were engrossed in making repairs to their gowns or their faces. Eleanor sat down on one of the stools in the corner of the room, leaning forward to look at herself in the mirror. Close enough, even for her, to see her face.

Not that she wanted to spend time looking at her face in the glass, but it was preferable to staring hazily at the crowd of people who might all be speculating on her family. If they cared enough, that is. She knew most people just cared about themselves, spending time on others if it seemed that there was something worth noting. She hoped that Lady Vale and the others who might have been talking about Della would find things in their own lives to talk about.

"Good evening, my lady." Eleanor winced as she heard Lady Vale's voice. Why had she turned up here also? Thank goodness it seemed as though the woman hadn't noticed her; she was addressing the lady at the other end of the room. Eleanor lowered her head and pretended to fix something on her gown so hopefully the woman wouldn't notice her at all.

"Good evening," the other woman responded. "You are looking in health this evening."

Even Eleanor could see how Lady Vale preened at the compliment. "Thank you. My husband is in the country dealing with some business on his estate." As though that were the reason for her being in health.

And this was the state her parents wished to push her into? Marriage with a person where your respite was when they left town?

"You are finding entertainment, then?" the other woman said in a knowing voice.

Lady Vale laughed throatily. "Indeed. Although the entertainment is not as vigorous as some other."

Now Eleanor was intrigued. What was she talking about? Did Lady Vale have her own list?

And how much longer could Eleanor listen without anyone noticing her?

Well, that latter question she could likely answer. Forever, if she were to gauge by her previous ballroom experiences. It seemed she had the ability to fade into the background, unnoticed by anyone until it came to asking her to dance. Or to marry them.

If only a pronounced skill at being invisible was something she could do something with.

"What other entertainment do you mean?" the lady asked.

Lady Vale glanced around the room, but didn't seem to see Eleanor. Of course. "Lord Alexander Carson. Very entertaining indeed."

The tree? And what kind of entertainment did she mean? Although Eleanor could likely guess, given the lady's tone of voice. And his choice of reading material.

"I have heard that," the other woman replied. "Lord Alexander appears to have gotten himself quite a reputation. For entertainment," she said, stressing the final word.

Eleanor bent her head down lower, trying to make herself even more invisible. She shouldn't be here, shouldn't be listening to this ribald conversation about a gentleman she already knew was scandalous, but she couldn't seem to stop herself.

"Yes, he has a certain type of imagination that is quite entertaining," Lady Vale said. "My current entertainment is not quite that innovative. But satisfying nonetheless."

"I am so pleased you have been able to fight the boredom that occurs when one's husband is away."

"Indeed," Lady Vale replied in a satisfied tone. "And I have heard that Lord Alexander has been seen at various social events lately. I am hoping to run into him at some point, accompanying his older brother in his courting of the Duke of Marymount's oldest daughter. As dull as her mother—if it weren't for the scandal of that one daughter running away, I would imagine we would never hear about any of those girls."

Now Eleanor absolutely could not reveal herself. Would it be possible for her to curl over and hide under the table?

"The Duke's Dull Daughters?" the other woman said with a derisive chuckle. "Thank goodness those girls have dowries or no one would pay attention to them."

"They're barely paying attention as it is. I just spoke to the oldest one, and I swear I nearly fell asleep."

Eleanor wished she could show this Lady Vale just how boring she was, perhaps yawning as she punched her, but that would cause the kind of talk Della had already stirred up with her elopement.

Was there something to be said for being dull? At least nobody would accuse her of causing a scandal. Of course, they also would not accuse her of being anything more than the sum of her birth—the duke's eldest daughter, the first in a long line of females whose pedigree was the most important thing about her.

Just once she wished she could do something that would make her, at least, stand up and take notice. Feel something more than what she was supposed to do, or more importantly, what she was not supposed to do.

Find someone as entertaining as Lord Alexander the Tree.

"MOTHER SAYS YOU are just playing coy," Olivia said, walking to the right of Eleanor.

They were in the newly opened Victoria Park, a place their parents had deemed acceptable for their daughters to walk in, provided they had proper accompaniment.

In addition to Eleanor and her three sisters, therefore, they were joined by Cotswold and two footmen who appeared to have been chosen for their breadth.

Eleanor swallowed. This was the hardest part. Justifying her answer to her sisters, who were dependent on her actions for their own. And she didn't have a good reason beyond that moment when he'd asked and she'd felt a frozen sort of fear gripping her. That wasn't a good enough reason, not according to her parents, who'd both been furious with her in their own respective ways.

"Eleanor does not play coy," Ida said in a dismissive tone. "If she said no, it is because she had a good answer."

Eleanor wished Ida weren't quite so helpful. Or so condescending.

"What is the answer, then?" Pearl asked in a quiet voice.

Eleanor took a deep breath. "I don't know how,"

she said. "I wish I did. It is just—" She paused, wishing she could explain how the thought of marrying Lord Carson set her heart to pounding and her pulse racing and her breath coming fast, and none of that in a good way. More as though she had been locked into a too-small box and was pounding to get out, only nobody would let her.

"It's just that I want more time to get to know him." Her answer sounded weak, even to her ears.

"What else do you need to know?" Olivia demanded. "He is handsome, pleasant, wealthy, and the heir to his father's estates."

"That isn't all there is to marriage, you know," Ida said disdainfully. And then Eleanor was suddenly pleased their sister had decided to join them after all. "Marriage between two people is forever. What if it turns out Lord Carson doesn't read?"

Eleanor had to laugh at the horror in Ida's voice as she uttered the last two words.

"Pshaw," Olivia replied, rolling her eyes. "If you don't want to see one another after you're married, it's easy. Just look at Mother and Father."

Eleanor felt her throat close all over again. Their parents were—well, they did speak to one another, but they barely communicated. Their mother went on and on, and their father responded with a barely disguised measure of dislike. Occasionally a few grunted monosyllables. As though the years had worn away the patina of pleasantry. On both sides, actually. Their mother was hardly subtle in how she wished their father would be more engaged with things relating to the family.

It was ironic that he had stirred himself enough to arrange for Lord Carson to meet, and likely marry, Eleanor. The last time he'd reacted to anything in the family had been when Della had run off with Mr. Baxter, and all he'd done then was break a few vases and stomp around the house.

"Ida has a point," Pearl said in a slow, considering way. All of them stopped to listen since Pearl uttered her opinion so rarely. "It doesn't so much matter if Lord Carson does or does not read. What is important is that Eleanor knows these things about him. How can she spend the rest of her life with a man she doesn't know the first thing about?" She shrugged, offering a shy smile to her older sister. "It is not as though we could have made our debuts this year anyway. As long as Eleanor is married, or at least engaged, within a few months it will be the same as if she'd said yes yesterday."

That sinking feeling in Eleanor's stomach sank a bit lower at Pearl's words, correct though they were. She had a few months to find out what Lord Carson was like, to resign herself to marriage, no matter what she found out about him.

Wonderful. At least the noose lying in wait for her had a deadline.

"Good afternoon, ladies." The deep voice drew her out of her thoughts. And then plunged her back into them, since of course it was Lord Alexander. Mr. Tree out in the park. Fitting.

"Good afternoon, my lord," Eleanor replied. She indicated her sisters, all of whom were regarding him with a varying degree of interest. Ida, of course, was least interested, just looking down her nose at him—impressive for a girl who was a foot or more shorter than he. "Lord Alexander, may I introduce my sisters? This is Lady Olivia," she said, suppressing a smile as Olivia blatantly examined him, "Lady Pearl, and Lady Ida. We are taking a walk." Which was an idiotic thing to say—of course he could tell they were taking a walk.

"Yes, I can see that." Judging by his tone, he agreed she was an idiot.

So they had that in common.

"It is a pleasure to meet you, my lord," Olivia said, her eyes wide. "We are acquainted with your brother, Lord Carson." She wrinkled her nose. "You are altogether too tall, I think."

"Olivia!" Eleanor said, just as Lord Alexander laughed.

"You've noticed," he said, as Eleanor felt her face heat.

"I suppose it is practical to be that tall if there are apples to be picked," Ida observed.

Eleanor wished her sisters would just stop talking.

"You have to excuse my sisters," Eleanor said, glaring at Olivia and Ida. Pearl had stepped to the side, as though to remove herself from the fray. Eleanor wished she could do the same.

"It is that we are not out yet, you see," Olivia continued, as though it couldn't get any worse. "Until Eleanor is married, or at least betrothed, we are stuck waiting for our turn." Olivia crossed her arms over her chest and gave Eleanor an accusing look.

"Society is much the worse for not having your presence in it," Lord Alexander said, a gleam in his eye indicating how humorous he was finding all of this. "I wonder if I might speak to your sister for a moment?"

Cotswold cleared her throat behind the group, and Eleanor glanced her way. "Certainly, my lord," she said, narrowing her gaze at her maid. As though Lord Alexander was going to somehow have his way with her when they were out in the middle of the park. "Girls, how about you go feed the ducks?"

"That sounds wonderful," Pearl said, which made her sisters all turn and stare at her. She turned as pink as Eleanor knew her own face was. "Let's go," she added hurriedly, darting one last look toward Lord Alexander.

"I'll be just over here, my lady," Cotswold said. Eleanor didn't have to look at her maid to know the woman was highly suspicious of Lord Alexander.

If only Cotswold knew the circumstances of their first meeting she wouldn't allow Eleanor within fifteen feet of him.

"What do you wish to say, my lord?" Eleanor asked, lowering her voice to just above a whisper.

"My brother shared your answer to him with me." He'd moved closer, and Eleanor felt herself keenly aware of him. His whole self, his proximity to her. As though he were touching her, even though he was still a respectable distance away. And now, so close, Eleanor could see him clearly. Clearly enough to see that same unruly lock that fell over his forehead, and while he was impeccably dressed, something about the way he stood indicated a certain casualness. One she didn't think was as a result of anything, but just the way he was. The way he moved. "And I want my brother to be happy."

Did that mean—? "Do you think he will be unhappy with me?" Eleanor couldn't stop herself from uttering the words, even though she was horrified as she did so. Ladies did not ask direct questions like that. They didn't even hint that they wished to ask a direct question.

He made a sound halfway between a laugh and a snort. "I think if you are inclined to marry him he will be very happy with you." He raised one eyebrow questioningly. "But I understand you are not certain you will be happy, and since you are a lady, and one, so I understand, who is under considerable pressure to marry, I thought perhaps we should discuss your feelings on the subject before you commit to something that might be a terrible mistake. For both of you," he said in a sober tone of voice.

Well, she hadn't thought about Lord Carson making a mistake. He had, after all, proposed; but she knew it wasn't on his own impetus. He had been persuaded into it by his father, but she assumed he was just as sanguine about the plans as she'd thought she was. Even though it turned out she was not.

"Did he tell you it might be a mistake?" she asked. She heard her voice, high and strained. Why did it feel terrible to think someone she wasn't sure she wanted might not be sure about wanting her?

That was a paradox she would have to pose to Ida. Perhaps her clever sister could examine it further and help her deduce what made her so contrary. Because right now she wished she could march back to Lord Carson and say, "Yes," even though she was aware that nothing had changed since she'd asked for more time to decide.

"He would not have been so ungentlemanly," Lord Alexander said in a low, fierce tone. "I am the rude brother. Bennett is nothing but honorable." He shook his head in frustration, glancing over at where the girls were tossing bread into the lake. "The thing is, I owe it to my brother to make certain he is as happy as possible." He raked a hand through his hair. That one errant lock got pushed up, but settled back into its usual place. Which was not where it was supposed to be, but where it looked the best.

"I apologize," Eleanor said in a quiet voice. "I did not mean to be impolite. Or improper." She raised her eyes to his face. "It seems as though I have been nothing but both of those things since we were introduced."

His expression froze, and Eleanor felt as though she were moving in slow motion again, that spun-sugar feeling catching her limbs and making it impossible to move. As though there were only the two of them in this world.

"I came here to offer you a bargain," he said after a long moment of silence.

"A bargain?" Eleanor repeated, sounding stupid even to herself.

His expression changed then, a flash of dismay or disappointment or something else entirely crossing his face so quickly she was nearly sure she'd imagined it.

"Yes," he said. "A bargain."

"What sort of bargain?" she asked. At least she wasn't just parroting his words back at him anymore.

"The kind where I discover what would make you accept my brother's suit."

She frowned as she processed his words. And he wondered, again, if she was stupid or just—different.

"Why wouldn't Lord Carson want to discover that himself?" she asked, not unreasonably. Not stupidly either.

This was the tricky bit. The part he knew he couldn't quite articulate, not without making Bennett sound cold and businesslike when his temperament was exactly the opposite. He wished he could just tell her the truth: *My brother has an outsized sense of responsibility, and so he agreed to marry you without knowing if it would make him happy. Because of that responsibility, he cannot spare time now*

*to discover that for himself. Not only that, he is antici-
pating a marriage without happiness, and the least I
can do is to ensure his bride is a reasonable person who
is capable of recognizing others.*

But he couldn't say that. Not without offense.

"Er, it is just that my brother is so preoccupied
with the family's business." He spread his hands
out, curling his lips up into what he had been assured by many ladies was a charming smile. "I
am the second son. My only duties lie with myself
and my interests," and at that a slow blush began
to heat her cheeks. He paused, wondering what
was causing her to turn pink like that, and then
he realized it was that she thought his "interests"
was a delicate way to indicate his particular taste
in literature.

Not that she was wrong.

But she was replying now, and he couldn't
spend time thinking about any of that. Or how
pretty she looked when she was blushing.

"So you are proposing we, what—spend time
with one another?" She lifted her chin and tilted
her head. "Are you certain that is wise? Given how
we first met? I don't think"—and here she lowered
her voice into the barest whisper—"that you are at
all respectable."

Or that perhaps she wasn't stupid after all.

"I'm not," Alex said. "But what I am is my
brother's—er, *brother*."

Now he sounded stupid.

"Yes, I had noticed that," she said in a wry tone.

"Bennett is important to me." He let the words

hang there so she might understand how true they were. "I don't want my brother to be unhappy, and you don't want to be unhappy either, which is entirely reasonable, so we should take steps— whatever steps those are—to see if happiness is possible." He wished he could take her hand, to impress upon her how important this was. But if he did that, her dragon of a maid would be on him, and the chance would be lost. "Bennett is exceedingly busy"—he'd said that already, damn it—"and I know both of you are under pressure to at least get engaged. If our families think you are moving toward that goal there will be less . . ." and he paused, searching for the word.

"Fussiness?" she said, the hint of a smile on her mouth.

"Precisely."

He saw her look over at her sisters, her face tight- ening into what he thought might be a worried ex- pression. Although her eyes were narrowed, once again, she looked . . . lost. And then she returned her gaze to him, and he saw that she was going to agree to this bargain, whatever the bargain was.

"In return, you will have to do something for me."

That raised all sorts of intriguing thoughts. Al- though they were also dangerous; the last thing he could do was to become somehow entangled with this proper, possibly not very intelligent woman who was supposed to marry his brother. There were so many ways that would be wrong.

More correctly, there was no way that would be right.

He folded his arms over his chest. "What is that?"

"I want to feel overwhelmed." That was not what he had expected. *Dance with me at the next ball. Rescue my sister's kite from a tree.* Something like that. Not something so amorphous, yet so descriptive.

What was she asking for, precisely?

She accompanied her words with a lift of her chin, as though aware she was being—not proper. And all of his senses, damn them, fired to life.

She was not stupid. He didn't know what she was, and that was perhaps the most dangerous thing of all—he felt a keen interest in unlocking that mystery, and he knew full well what that would entail. For him, at least.

"Overwhelmed," he echoed, aware that he was doing just what he'd been dismissive about in her. Now perhaps she would think he was unintelligent.

"Yes." A flash of frustration crossed her face. "I don't have the freedom you likely take for granted. Less so now that—" and then she stopped speaking, her expression closing. "Never mind that." A pause as she thought, and then she shook her head. "The thing is, I didn't reject your brother outright. I just want—I just told him I needed some time."

"To be overwhelmed," Alex replied.

"Yes." She drew a deep breath. "Once I am satisfied in that, I am certain your brother and I can come to an amicable agreement." She looked at him directly, having to tilt her chin back in order to stare into his eyes. "Are you able to overwhelm me, Lord Alexander?"

Well, that was a question he could answer. Whether or not he should was an entirely different matter—one which he also thought he knew the answer to.

And what that would all look like—well, that was very dangerous territory.

"It would be my pleasure, my lady," he said, bowing.

Knowing he was walking on a very thin edge of danger, but impossible to deny his brother's plea. Or the walking contradiction that was Lady Eleanor Howlett.

Lady Eleanor's Good
List for Being Bad:

Be honest. Be forthright.
Be <u>noticed</u>.

Chapter 6

$\mathcal{G}$ood afternoon, Mr. Woodson." Alexander nodded to the bookshop owner, his gaze taking in the few patrons browsing the shelves.

"Good afternoon, my lord," Mr. Woodson replied, a warm smile creasing his face. "I was hoping you would stop by. I want to ask for your advice."

He stooped behind the counter and withdrew a small dark decanter that held the worst-tasting cordial Alex had ever had. But Mr. Woodson's wife made it, and the man himself was so proud of Mrs. Woodson's creations that Alex didn't have the heart to share what he really felt, his bluntness giving way to his wish to not hurt his friend's feelings—since Mr. Woodson had become a friend, at least as much as a marquis's son and a shopkeeper could be friends, in the months since Alex had made his first purchase.

Mr. Woodson was just the latest in the coterie of unlikely friends Alex had made over the years—from the family's steward and his children, to the lamplighters who recognized him after a long night out, to the various shop owners where he did business. He couldn't just stay still and let others do things for him—he needed to be there himself, and wherever he went, he found friends.

The only person, it seemed, who was immune to his charm was his father. But that was a fair exchange, since Alex held no respect for that gentleman.

"What do you need help on?" Alex asked, holding his breath as he took a deep swallow of the cordial. It didn't necessarily remove the taste, but it ameliorated it somewhat.

"I am thinking of taking some advertising for some of the books I sell here," Mr. Woodson said in a pointed tone. Oh, *those* books. The ones that Alex bought and that certain young ladies turned bright red over seeing. "And I wanted to know which papers would attract the most likely customers."

"People who can afford to purchase your discreetly offered books?" Alex replied with a smile.

"Yes, precisely." Mr. Woodson finished his cordial, and then immediately filled up his glass again, tilting the bottle to Alex to ask if he wanted more.

"No, thank you," Alex replied. "Yes, I can certainly make a list, and I can help you with the wording of the advertisement as well."

Mr. Woodson beamed. "Well, isn't that a generous offer, my lord. I can offer you a percent—" He stopped speaking when Alex held his hand up and shook his head.

"No, I would not take any of your hard-earned money," he said. "I just want to help."

And he did. Help his friend, help his brother, help his mother. But he wasn't always allowed to, so he did what he could; drank the cordial, assisted with reaching the correct people, helped his brother woo his bride-to-be. The things he could do.

"GOOD AFTERNOON, MY lady," Lord Alexander said as Eleanor descended the stairs to where he stood in front of a carriage led by two brown horses. There was probably a name for their color, a horse-specific name, but she didn't know enough about horses to be aware of it.

Which just reminded her how ignorant she was of so many things.

"Good afternoon," Eleanor replied, squinting up at the seat of the vehicle. She heard Cotswold make a harrumphing noise behind her.

It was very high. And the horses seemed very spirited. Perhaps she shouldn't have wanted to be overwhelmed? Or at least not so vertically?

And there was certainly no room for Cotswold. She would be alone with Lord Bennett's brother. The final version. The handsome tree.

Her mother had agreed to the unorthodox adventure since, in her words, "It is not as though we don't know you are to be engaged to Lord Alexander's brother, even if you were foolish enough not to confirm it at this time." And then she added many more words, all of which meant the same thing. Her father just grunted in an approving way.

So apparently it was perfectly respectable to

drive out with a gentleman so long as the gentleman's brother planned to marry you. Something she'd missed during etiquette training.

She didn't think the situation was specifically covered in manuals that purported to detail a Young Lady's Proper Decorum and Such, but apparently her mother's blithe approval superseded such rigidity.

"Bennett lent me his curricle for our drive since I didn't think we would want to be cooped up in my carriage. He said to pass along his regrets that he couldn't join us." Lord Alexander accompanied his words with a wink, a sly acknowledgment that Lord Carson had never had the intention to join them, since he was far too busy with whatever he was busy with.

What was he busy with, anyway? And if they were to be married, would that busyness continue? Would she ever see him?

Why did she have so many questions? She'd gone twenty-one years without having more than the usual amount of questions, and yet here she was, apparently now a walking question mark.

"Allow me, my lady," Lord Alexander was saying, holding out his arm.

"Are you certain?" she said, peering at the curricle. It looked very fast. And tall.

Rather like Lord Alexander, to be honest.

"You did say you wished to be overwhelmed," he said in a low tone, low enough that she knew Cotswold couldn't hear, no matter that she was probably straining her ears at that very moment. As he spoke, he took her hand and looped her arm through his. "It is difficult to be overwhelmed with an audience," he added, tilting his head in her maid's direction.

Why did that sound so . . . scandalous?

Because it was him, and she knew things about him. Things that no young lady should know about a gentleman. So why did she ask him the overwhelmed question?

But she knew that already. Because she knew he did know about . . . overwhelming things, and she just couldn't seem to stop the words from leaving her mouth. And now what must he think of her? What did she think of herself?

This really was a situation of her own making. She hoped it wouldn't lead to her undoing as well.

She allowed him to assist her up into the curricle, which was, indeed, quite high. She heard her breath hitch as she looked down—and down some more—to the ground. Which she couldn't see very clearly, given how far away it was and how difficult it was for her to see.

She wished there was some dispensation for wearing her spectacles when she was in the company of a man who definitely would not be marrying her at any point in the future.

But there was not.

Just in case, however, she'd brought her spectacles along. She had gotten adept at slipping them on when nobody was looking at her, which was depressingly frequent. But then she could see everyone not looking at her, which was better than the alternative.

He vaulted up beside her, his leg only a few inches away from hers on the small seat.

"Unless you have any other ideas, I thought we would go for a ride in the park," he said, taking up the reins and setting off.

"That doesn't sound very different from what I have done before," Eleanor replied in what she knew was a prim tone of voice.

He leaned over slightly, enough so that his shoulder brushed hers. "Oh, but you haven't experienced the park with me before, my lady."

She swallowed hard at the feelings that comment engendered. She should not be so absolutely and entirely thrilled to be seated beside him. It wasn't as though he truly wanted to be there; she'd made it a point so that he could persuade her to say yes to his brother.

But she was absolutely and entirely thrilled. And it wasn't just because of him; for one of the first times since she'd made her debut, she was without a chaperone. The weather was surprisingly pleasant, she had yet to be forced into a marital commitment, and then, yes, there was him.

His presence wasn't the only thing that made her thrilled, but it definitely helped. She couldn't see being nearly this enthusiastic about going for a ride in the park with her cousin Sir Reginald, for example, a gentleman whose only conversation was about hunting and his dogs.

"I understand your brother is very busy"—*doing*

heaven knows what—"but what do you do with your time?" she asked, then felt her eyes widen as she realized she knew one of the things he did.

Thankfully, he didn't reference his choice of reading material in his reply. "I am of not much use to anybody," he said in a remarkably cheerful tone, considering his words. "I lounge about, I drive in the park"—at which point he gestured to the horses—"I encourage my brother to stop taking everything so seriously, and I gamble on occasion."

"You and I have much in common, then," Eleanor replied. He glanced over at her, a wry grin on his face.

"You gamble as well?"

She couldn't suppress the burst of laughter that emerged from her mouth. His grin grew wider, and his eyes warmed.

Oh dear.

"No, I do not gamble." Although this bargain they'd made was a gamble of sorts, wasn't it? *Show me enough fun for a short period of time so I will agree to marry your average brother and have an average life without regrets.*

Not really a gamble she wished to make, but here she was anyway.

At the very least, she could put it on her list.

"I could take you to a gambling den. If that is the sort of overwhelming experience you'd like." She felt his gaze on her, her cheeks heating at the scrutiny.

Her lips were suddenly dry, and she darted her tongue out to lick them, his eyes narrowing at the movement. He snapped his head back around again and she felt the loss of his regard like a tangible thing.

This was not at all the type of thing she should be feeling. Not with the brother of the man whom she'd told "not yet."

But—"A gambling den?" That sounded quite overwhelming, and precisely the kind of adventure that she was longing for. Well, both longing for and dreading. It definitely belonged on the list.

"Yes. There are a few that are respectable enough for a lady such as yourself, provided we disguise your—your . . ." and his fingers waggled in the air as he tried to find the word. Her mind hunted frantically for what he might possibly be trying to say, only all of the things she thought of—gentle breeding, naïveté, virginity—all sounded dismissive and far too blunt.

Although Lord Carson had said his brother was remarkably blunt. Goodness, there must be something she hadn't even thought of that he was trying to avoid saying.

"White gowns?" she supplied. "I do have other colors, I am certain I can contrive to look less of whatever it is you wish me to look less of."

That got a surprised snort from him, and she felt herself relax a tiny amount. Perhaps this wasn't the most foolish, ill-considered thing she'd ever done. Maybe there was a chance that he would do what she'd asked, and then she'd settle down into marriage with his much less intimidating brother.

Perhaps it wouldn't be too terrible.

"WE'RE ALMOST THERE," he said after about ten minutes of silence. Eleanor had spent the time glancing about as the park's gentle trees and rolling slopes gave way to a more ragged area, one where there were brown patches of dirt mixed in with the lush greenery.

"I've never been to this side of the park before," Eleanor admitted.

He glanced toward her, a crooked grin lifting one side of his mouth. "I did say you'd never been to the park with me before, didn't I?"

And then that fluttery feeling returned, only this time it was accompanied by something that felt almost bold, roiling inside her.

"Where are we going?" she asked. There were no other carriages in sight, although a few groups of people were on foot in the distance. Not that she could make them out, but she could distinguish a clump of people from a clump of trees. Especially when they were wearing non-tree colors. It did feel exciting, actually, to be in a new place.

And then he answered her question.

"A cricket match."

"A—a what?" she said in a confused tone.

"You have heard of cricket, haven't you?" he asked, his mouth now turning down in what appeared to be dismay.

"Of course I have"—*because I've overheard the*

servants speaking of it—"but I've never attended a match before. I didn't know it was even called a match, honestly."

"Good, then. This is your first adventure," Lord Alexander said in a curt tone as he turned the carriage toward a wide-open field where there were many non-trees running about.

ALEX FELT WOBBLY and uncertain, something he hadn't felt since he was shorter than Lady Eleanor. Or shorter even than one of her younger sisters.

But she kept surprising him. Was she the lady he'd first met at the bookshop, the sharp, snappish one, or the female who'd been so demure at the ball—until she was not?

He didn't know which version he wished for; either she was intriguing, in which case he'd be intrigued, or she'd be a demure, modest wife that would be the partner it seemed Bennett wanted, which made Alexander angry, no matter how many ducal ducats she brought to the family.

Ducal ducats. He glanced over at her, opening his mouth to share the joke, only to realize of course he couldn't. For once, he could not be blunt and direct, because no matter what he was being blunt and direct about—either because he found her attractive and he wished to bed her, or because he found it abhorrent to consider she would be marrying his brother—the truth would not be borne.

He'd have to get better at diplomacy, like his elder brother.

"We're here," he said, pulling on the reins to

stop the horses. They had arrived at the edge of a flat field, one showing the wear of frequent usage. There was a game ongoing, as Alex had known there would be, although he honestly had no idea why he thought taking Lady Eleanor to a cricket match, of all things, would be overwhelming for her.

Just, perhaps, that he didn't want to overwhelm her too much with, say, a visit to a gambling den. Or a clandestine interlude in a pleasure boat, all alone in the middle of the night.

Thoughts of which were far too interesting and overwhelming, he'd have to say, to his body, which was reacting in a predictably male way to the idea.

"This is—cricket?" she said, sounding skeptical.

"What did you imagine it was? Unless you thought the actual insects were wandering about playing some sort of organized entertainment," he said, raising an eyebrow at her as he spoke.

She looked at him, her blue eyes wide, and then they narrowed and her words emerged before, he would guess, she had time to consider what she was saying. And the lady from the bookshop reappeared.

"You seem to think I am so idiotic that I would possibly imagine that insects would be engaged in a sporting activity." Her tone dripped with icy disdain, and he felt himself heat at the sight of her enraged. "I assure you, my lord, that simply because I have not yet had experience with things that I am not entirely stupid." She glared at him, her eyes narrowing even more. "That is what you believe, isn't it? That I am unintelligent?" She focused her attention on a small purse she'd brought along with her, opening it with shaking fingers. "I am many things, or not many things, depending on what your perspective is, but I am not stupid." She withdrew a pair of spectacles from her purse and placed them on her face, settling the wires behind her ears. And then she looked at him again, raising her chin in a defiant pose. "As it happens, I am poorly sighted. That much is true." And she resumed glaring at him from across the seat. "Likely you have misjudged my expression because I have a lack of vision. But since you don't seem to think very highly of me in the first place, I might as well wear my spectacles so I can see your disdain."

He wanted to both applaud and kiss her all at the same time.

The glass of the spectacles made her eyes appear even larger, and he could see the sheen of moisture in her eyes. And then felt horrible about himself. His derision had made this woman, a woman who only wanted to experience a bit of life before surrendering to what he knew—from the reports of the married ladies with whom he'd dabbled, so perhaps not a fair measure—was a life of thankless boredom, enhanced only by the prospect of illicit activity.

Although he would not allow her to be illicit if she was married to Bennett.

When she was married to Bennett, he corrected himself.

He took her hand in his, noting how she drew her

breath in sharply at the contact. Of course, the holding of hands wasn't something gently bred young ladies generally did. Imagine if he did what he'd wanted to a moment ago; reached out to gather her into his arms, to press her lovely, curvaceous body against him as he kissed her senseless. Or senseful, actually. Since he now knew she was not without sense, she just wanted more.

"I am truly sorry," he said in a low voice, seeing her pulse flutter at her throat. "I didn't mean to imply . . ." he began, only to have her withdraw her hand.

"But you did." She bit her lower lip. "You don't have to show me anything if it is so unpleasant for you." Her voice was flat, as though she were tired. "I just thought that if I could see what I would be missing, to experience it myself, even for just a short time, that I could . . ." And then she stopped, shaking her head and looking down at the ground. "Never mind."

"That you could what?" His whole self longed to take her hand again, to reassure her with his touch. Or perhaps the touch was to reassure him.

"That I could do what my father wants me to. What my entire family wants me to, even though I barely know myself, much less your brother." She lifted her head and gazed at him. "But you can take me back home, Lord Alexander. I believe you have overwhelmed me enough."

Her voice wavered, but her gaze didn't, and he found himself admiring her spirit. That she understood what was likely to happen to her, that she accepted it as her fate, but that she was intelligent enough to know that there were other things out there—there were many people in their world who had no idea that other experiences were possible. Or if they did, they assumed the other experiences were lesser because they weren't part of the rarified world they inhabited.

She didn't dismiss things because she didn't know about them. On the contrary, she wanted to know what they were precisely because she didn't know about them. She wanted to see them, in all sorts of ways, from the mundane act of seeing to the higher levels of understanding.

"No, I won't take you home now." His refusal seemed to startle her, since she sat straighter in the seat and gaped at him as though she couldn't believe he had said the words.

He could well believe he'd said the words, given how accustomed he was to stating his thoughts without concern about the listener.

"I brought you here to show you something I hope you'll find enjoyable. Overwhelming, perhaps." And he allowed himself to grin at her, hoping she would respond.

Her expression wavered between anger and a glimmer of what he thought might be humor, and then she rolled her eyes—still behind her spectacles—and flung her hands up. "Fine. You can show me the cricket game." Her tone was sulky, but not as dispirited as it had been a few moments before. "The game without insects," she added.

He vaulted out of the carriage seat and held his

hand up for her to take before she changed her mind. She allowed him to help her out of the carriage, only clutching at his shoulder once as she descended.

"You're not going to attempt to explain the rules to me, are you?" she asked as they began to walk to the edge of where the players were playing.

"Uh, no, of course not," Alex replied, quickly revising his idea of doing just that.

"I would not be overwhelmed, but I would be overwhelmingly bored. My sister Ida tried to tell me all about Galileo's grand idea of something or another, and all it did was make my head hurt, and then I fell asleep. I did sleep quite soundly that evening, so perhaps I will ask you to come explain the rules of cricket while I am in bed."

It seemed she did not consider her words that well either, because now the last two words—*in bed*—hovered between them, making the silence edgily uncomfortable.

"That is, I wouldn't find you entirely dull if—oh, bother," she muttered, walking more quickly toward the field.

Alexander lengthened his stride as well, suppressing a chuckle as he followed her.

*Lady Eleanor's Good
List for Being Bad:*

---

*Ride in a curricle with a
gentleman, provided the
horses are not too large.*

Chapter 7

$\mathcal{I}$t felt so freeing, Eleanor thought, to speak her mind. No wonder nobody wanted her to do it. It was as though she had unstoppered herself, and her emotions were tumbling out, her anger and frustration and interest and desire all mixing together in a passion-fueled torrent.

And so far she had only rebuked Lord Alexander for implying she was stupid. Imagine what else she might say, if given the chance.

She drew up at the edge of what she presumed was the playing field, aware that Lord Alexander was directly behind her. Conscious of him, even though he wasn't in her direct line of vision.

And speaking of vision, she could see. It was marvelous wearing her spectacles outdoors, being able to see the individual men scampering about, even if she had no idea what it was they were attempting to do. That too felt freeing, as though perhaps she could actually know where she was going instead of being shepherded about like a duke's dutiful daughter.

The duke's dutiful daughter was only slightly

less damning than the duke's dull daughter, as she'd been referred to by that Lady Vale. The one who found Lord Alexander so entertaining.

"So this is cricket," she remarked as Lord Alexander came beside her. The players were all wearing white clothing—rather like a debutante, she thought wryly—that showed the various and sundry marks of dirt and grass. She turned to him. "And why did—?"

"Alex!" a voice called out, one of the players trotting off the field toward them. It was a man who was older than Lord Alexander, a few streaks of grey at his temple, a full beard hiding the lower half of his face.

Lord Alexander stepped forward, a grin splitting his face, and shook the man's hand. "Charles, a pleasure. I hadn't thought you'd be playing today, I assumed you'd be at the factory." He turned to Eleanor. "My friend Mr. Powers here is a part owner of the Powers and Smith Railway." He returned his attention to his friend. "Does this mean that British industry is grinding to a halt?"

Mr. Powers laughed, a laugh that made him lean back and open his mouth wide. Eleanor envied his emotional exuberance.

"No, my partner is keeping things chugging along, so to speak," he said, winking in Eleanor's direction.

She groaned in response before thinking about how proper ladies, dukes' demure daughters, were not supposed to groan, no matter how bad—or how splendid—the pun was.

"Introduce me, Alex?" Mr. Powers said, nodding to Eleanor.

"Of course. Lady Eleanor Howlett, may I present Mr. Powers, currently—so to speak—of the Powers and Smith Railway company."

"Charged, I'm sure," Eleanor replied, holding her hand out to Mr. Powers. She might as well be who she was, for now at least.

His expression was puzzled for a moment as he shook her hand, then he burst into another envy-inducing guffaw. "Excellent, my lady." He poked his finger at the side of his head. "Got to keep the wheels turning is what I say."

"Don't stoke the fire, my lady," Lord Alexander said. "Charles here is just on track to outpun us all."

Both Eleanor and Mr. Powers groaned at that, while Lord Alexander just grinned delightedly.

She hadn't expected him to appreciate a good pun. A slow warmth spread over her that had nothing to do with the sun overhead.

"Care to play, Alex?" Mr. Powers said, gesturing to the field. "Bob there has to run home to his wife, and we're already down one fielder."

Lord Alexander glanced over at Eleanor. "I don't think—" he began.

"Oh, go ahead. This will be a new experience for me," she said. Besides, now that she had her spectacles on, she thought it would be delightful to watch Lord Alexander engage in an athletic pursuit.

If she were admitting things to herself, like a duke's disgraceful daughter would.

"All right then," he said, beginning to remove his jacket. He handed it to Eleanor, who froze before taking it.

That was a new experience as well, having a gentleman hand her his jacket. The gentlemen of her acquaintance generally wouldn't even dare to be seen in her company without a jacket on, much less hand her the one they'd just removed.

Lord Alexander didn't seem to notice her shock, however, only rolling up his sleeves, exposing his wrists and forearms.

Eleanor felt overwhelmed, to be sure, by the sight of everything. By being able to see things, thanks to her spectacles, and also by what she was seeing. Lord Alexander's strong wrists, his stronger forearms with intriguing lines running up them, sprinkled with a dusting of golden hair.

His arms looked so different from hers, so male, she felt herself start to lean forward for a closer examination, only to jerk back in horror. She wasn't supposed to be examining Lord Alexander's forearms, for goodness' sake. She was only here to experience new things, and new things did not include a man's body parts.

At which point she felt as though her corset was suddenly tighter, her stays digging into her side as she took a deep breath.

"Wish me luck, Lady Eleanor," Lord Alexander said before loping onto the field.

She took a moment to admire his long legs striding across the field before resuming her rebuke of herself. While also still enjoying the view.

"Yes!"

At the call, Alexander took off running, relishing the feel of his breath coming fast and hard in his lungs, his leg muscles straining as he pounded over the field's dodgy surface.

It was exhilarating, engaging in this kind of all-out physical activity, something he'd only discovered one day when Bennett had dismissed him from their parents' house, saying he was driving him crazy with his pacing.

Alex had walked through the park at a furious clip, merely nodding to the people of his acquaintance who bid him good-day. Eventually he'd wound up in this part of the park, where nobody he knew would venture since it was so unfashionable.

And it was here he had found Charles, and the other cricket players, engaged in one of the most intense games he'd ever seen. Afterward, Charles had come up and introduced himself and invited Alex to join them in a future game. It was the only thing he'd found—besides his various romantic activities—that could calm his mind and his body so he could sleep and think without distraction. The men he played with came from all walks of life, from butchers' assistants to industry types such as Charles, to a few other third and fourth sons of aristocratic families. All of them united by the desire to have a good game. As simple as that. Which was entirely refreshing, and Alex had found himself collecting more friends and acquaintances.

This game wasn't quite as intense as that first one; there weren't enough players, as Charles had mentioned, and the heat of the day made them all more languorous. But not Alex, who wanted the exhaustion of the exercise more than staying cool.

He'd sweated through his shirt, forgetting Lady Eleanor was there when he drew it up and over his head, tossing it to the ground as he prepared to take another swing.

It was only when Charles nudged him in the ribs that he remembered. "Your lady over there looks as though she's imitating a hot piece of coal, she's so bright."

Alex turned his head slowly to look at her. Yes, she was the chaise-longue color again, but this time he couldn't fault her for it. It wasn't as though she had likely ever seen a gentleman's upper body before. At least he was surmising she hadn't.

He wondered if she was overwhelmed at the sight, then shook his head at himself. Of course she was, but he hoped she wasn't regretting agreeing to this bargain, recalling their first encounter in the bookshop.

When they'd seen that drawing of a bare-chested Hercules fucking his woman so thoroughly.

Damn it, and now he felt warm throughout. He wished he could separate his natural inclinations from the task of convincing Bennett's bride-to-be that she would be his bride, but he found it nearly impossible. Especially now, standing there at the edge of the playing area, those quirky spectacles perched on the end of her nose, her entire face rosy from whatever she was feeling.

Knowing, too, that Bennett didn't seem to care one way or the other.

"I'd better take her back," Alex muttered, grabbing his shirt from the ground and pulling it back over his head as he marched to her.

"I think that's enough overwhelming for today, don't you?" he asked as he took her arm and led her back to the curricle.

"You brought her to a cricket match?" For once, Alex knew precisely what his brother was feeling, since his tone was entirely and uncompromisingly bemused.

"I did." He shrugged, wishing he could just return to his room and strip down for a bath. Lady Eleanor hadn't spoken much on the drive home, while Alex had searched his mind frantically for appropriate topics, none of which he could come up with. Asking her, "Did you like what you saw?" and, "How about that pitch?" were both too vague and horrifyingly specific.

Instead, he'd spent the time noticing how her hands were clasped tightly in her lap, and how pretty her eyes were behind the glass of her spectacles. And that her mouth was full and her lips looked appealing, even though he knew he should absolutely not be thinking of her that way.

But he was Lord Alexander Raybourn, whose only skills were athletic in nature, whether on a cricket field or in the bedroom, so he couldn't help but think of those things.

He nearly laughed aloud when he thought about combining the two. And then spent the remainder of the ride figuring out the rules for such a game of cock-cricket or whatever it would be called.

"And you thought taking her to see a group of men running about a field of grass fussing about a ball would convince her to marry me?" Bennett continued. Engrossed in his own thoughts, Alex had forgotten he was there. He hadn't told Bennett about Lady Eleanor's request to be overwhelmed, because it sounded odd, even in his own head. As though it meant something entirely different.

"Well, I have to think marriage to you is more appealing than watching a cricket match." Alex wanted to wince, his explanation was so appallingly bad.

Bennett snorted. "Thank you, brother. Your support and admiration of me and my character is remarkable."

"But the thing is, Bennett, I think you should be the one to take her about. It's you that's going to have to marry her, after all." As though it were a chore. Which made Alex want to wince all over again.

"I don't have time. Nor, honestly, do I have the inclination." Bennett spoke as bluntly as Alex usually did. "She's perfectly pleasant. She has a substantial dowry, and appears in good health." As though he was discussing his favorite horse, only he spoke more enthusiastically about the four-legged creature. "She seems to need some attention I don't have time to spend on her." He shrugged. "So I want you to continue to try to persuade her to marry me. By taking her somewhere other than a cricket match." He paused, and tilted his head to look at Alex's face. "Actually, never mind that. Just do it however you want to. I haven't got time to fuss over where you are taking the woman who has de-murred at becoming my bride. There are more important things to worry about."

More important than the decision of who you'd spend the rest of your life with? Not for the first time, Alex was grateful he was the second and less responsible son. Of course that meant he was now the one to discover more about Lady Eleanor.

ELEANOR FOCUSED ON keeping her lips pressed to-gether as she entered her house, merely nodding as Cotswold exclaimed over the state of her hair and the grass stains at the bottom of her predictably white gown. Because if she did allow herself to speak, she was fairly certain all she would be able to say was, "I've seen Lord Alexander's chest, and it is magnificent!"

And that wouldn't be appropriate for so many reasons.

"My lady, your mother and your sisters are tak-ing tea in the Purple Room"—so named because her mother had insisted on decorating it in all the shades of that color she could find—"and they asked you to join them when you return."

Eleanor nodded in an automatic response, then shook her head vigorously. "Not yet." *I need time to stop thinking about the way he looked, how the muscles in his back shifted as he ran.* "I just want to go wash my face."

Maybe while she was up there she could give her brain a rinse as well so she could wash the images out of her head. Only she doubted there would be anything to chase those pictures away. Much like the Hercules and Dejanire picture, she thought how he looked running up and down that field would forever be emblazoned in her memory.

"Where did you go with Lord Alexander?" Olivia demanded as soon as Eleanor entered the room. She had washed her face, but her mind was still ruminating on everything she'd seen and done, with the emphasis on the *seen* part.

"Come sit here, my dear," their mother said, patting the sofa seat next to where she was sitting.

Eleanor stepped over Ida, who was engrossed in building some sort of mechanical thing on the floor, smiling at Pearl who was curled up in one of the far chairs, her feet tucked under her.

"Thank you, Mother," she said, taking the cup of tea her mother had prepared. Eleanor took a sip, wondering if this would be the day her mother remembered how her eldest daughter took her tea.

Too much sugar, no milk at all. Today was not the day.

She glanced at Olivia, wrinkling her nose. Olivia put her hand to her mouth suppressing a giggle. It was a bet among the four sisters—five when Della had been living with them—as to which daughter's tea their mother would finally get correct.

Thus far, the closest was Ida, simply because she took her tea with nothing at all, and their mother had come very close to completely forgetting to do anything to the tea once she'd made it. But at the very last minute, just as Ida was beginning to allow a triumphant smile to cross her face, their mother had snatched a piece of lemon and squeezed it mercilessly into the cup.

"We went to the park. In Lord Carson's curricle," Eleanor replied, keeping her gaze fixed on the leg of the chair Pearl sat in. She didn't want to reveal anything that might make her sisters ask even more questions, or to admit to anything shocking. Even though there was plenty to admit there, and she knew her sisters would find the entire afternoon fascinating.

Her mother wouldn't recall anything, so she could have told her about Lord Alexander and the Discarded Shirt, but the Duchess of Marymount had a disconcerting habit of occasionally surprising everyone with blurting out a particularly odd and out-of-context detail. "My daughter Lady Eleanor very much enjoyed seeing Lord Alexander Raybourn's vast expanse of chest," for example. Told to a group of matrons whose daughters were jockeying for position in the marriage mart, eager to find anything that would discredit one of the other competitors. Probably with Lady Vale there, just to make things even more horrible.

Not that marriage was a competition; if anything, Eleanor would have to say she regarded it more like a prison sentence, one that would only be cut short by death.

And now she had chased away all of her indecent thoughts regarding Lord Alexander because she was currently envisioning herself trapped in a tiny cell with Lord Carson, and nothing to do but stare at one another. That might be tolerable if it were Lord Carson's brother, or at least tolerable for longer, but she couldn't imagine it was a future worth looking forward to. No matter who was in the cell with her.

"The park sounds boring," Olivia said. "Although that curricle was stunning. That is Lord Carson's, isn't it?"

Ida looked up from whatever she was building, her eyebrow fully raised. "You know perfectly well it is—you went and spoke to the coachman all about it. And I believe I saw you look around as though you were going to hop up into it."

"Hmph," Olivia replied, thereby confirming what Ida had said.

"It is Lord Carson's curricle, yes." Eleanor smiled at Olivia to let her know she was fine with whatever girlish passion her sister had for her not-yet-husband. Girlish passion, or womanish passion, for that matter, was fine as long as it was not acted upon.

Which of course brought her mind back to Lord

Alexander and his Handsome Chest. She hadn't done anything, after all; she'd just looked. Thoroughly.

"What else did you do? Unless you just drove around the park for the hours you were out."

"We—" Went and saw a cricket game? How did that sound? Did it sound as shocking as it was? Likely not. And here she was again, asking questions when she'd gone so long without asking any. "We went to a playing field where we watched some men playing a game. Cricket."

"Cricket!" Pearl echoed, making everyone in the room stare at her. She promptly shrank back into her chair turning a bright pink color.

"Do you like cricket, Pearl?" Eleanor asked gently. Perhaps Pearl could explain the rules, even though that held even less appeal than Lord Alexander doing it.

"She does. She likes to whack the ball back and forth when nobody is about," Olivia said in a dismissive tone. "It sounds as though she and Lord Alexander have something in common." She accompanied her words with a scornful eye roll that left no one in doubt about what she thought about that.

"I hope Lord Alexander was able to talk some sense into you regarding his brother's suit," the duchess said. "I presume that is why he asked you to go for a drive."

"He did mention his brother, yes, Mother," Eleanor said. She'd have to walk a fine line between sharing enough information to persuade her mother to allow her to spend more time with Lord Alexander, yet not so much that her mother saw the encounters as possibly dangerous to the potential engagement.

It was a conundrum she wasn't sure even Ida's impressive brainpower could solve.

"I still don't understand why Lord Carson isn't taking you out himself if it's him that wants to marry you," Olivia said, getting to the heart of the matter right away.

"Lord Alexander mentioned that Lord Carson is very busy with some family business dealings." It did sound weak, didn't it? And it definitely did not bode well for their future together. Although perhaps that meant they'd be occupying separate prison cells? *Something to look forward to*, Eleanor thought ruefully. At least she'd have some time to herself.

"Nothing should be more important than love," Olivia proclaimed, her tone as earnest and fervent as a young girl's could be. Which was a remarkable amount.

"Love doesn't enter into this equation," Ida said, glancing up from her project. "This is a matrimonial enterprise, where one side gains something from the other, and vice versa."

"Someday, Ida, you are going to fall head over heels in love, and you'll find yourself as confused and foolish as anybody," Olivia declared.

Ida only shrugged in doubt.

"Eleanor will be seeing Lord Carson at the Lindens' tonight," her mother said complacently. "He will find time to speak to Eleanor about his suit. I am certain that her refusal is only nerves. I refused your father three times before I finally agreed, and look how well that turned out!"

At least their mother was so oblivious to other people she didn't see the looks of dismay the sisters shared.

But that meant Eleanor would also likely see Lord Alexander tonight. Fully clothed, but not less compelling, and dangerous to her state of mind.

Lady Eleanor's Good List for Being Bad:

Welcome the opportunity to see underneath a gentleman's jacket and shirt, particularly if the gentleman in question is of an athletic persuasion.

Chapter 8

*E*leanor couldn't help but locate Lord Alexander in the crowd at the Lindens'. She told herself it was only because he was so much taller than everyone else, and even her poor eyes could find a gentleman who towered over the crowd, but she also had the suspicion she wanted to find him.

Just so she would know where his brother was also, she tried to lie to herself, but she couldn't quite manage that, even inside her own head.

Bother. She liked Lord Alexander; she wanted to speak frankly with him about all sorts of things, including mythological stories of gods and demigods doing reprehensible things, the joy of athletics, and the glee in making someone groan through a pun.

"He's over there, your Lord Carson," her mother said, poking Eleanor in the side and pointing with her fan.

"I see," Eleanor replied, even though of course she couldn't.

Lord Alexander hadn't seemed to mind when she wore her spectacles; why would it be so terrible for her to do so in public? It would certainly make things less . . . fuzzy.

Although if she were to see things more clearly, perhaps she'd decide she didn't want to be where she was at all. She was already close to wanting that now, even with her poor eyesight.

"Your Grace, Lady Eleanor." The ladies turned at the words, and Eleanor was able to see it was their hostess, Lady Linden, an elegant woman whose appearance hid her gentle manners and kindness.

"Thank you for the invitation, my lady," Eleanor said, offering a brief curtsey. "It is a pity it is looking to rain."

Lady Linden waved her hand in dismissal. "Ah, rain. The curse of the London hostess, but at least there is plenty of room inside. I will be surprised, my lady, if you are not asked for every dance. You are looking remarkably pretty this evening."

"Thank you," Eleanor said, smiling in satisfaction as she gazed down at her gown. Cotswold, prodded by the extremely supportive twins, had agreed to let Eleanor add some color, in the form of ribbons, to her cream-colored gown. Eleanor had chosen burnished gold ribbons to put in her hair and at her waist.

The color was remarkably close to Lord Alexander's hair color, but she hadn't thought of that when she'd chosen them. Of course not.

The ribbon in her hair brought out the golden highlights in her own brown hair, making it look more lustrous, while the ribbon at her waist brought attention to her curves. With any luck, she might be able to persuade Cotswold to let her wear a light pink in a few months.

Just in time to get betrothed, eventually to be married, and therefore be able to wear whatever color she liked.

"Good evening, Your Grace, Lady Eleanor." Lord Carson's amiable tone snapped her out of her vision of entering her marital prison cell in a peacock-blue gown.

"Good evening, my lord," her mother replied, waving her fan. "I was just remarking to Lady Linden that it is a pity that the rain is coming, but that is the price we pay for living in the world."

"Exactly so, Your Grace," Lord Carson replied, sounding as though he knew what the duchess had meant. Was that a positive or a negative attribute? "I am hoping that Lady Eleanor will be able to spare a dance with me this evening? You are looking in excellent health, my lady. It seems your ride with my brother did not unduly affect you."

Not in any way I can possibly say, Eleanor thought.

"Yes, thank you, my lord. A dance would be a pleasure."

"And I will follow my brother's lead and ask you as well." Lord Alexander—because of course he was there, standing beside his brother, towering over him like an outsized . . . tower.

"Thank you, yes," Eleanor replied, keeping her gaze directed to the floor. She couldn't see the floor, of course, but it was safer for her to not see the floor than to not see him.

The music struck up, and Lord Carson's hand entered her field of vision. "May I claim my dance now, my lady?"

She looked up at him, wishing that the sight of him made her heart race in any kind of way. That she didn't anticipate having an average and dull life with him in their respective prison cells.

That her family didn't require her to enter into prison so soon after entering the world.

"Yes, thank you, my lord," she replied, taking his hand.

ALEXANDER FELT HIS chest tighten as he watched Bennett take Lady Eleanor onto the dance floor. He wished he didn't feel this need to—to *claim* her, that he wasn't absolutely certain that he knew her best among all the people here. And he barely knew her at all, but he did know her somewhat. He knew she had a temper when provoked, he knew she enjoyed bad puns, and he knew she wanted to be overwhelmed. That nothing in her life thus far had given her the excitement she craved.

He wished he didn't know so quickly just what type of excitement he could provide.

The duchess kept up a steady monologue beside him, nothing that required him to do more than murmur a few "yes, Your Grace"s or "of course, Your Grace"s. His toe tapped to the music, his whole self yearning to go and thrust Bennett out of the way and take her in his arms.

But that was not what his father wanted, and more importantly, it wasn't what Bennett wanted.

What the family needed. Because Bennett didn't actually want her. He just needed her as a means to an end, a way to prop up the family's fortune.

He didn't think the Duke of Marymount would want to dower his daughter quite so well if she wasn't marrying the heir to the title. Wasn't marrying the responsible one who hadn't spent most of his life in the pursuit of pleasure. Namely his, although he was glad to share his pleasure along the way with whomever happened to be with him at the time.

Although—? No, he couldn't even think of that.

The dance ended, and he tried not to be quite so glad when Bennett and Lady Eleanor returned to where he and the duchess stood. There was something different about Lady Eleanor tonight, something that seemed not quite so pale and indistinguishable as the night he'd first met her, just another female in the cluster of virgins. Her cheeks were pink from the exertion of the dance, and her eyes sparkled, even though he knew she couldn't see everything in the room, which made him wonder just what she could see, and how close she'd have to be to something to see it clearly.

Not something he should be thinking about at all.

"That was lovely. Thank you, my lord," Eleanor said, inclining her head. She looked over at Alexander, a clear question in her gaze, and he stepped forward, holding his hand out.

"And this is my dance, is it not, Lady Eleanor?" Alexander asked.

"Yes, thank you," she replied, hesitating only a

moment before taking his hand and letting him lead her out onto the dance floor.

The music struck up, not a waltz, damn it.

"I have to ask," she began, only to be separated by the movement of the dance, "why it is," pause as he bowed to another lady in the set, this one a petite woman who stared up at him as though he were going to crush her, "that your brother," pause, this time to bow to the tiny woman's partner, an equally small gentleman who looked equally terrified, "has time to," and then Alex couldn't stand it any longer. He took her hand and led her off the dance floor, walking swiftly to the doors that led out onto the terrace.

"But—" she began, only to stop speaking as he dropped her hand to shut the doors behind them. "It's beginning to rain," she pointed out, moving to the door.

"Wait," Alex replied, taking her wrist in his fingers. Moving her beyond the doors so they couldn't be seen. "This could be another one of your overwhelming experiences—have you ever done this?"

"Been outside in the rain?" she said in a dubious tone of voice. "We live in England—rain is a constant."

"No, not that," he replied, now wishing she weren't quite so clever. "Spent time outside in the rain when there is nothing keeping you from going back in. When you relish the feeling of it, savor the moisture on your face, the fresh, clean scent of the rain tickling your nose."

She tilted her head and peered up at him, squinting. Of course, she couldn't see clearly. "You are right. I have never done that." She kept her gaze on him for a few more moments, then nodded. "Fine. I'll stay out here in the rain, but if it starts to rain very hard, I will have to return." She glanced down at her gown. "I cannot risk what it might do to my reputation if I get soaked."

"So you can relish the feeling of it within moderation," Alexander replied with a grin.

"Yes, that," she said, returning the smile.

The rain was only a light sprinkling, and they stood side by side in silence, both of them lifting their faces toward the sky.

If anyone but Bennett had ever paid attention to him in his family, his love of the rain would have become a family legend. But only Bennett noticed, and he just shook his head whenever Alex deliberately went outside during a storm. There was something so powerful about what nature could and would do to the world's inhabitants, something that couldn't be controlled no matter how much prestige and money a person had.

"This is nice," she said in a surprised tone of voice. He glanced over at her; she had her eyes closed, her face still lifted. "I have never done this before. Usually my mother is fussing about umbrellas and wet boots and overly curly hair. I've never just been out in the rain without purpose." Now she opened her eyes and looked over at him, a delighted expression on her face. "Thank you."

"You are entirely welcome, my lady. I am determined to allow you to experience as many new things as you can while we are agreed to our bargain."

"Yes, you most definitely are," she replied.

And then, to his surprise, she grasped his shoulders and pulled him down toward her for a kiss.

SHE HADN'T MEANT to kiss him. What with his not being even close to a possible suitor for her, and his making it clear earlier in the day that he had initially judged her as being not very smart. Those two things alone should have stopped her, but somehow, with them standing together in the rain, the light from the ballroom casting a faint yellow glow onto the stones of the terrace, the feel of the rain on her face—everything blended together in a grand overwhelming of feeling, one that she could only savor through kissing him.

Not that she knew any of this when she'd grabbed hold of his shoulders to lower his mouth to hers; she just knew that she was here, as was he, and the thing she most wanted to do was kiss him.

His mouth was warm, warmer than the night air outside. His shoulders, the ones she'd first grasped at the bookshop where they'd encountered one another, were strong and hard under her fingers. She found herself gripping them, raising up on her toes so as to get better leverage.

"Mmm," she murmured, beginning to remove her mouth from his when he grasped her firmly around the waist and hauled her against his body, making it easier for her to stand on her tiptoes.

His mouth returned to hers, the faint scratch of the stubble on his upper lip scraping her skin in a most delicious, enticing way. He was kissing her in earnest now, his lips nibbling at hers, his fingers splayed against her back.

It felt intoxicating. It was the most feeling she thought she'd ever felt, of pleasure, at least; she had felt plenty when she had been the one to discover her sister Della had eloped.

But this affected her body all over, making her want to squirm inside her skin. Her breasts were pushed against his chest—the chest she'd been admiring—and they felt tender and aching, somehow.

And then he did the most unexpected thing, and slid his tongue into her mouth. She was so startled she nearly bit down, but then his tongue found hers, and he began to lick and suck on it, and she melted.

She felt the muscles in her calves strain, but that discomfort was nothing compared to how the rest of her body felt. She reacted naturally, sliding her own tongue over his, widening her mouth to allow for as much contact as possible.

And then he groaned, low in his throat, and the hand at her waist held her fast against him, so close she could feel how his breath rose and fell in his chest.

The rain slid between them, a few drops running down her face as they continued to kiss.

And it felt like she couldn't breathe, but she didn't want to stop doing this. Ever.

Until he leapt back, his hands dropping from her body, his expression aghast.

"Dear God," he said, shaking his head, "what have we done?"

She couldn't answer, not with her breath still coming fast and shaky in her lungs, not with the sting of his kiss still upon her lips.

Not with how she wished he was anyone but who he was, and she was anyone but who she was so they could continue doing what they were doing, continue getting to know one another set on an overwhelming course.

"I will return to my mother," Eleanor said at last. She was relieved she could manage a reasonable tone of voice. "Thank you for the dance." And she turned to the door as quickly as she could, twisting the knob and slipping back into the ballroom before she could hear what he might say next.

Because if it was something such as, "This is the worst mistake I've ever made," or, "I have to tell my brother," or worse, "You are a terrible kisser," she might just crumple down on the terrace floor and cry.

*Lady Eleanor's Good
List for Being Bad:*

*Kiss someone who is not related
to you who would be
pleasant to kiss.*

Chapter 9

$\mathscr{K}$issing her was clearly not going to persuade her to marry Bennett.

Unless she loathed the experience so much she would do anything to avoid it occurring again. But judging by how she held him, how her body practically melted against his, and how quickly she learned what to do when his tongue entered her mouth, he didn't think that was a possibility.

But if there was a ranked list of Things to Do to Persuade Lady Eleanor to Marry Bennett, he'd be tempted to put "kiss her on a rainy terrace" as the number one entry. And a part of his mind was already strategizing how to topple that number one with an even more outrageously enjoyable adventure.

Damn his mind, at least the part that had that sort of imagination.

"There you are," Bennett said, clapping his hand on Alex's shoulder. The shoulder that could still feel the grip of her hand. "I was hoping you would join me in speaking to the Duke of Lasham about improvements for the working poor. He and his wife have been very involved in a variety of activities."

"You know I know nothing about anything, Bennett," Alex said in his normal bantering tone, only now it felt edged with a hard, savage truth that hurt. Hurt himself only, but still. A hurt that burned inside.

"You say that, and yet you are the person I talk to about everything," Bennett replied, tugging on his arm to guide him to a corner of the ballroom.

The opposite corner from where she stood, he couldn't help but notice.

"I don't listen," Alex said in a short tone of voice, his gaze still on her. Even from here, he could see her heightened color—not quite chaise-longue color, but a bright pink—and that she kept touching her mouth. It was likely bruised from his kiss, and even though he felt profound regret at it having happened, he also couldn't help but be proud he'd affected her so.

"Stop saying things like that," Bennett continued, still exerting force to make Alex move. "You listen more than you know. You don't give yourself enough credit, brother." And with those words, Alex felt as though Bennett had inadvertently kicked him in the stomach, fresh from the betrayal of kissing Lady Eleanor on the terrace, guilty for doing it, and even guiltier for wanting to do it again.

All while Bennett was complimenting him, saying he didn't take enough credit for himself.

If the credit was "who could be the biggest scoundrel of a brother while still having his brother admire him," then yes, he would take all of the credit.

They reached the corner where two people, a man and a woman, stood. The man was striking, an eye patch over one eye; his height not as great as Alex's but his width was broader. His wife—since Alex presumed this was the duke and his wife—had a mischievous smile on her face, and her hand was tucked into her husband's arm.

"Good evening, Your Grace, Your Grace," Bennett said to the pair. Both of them nodded, with the lady looking with quick, curious eyes toward Alex.

"Allow me to introduce my brother, Lord Alexander," Bennett said, gesturing to Alex, who bowed.

"What is this bill you wish me to support?" the duke said bluntly. Nearly as bluntly as Alex spoke, which immediately made him like the other gentleman.

"Goodness, Lash, allow there to be some semblance of niceties," his wife said, rolling her eyes at her husband.

"No, your husband's directness is appreciated," Bennett said, smiling. "As it happens, I am working on a bill to regulate more of the working conditions in the factories of London. There is a great need for funds to support those families who might be suffering hardship because the men of the family are injured or can't work."

This on top of what he was doing for their family? Alex swallowed against the waging emotions of pride and shame he felt at hearing just how much his brother was doing—and what Alex himself had just done.

"I've reviewed your bill, my lord," the duchess said, "and I have a few questions."

Alex hadn't lied when he told Bennett he didn't listen; as the duchess peppered his brother with questions, he found his mind filled with recollections of how Lady Eleanor felt, and what they'd done, and whether or not he should tell Bennett, not paying attention to the conversation happening outside of his head.

If he were an honorable person, he would tell Bennett. But then that would mean that Lady Eleanor would not even have a chance to marry Bennett because Bennett would—likely as not—withdraw his courtship of the lady. Not because Bennett was piqued, or petty, but because he would not want to force his suit on a woman who was not receptive. And Alex was fairly certain Bennett would define "not receptive" as "willingly kissing another man, in fact instigating the kiss."

He wouldn't mind so much if their father had to curtail his lifestyle because the marriage didn't occur, but their mother was already ill, and any change in her life would likely make her dose herself with even more laudanum. And Bennett himself would view his actions as having been a failure, when actually it would be Alex's failing. His inability to keep himself from attempting to seduce an attractive woman, even though that woman was supposed to be off-limits to him.

So he would have to keep his hands off Lady Eleanor while still spending time with her to convince her to accept his brother's hand in marriage.

The next time he saw her, he should ask her about Hercules's labors, and not the ones involving his wife and his cock.

Thus settled about what his own labor would be, he returned his attention to the conversation, which appeared—thankfully—to be finishing.

"Thank you so much for your support, Your Grace, Your Grace," Bennett was saying, shaking the duke's and duchess's hands.

"You are most welcome. It is the least we can do for your efforts," the duchess said, while the duke nodded his agreement.

"It has been a pleasure to meet you," Bennett said, executing a final bow, Alex following his example, before they left the pair.

"Thank you for accompanying me. I have to admit to finding the duke rather fearsome, and knowing you were beside me helped."

"You're welcome," Alex said. "What other help is needed for this bill of yours?"

Bennett halted in his progress and looked at Alex with a proud smile. "See, you were listening."

Not really, Alex wanted to reply. *Mostly I was thinking about kissing your Lady Eleanor, who isn't yours yet, but she most definitely is not mine.*

"We need funds, of course, and people to know about the bill who can speak intelligently about it to people who matter." Bennett tilted his head as though he'd thought of something. "You would be excellent at that, given your own skills of persuasion." At which Alex felt guilty all over again. "I could use your help."

"Persuading people to support it?" He could do that, he thought to himself. It might make him feel not quite so guilty.

Bennett nodded, his expression tightening. "There is so much to be done, and as you know, I am stretched to my limits with these familial obligations. We need more money, which I also don't have."

"I'll think about how I can help," Alex replied, as sincere as he'd ever been. Perhaps if he were able to do some good to mitigate the wrong he'd done, he wouldn't feel so terrible about himself. Perhaps he could use his skills of persuasion for more than just coaxing women into his bed.

Although that held no allure now, not when there was only one woman he wished to persuade into anything.

Which did not mean, a stern voice said inside his head, that he should allow himself to kiss her again.

"WE WAITED UP for you, even though Mother said we'd be haggard in the morning," Olivia chirped as soon as Eleanor walked into her bedroom.

Pearl sat beside her twin, stifling a yawn. They were sitting on Eleanor's bed in their nightgowns,

Cotswold seated in the large armchair at the corner of the room. She rose as Eleanor walked in.

Eleanor nodded at her maid, who came over and began to undo the buttons at the back of the gown. "You can stay as I get ready for bed, and I will tell you everything about the evening," she said, even though she knew she wouldn't tell them *everything*.

"Who did you dance with? Were there ices? Is Lady Linden nice? Was the party crowded? How many times did Mother point out where Lord Carson was?"

"There are far too many questions for me to answer all at once," Eleanor chided. Thankfully Olivia hadn't thought to ask, "Did you kiss anyone tonight?"

"Start at the beginning, then," Olivia said, her tone exasperated.

"Let Eleanor get into her night things at least, Olivia, before you start peppering her with questions," Pearl admonished. "Though we do want to know everything," she added in Eleanor's direction.

Cotswold assisted Eleanor out of her gown, then quickly undid her stays and corset, leaving her in just her shift. Her sisters made an exaggerated motion of looking away so that Eleanor could have a pretense of privacy as Cotswold got her into her nightgown, a cotton garment with a ribbon at the neckline.

White, predictably, as was the garment itself.

"That will be all, Cotswold," Eleanor said, dismissing her maid.

Cotswold curtseyed and left, closing the door behind her.

"Now you have to tell us everything," Olivia demanded.

"Fine." Eleanor joined her sisters on the bed, stretching out with her head on her pillow, the girls on either side of her. "Lady Linden is a nice person and an excellent hostess. There were three different types of ices."

"Three!" Olivia exclaimed, before Pearl hit her on the arm.

"And I danced with Lord Carson, his brother, our cousin Lord Reginald, and some other gentlemen I met this evening."

"Ohhh," the girls said in unison.

"Did Lord Carson ask you to marry him again?" Olivia asked.

No, but his brother kissed me, Eleanor thought.

"No, he didn't. It was only a few days ago that he asked the first time. It would seem odd if he asked so soon." *Please don't let him ask again, not for a while*, Eleanor thought in her head. She knew she would have to agree eventually, but not until she'd been thoroughly overwhelmed.

And tonight did not count. It was wonderful, it was overwhelming, but it just left her with a desire for more.

"What else happened?" Pearl asked, her gaze narrowing. "You look as though something else happened." At which both of her sisters looked at her in surprise, although Eleanor's surprise was colored by a substantial amount of guilt.

"Nothing—why do you say that?" she replied, trying to keep her voice as neutral as possible.

Pearl shrugged, her expression still suspicious. "Because you just look odd, that's why."

"Probably because she knows we're just dying for her to say yes to Lord Carson," Olivia responded.

Right. And there it was, the reason she couldn't think about kissing Lord Alexander, or even the possibility of kissing him. Because her entire family, most especially her sisters, needed her to get respectably married or they would never have their own chances at happiness in love.

Instead, when their father died, their cousin Reginald would inherit and dispossess all the female members of the family from the house, leaving them in even further disgrace because they hadn't managed to get married.

That was a lot of responsibility resting on her white-clothing-covered shoulders.

"Enough about my evening, I don't want to be haggard just in case Lord Carson does come to propose tomorrow." He wouldn't, but they didn't know that. The very mention of Lord Carson sent them scurrying out of her room, which was good, because otherwise she'd likely be up until dawn reliving the entire evening.

Not that she had any expectation of sleep, since she would be reliving the entire evening, now that she finally had a chance to be alone with her thoughts.

He'd felt horrible about it, she knew, but it wasn't his fault, something she would tell him at the next possible opportunity. She had kissed him, so all the responsibility fell on her.

And what a kiss it was. Not that she had anything with which to compare it; the closest to an actual kiss had been one time under the mistletoe with her cousin Reginald, and that was only a pressing of his moist lips to her cheek. And while she could recognize that a kiss could be better than the one she'd had this evening (though she couldn't imagine how) there was no denying that it was a fabulous kiss, and that she had enjoyed every minute, right up until he'd had his crisis of conscience and withdrawn.

If he hadn't, she wasn't entirely certain she wouldn't still be standing on that damp terrace with him. Kissing him as thoroughly as he had kissed her.

She heard a loud sigh emerge from deep inside herself and rolled onto her side, pillowing her head on her hand. Why did it have to be Lord Carson's brother? Why did she have to be so intrigued by him?

Why was she currently recalling the picture she'd seen at the bookshop and wondering how it would look if it were her and him rather than Hercules and Dejanire?

And why hadn't someone burst through her bedroom already to accuse her of thoughts entirely unbecoming to a duke's dull and dutiful daughter, the one who was tasked with the job of saving her family's reputation?

What if she was actually the duke's dangerous and not-at-all demure daughter?

And what was she going to do with all these thoughts and emotions? She couldn't just write everything down on her list and hope that would make the feelings go away.

Lady Eleanor's Good
List for Being Bad:

---

*Admit to feeling things a young
lady is not supposed to feel.*

Chapter 10

"It was my fault."

Eleanor glanced up at Lord Alexander as she spoke the words, wishing he were slightly less tall so she could see his face more clearly.

They were walking in the park, his having arrived earlier that day with a bouquet of flowers purportedly from his brother, as well as an invitation to go for a stroll that afternoon. That invitation had come from him, not from his brother.

It had been nearly a week since the last time they'd seen one another, although Eleanor had seen his brother at a few of the events she'd attended. But no Lord Alexander; she hadn't wanted to ask Lord Carson where his brother was, since she definitely did not want to indicate to anyone, much less herself, that she actually cared.

Even though she did.

"It wasn't," he replied in a fierce tone, not even pretending that he didn't know what she was talking about.

"I kissed you," she pointed out. She was holding his arm as they walked, and she felt his arm muscles tighten.

"And I continued the kissing." A pause, and he walked more quickly, as though propelled by his own emotion. His own guilt.

"It can't happen again." And then he stopped short and turned to face her. Even with her weak eyes she could recognize the ferocity of his expression, the resolute set hardness to his features. "It won't happen again, no matter how alluring you might be, or how much I enjoyed it."

Alluring? Enjoyed? Eleanor had to repress the immediate desire to just do it all over again, reach her hands up to his shoulders and bring his face down to hers, kissing him, only this time jumping straight to the interesting tongue part.

Instead she nodded in agreement. "It won't happen again," she said in a firm tone of voice.

"What will it take for you to agree to marry Bennett?" he said, turning back around and tucking her hand back in his arm as though the whole kissing discussion was entirely over.

She felt befuddled by the quick change in conversation—not just because she wanted to hear more about how alluring she was—but she wasn't going to keep talking about it, in case she was overwhelmed (so to speak) with wanting to kiss him. Again, and more thoroughly this time, since she knew better what to do, and could jump right into it.

Not that she was thinking about it, of course.

"I don't know anything about him. I know more about you than I do your brother," she added.

"What do you know about me?" he said in a disbelieving tone.

This was a challenge she could take up. "I know that you don't think you are worth much, I know that you enjoy books of a certain type, I know that you like to compete in athletic pursuits, I know that you enjoy a good—or terrible—pun, and I also know that you are a kind and loving brother."

"Oh." He sounded chastened, and she was pleased she'd been able to be so on the mark about him.

"The only thing I seem to know for certain about Lord Carson is that he is terribly busy, too busy to find out more about me. That doesn't augur well for a happy marriage." She paused as she considered it. "Perhaps it augurs well for one that isn't troublesome, but that isn't a goal to which I wish to aspire—to marry so I don't have to bother too much about my husband." Her parents did that now, and she didn't think either one of them could be said to be happy.

"What do you think makes for a happy marriage?" he asked. Now he sounded genuinely curious, although Eleanor was keenly aware that this was a dangerous topic.

She considered how to answer as they passed by a family, the youngest of whom was determined to run off to the nearby pond where there were ducks walking about, the father of whom was equally determined not to let him. They both watched, and she felt a smile curl the corners of her mouth.

"I think a happy marriage is one where the two people know about one another," she began, conscious that she'd just told *him* exactly what she knew. "And that there is mutual trust and respect. For my own marriage, I would want to be a partner to my husband, helping him to achieve the goals we've decided on together." She uttered a rueful laugh. "That doesn't sound as though it is too much to ask, but I doubt there are many such examples of marriage in our world."

He didn't reply, not at first, and she wondered what type of marriage his parents had—she'd met his father, but she didn't recall ever meeting his mother, though she knew the marchioness lived in the London town house with her family.

"If you were to marry Bennett—*when* you marry Bennett—I hope that is the type of marriage you will have." His tone was fierce, as though he was trying to convince both of them.

"I know there are reasons why I should accept your brother. And why he is being pushed into marriage with me." Eleanor spoke in a soft voice. She had never spoken so directly to a gentleman before, especially since she'd fallen out of the habit of confiding to anyone since Della, her best friend and now hopelessly lost sister, had left. "It just doesn't seem fair to either of us, that we should have to suffer one another for the remainder of our lives because of these external forces."

"You wouldn't suffer. I promise you that." He spoke as fiercely now as he had a few moments ago.

"I wish I could believe that," she replied, squeezing his forearm. "But I suppose, given all those other factors, that I will have to compromise my hopes for my future. I just want to extend this time for a bit longer. I want to know more about the man whom I am to marry"—*I want to know more about you*—"and I want to know more about myself."

"So we're still set on our bargain? You wish to be overwhelmed?"

"I want more than that," she said, surprising herself with her words. "I want to find a way to be happy, no matter what circumstances I find myself in. I want to make some sort of difference. I want to—I want to do more than wear white gowns and curtsey appropriately. I want to find my joy." She glanced up at him, appreciating how he was looking intently down at her, as though her words were important. "I have no idea why I've come to be speaking like this to you. Perhaps it was the kiss," she said, and she felt guilty for bringing it up, again, but she couldn't pretend it hadn't happened. "Or how we came to meet, which was the most shocking thing that has ever happened to me. I think that you might be the person who can help guide me. Not least because I am too poorly sighted to find the way myself," she added in a rueful tone of voice.

"Make a difference, hmm?" he said, turning his head to stare off into the distance. "I might know a way." And then he looked back down at her, a sly grin on his face, and she felt both terrified and excited. Which was more than she had felt in all of her twenty-one years.

IT WAS TERRIFYING, how similarly they seemed to feel. That they both wanted to make a difference, that neither one of them knew how, that both of them were frustrated by the constraints of their limitations—her of being a duke's daughter, and female (obviously), him by being the second son from a feckless family whose only attribute appeared to be the persuasion of ladies into doing things.

And a profound appreciation for certain types of literature.

"You are proficient in Italian?" he began, hoping she wouldn't scream or faint when he made his suggestion.

Her mouth curved into a shy smile. "I am quite fond of the language, yes. I am familiar with French and Spanish as well, but Italian is my favorite." She raised her eyes up to his face and now her expression was rueful. "It was my fondest wish to go to Italy and study the culture and the people myself, but of course that was not possible."

Constraints. Binding them as thoroughly as the strongest of ropes.

"I have a project I am hopeful of undertaking." Which sounded vague and indefinite, not something he was used to sounding. "That is, that book—the one we met over, if you recall it?"

Judging by the way her cheeks had turned chaise-longue red again, she did recall. She neither screamed nor fainted, however, so he took it as a win.

"My brother is involved in many charitable pursuits," he began, only to feel his own face flush—and when had that ever happened?—as he realized how she might interpret his unclear words.

"The thing is, I am thinking that if I can have that book translated into English, I could sell copies of it to people who would be interested, and I—that is, we—would contribute the proceeds to help Bennett's cause."

There. That was suitably direct.

"Oh," she said, her eyes wide. He doubted whether anybody had ever suggested she translate erotic poetry written in Italian from a few centuries ago. So at least he was overwhelming her, if not entirely in the right way.

"The book, the writing—is it as . . ." She hesitated before she spoke, her tongue darting out to lick her lips. "Is it as shocking as that picture?"

Alex held his hands out, palms up. "I have no idea. I don't read Italian, you see." It wasn't something his father had wanted to waste money on, and he saw anything more than rudimentary education as a waste when it came to Alex. "I do know the poetry was banned by the Catholic Church—the book I purchased is exceedingly rare. I would guess it is, so if you wish to decline, that would be entirely understandable."

"No, it sounds . . ." and she paused, and he held

his breath. Sounds horrible? Sounds ridiculous? Sounds like I might both scream and faint at the prospect? "Intriguing," she finished at last, and he exhaled.

"*Intriguing* is one word for it," he said with a return to his old self. At least, the old self that existed before a few days ago. Now it seemed he was someone who would do the right thing to aid his brother, had a heart that wanted to do good, and was considerate of a young lady's feelings.

Things he didn't think he had ever been before.

"How shall we do this? It is not as though you can arrive on my doorstep with that book and sit down in the library with it."

"Mmm. I hadn't thought of that." He had never had to be discreet before. So now he was experiencing some new things as well.

"If I say I am going to the bookshop—the one where we met—my family will not think anything of it."

"You spend a lot of time there, then?" Why hadn't he seen her before?

Most likely because Mr. Woodson had a special room for his special books—and that is where Alex spent his time when there.

She nodded. "Yes, but it is not just that. Since my sister—since my sister left rather suddenly, my parents have been otherwise preoccupied in shoring up the family's reputation. That means paying more social calls than usual, showing up at the House of Lords, and ensuring that newspaper columnists say the right things at the right time. That doesn't leave a lot of time for their daughters who haven't eloped."

His heart pulled a little at how lost she sounded. He hadn't considered that there was something she would gain if she married. Her freedom, at least more than it was as an unmarried young lady. The ability to do and say what she wanted, within reason. Bennett wouldn't try to curb her interests; he'd probably encourage her to form an Italian speaking club or purchase books of mythology for her.

"I didn't realize your sister had eloped," he replied.

"You might be the only one who didn't," she retorted. "Why else are my parents so desperate for your brother to marry me?"

"And my father is desperate for your dowry."

"Ah, I didn't know that. That is, I suspected, since why else would your brother have asked? It is not as though he knows me." She raised her gaze to his face. "Perhaps if ladies were kept less in the dark about what kind of world they were entering, they wouldn't do foolish things like run away with the dancing master." Her lips were pressed together, and her whole self radiated a self-righteous anger that was oddly appealing. "Or have a need to know things about the world and themselves. They would just . . . know it."

"It isn't fair," Alex said, surprising himself with how quickly he agreed with her.

"So that is why your father is so set on your brother marrying me. For my dowry. I knew it wasn't because Lord Carson chose me on his own." She spoke in such a matter-of-fact tone, one that belittled herself, that he just wanted to gather her up in his arms and kiss her.

Or, to be perfectly honest, he just wanted to kiss her anyway.

"My father has made many poor investments over the years," he explained. "Your dowry will infuse some much-needed funds into the family's holdings, and Bennett has gotten my father's promise that he will be the one to manage the money from now on." Something his father had readily agreed to, particularly since it meant he could spend more time with Mrs. Cheslam.

"Oh. Your brother must be a good man," she said in a slow, considering tone.

"The best."

She raised her chin and met his gaze. "So why does his brother seem so much more appealing?"

He didn't have an answer for that question.

Lady Eleanor's Good List for Being Bad:

Translate Italian medieval erotic poetry.

(An entirely surprising entry, but it needs to be on the list for specific reasons.)

Chapter 11

"This is not at all proper, my lady," Cotswold said as they walked to the bookshop.

"It will be far less proper if you refuse to accompany me," Eleanor retorted. "Because I will do this, whether or not you approve."

"I didn't say I don't approve," Cotswold replied. "I just don't want you to be gossiped about." Any more than the Howlett sisters were already, Eleanor understood her maid to be saying.

Eleanor smiled and patted Cotswold on the arm. "I will be discretion itself."

If by being "discretion itself" one referred to translating shocking material in the presence of an even more shocking man.

"If only your sister hadn't run off," Cotswold began. Eleanor felt her chest tighten, as it always did when Della was mentioned. Why hadn't her sister shared what was going on? Why had she run off so suddenly, and with a man they all knew was a reprobate? Was her sister so unhappy that she would prefer marriage to a man of unstable reputation and means to staying at home?

Or was she so desirous of change that she couldn't resist?

And was Eleanor just following her sister down that very same path? Was Della happy now?

"We're here," Cotswold announced, just as Eleanor was beginning to consider the wisdom of the plan. Which wasn't much of a plan, to be honest; she would spend a few hours a day at the bookshop, translating Lord Alexander's book. Then he would have the pictures reprinted along with her translation and sell it—discreetly—to gentlemen who wished to have the book in their private collection.

Lord Alexander had explained it all, Eleanor blushing furiously throughout the explanation, on one of their trips to the cricket field.

The only thing keeping Eleanor from bursting into flames of embarrassment was the possibility of seeing Lord Alexander in all of his athletic exuberance again.

He had persuaded the bookshop owner to allow them the use of an even more private back room for the translation work, and had refused to allow Eleanor to do the work on her own.

Eleanor wasn't sure if that was to ensure she did the work, or so he would be able to watch her reactions to the pictures, but she knew if they were discovered, the resulting scandal would mean none of her sisters had a hope of finding their own happiness.

The bell on the door tinkled as Cotswold swung the door open, holding it so Eleanor could enter.

"Good afternoon, ladies," the shopkeeper said. "What may I—oh," he continued as Alex stepped up to greet them.

From the little she could see of his expression, what with it being so dark in the shop, plus his height, plus her eyesight, he looked—nervous.

It made her feel a little fluttery that he might've worried she wasn't going to come.

Or perhaps he was concerned he'd have to find another person to do the translation of obscene Italian into equally obscene English.

"Good afternoon, my lady." She saw his Adam's apple move as he swallowed. He was nervous.

"Good afternoon, my lord," Eleanor said, nodding the precisely polite amount required of someone like her to someone like him.

Even though there was nothing at all polite about the situation.

"Mr. Woodson has allowed us to use his office for our—" And then he stopped speaking abruptly, no doubt at a loss for words as to what to call what they were about to do. She didn't think she could supply the word either, and she was fluent in more than just one language.

"Thank you, Mr. Woodson," Eleanor said. She turned to Cotswold. "You can return in an hour," she said to her maid, whose expression revealed just what she thought of that plan. "It is the most sensible way to avoid gossip," she explained. "If anyone sees you here, they will know I am here, and if they don't see me, they will presume I have gone off and done something shocking." She paused to let Cotswold think about it. "But if you are not here, nobody will know I am, and so there will be no scandal."

Her maid's eyes narrowed as they darted between Eleanor and Lord Alexander, but eventually she sighed and nodded. "Fine. But I will return in one hour, and you will be ready to depart at that time."

"Two hours," Lord Alexander parried, an amused tone in his voice.

"An hour and a half," Cotswold conceded.

Eleanor glanced at the two of them, amazed that Cotswold had capitulated and that Lord Alexander had made it seem so—effortless.

Small wonder he was tasked with the job of persuading her to marry his brother. If he could get her fiercely determined maid to agree to something, he was quite talented.

"An hour and a half," Cotswold repeated to Eleanor. "And you be careful," she said in a lower tone of voice.

Careful of what? Eleanor wanted to ask. *That I might fling myself in Lord Alexander's general mouth direction? Or that I might ask him to overwhelm me right in Mr. Woodson's back office?*

Or that I might accidentally fall in love with the wrong brother?

She shouldn't even ask herself that question, since she was afraid she might already know the answer.

H<small>E HADN'T BEEN</small> certain she'd come, so when he saw her, dressed in the white that it seemed she disliked, he'd heard himself exhale in relief.

And he had to acknowledge he did wish to spend time with her, beyond doing good and benefiting people who were constrained by things like lack of money, or proper housing, or ill health.

Not ridiculous constraints like being of no use to one's family, or being forced to be a pawn manipulated into a marriage.

"This way," Alex said, sweeping his arm out to point toward a small door on the far back right of the shop. The bookshelves were tall, but his height made it easy for him to see over them, but of course she didn't have that advantage. Even if she could see well, the top of her head came up to the top of his arm, even with her hat on.

"You're going to have to lead me," she said in an irritated tone, taking his arm.

It felt right to have her there. He walked through the narrow aisles, with her just slightly behind, her hand on his sleeve.

"You must be a good customer," she said as they made their way to the back of the shop.

"You could say that," Alex replied. Mr. Woodson had been delighted that Alex had found a translator for the book. Less delighted when Alex had told him who it was, but by that time, Mr. Woodson had taken several orders for the book, which made it impossible to back out of the agreement.

They reached the door, and he swung it open, allowing her to step inside first. He'd arrived over an hour ago to ensure the room was tidy, and would meet the requirements any young lady would have when asked to translate a large amount of obscene material written in a foreign language.

And then had to stifle his inappropriate laughter at just what an odd situation he had gotten himself into. This was possibly the oddest, even including the time he'd managed to wheedle two ladies, married to brothers, into his bed. At the same time.

"The book is on the table," he said, pointing to where it lay. He hadn't opened it, so for the moment it looked as though it could be any kind of book, even a tedious, perfectly respectable one that detailed economies of agriculture, or uplifting essays written by people who'd long ago turned into dust.

Not scandalous poems illustrated by even more shocking pictures.

"Oh," she said, hesitating for a moment as though concerned the book might spring open and reveal its contents to her virginal eyes.

Which it would, of course, if she did what they'd agreed to.

"I suppose I will have to open it," she continued, sounding as though she were committing herself to battle.

He laughed at the thought. "You don't have to, you know," he replied, touching her on the arm. Keeping his hand curled around her elbow. "You can just turn around and walk out of here, and you will marry my brother and forget you wanted anything like to be overwhelmed or to make a difference or such like that."

She yanked her arm from his hold and turned to face him. Her eyes were narrowed, and he didn't think it was simply because she couldn't see clearly.

She looked furious. Nearly spitting mad, and it made the color in her cheeks deepen and her chest move up and down in a most delightful way as she breathed, and her mouth was pressed into a thin line, and all he wanted to do was gather her up into his arms and draw her toward him and lower his head down—and down some more—and kiss her thoroughly.

"Is that a challenge, my lord?" she asked, raising her eyebrow, just the one, as she spoke. "Because I am not going to withdraw from our bargain, no matter that looking at that book again"—and she punctuated her words by pointing an accusatory finger to the book in question—"is the most scandalous thing I have ever done." She stepped toward him so now if he wanted to—which he did—he could easily draw her into his arms and kiss her.

But he did not.

He held himself still, his fists clenched at his sides, willing himself not to act on his own instincts, which were to take this woman and brand her as his own. He'd never had to not do what he wanted to, and it was only the image of his father's tenants starving and regarding him with accusatory eyes, as well as how Bennett would look, that made him freeze in place, every muscle rigid with the need to move. To sweep her into his arms and kiss her and touch her soft curves.

"You'd best get working then," he said, the words emerging from his clamped jaw.

AN HOUR INTO the work and Eleanor was regretting agreeing to Lord Alexander's bargain.

Not because she was shocked, though she certainly was—she didn't know human beings were quite so creative as well as flexible—but because translating medieval Italian was nearly as boring as listening to Ida discuss ancient druidic rituals.

Which is to say, very boring indeed.

She dropped her pen on the table, removed her spectacles—they'd long since passed the time when it mattered, given what they'd seen and done together—and rubbed at the spot between her eyes. Lord Alexander was seated opposite, his long legs stretched out in front of him, his feet nearly touching hers.

She knew that because she'd stretched her toes out at one point and come into distinct and unsettling contact with him.

It hadn't helped that he'd raised a brow and given her a sly look when she yelped in surprise.

"How is it going?" he asked.

She shook her head and put her spectacles back on.

His lips drew together into a thin line as his gaze traveled over her face. "If this is too much, if the work is too difficult . . ." he began.

"No, it's not," Eleanor said, her words clipped.

She dropped her hand onto the table. "It's just that I never thought such scandalous material would prove to be so onerous."

His mouth curled up into a smile, and she was transfixed at the sight. That mouth, those lips, had been on hers. And she couldn't stop thinking about it, not even when she was wrestling with the proper translation for a body part she shouldn't even know about, much less in a second language.

That was probably why the work felt dull. She would much prefer to be walking somewhere with Lord Alexander, having his looming presence near her, finding out more about him. And his brother, of course, she added hastily.

She sighed at that thought, picking up her pen again. She was here to do something good, even though this was an oddly circuitous way to go about it.

"You really don't have to do this," he continued in a soft voice. He moved his hand, which lay on the table, forward as though to take hers, but stopped a few inches shy of where her hand lay. "It was a whim. I am not one who plans ahead very often. That is, ever," he said, punctuating his words with a self-deprecating chuckle.

"Whereas I don't even know how to plan. I would never be allowed to, you see," Eleanor replied, putting her pen down again. It seemed she was going to continue to be distracted by Lord Alexander—she should just succumb to it, since her brain was so determined.

"I've never thought of how hard it must be to be

female," Lord Alexander said in a musing tone. "To be squired about constantly, to have one's movements always monitored." A pause. "To have to wear a certain color because of one's status in society," he added, gesturing to her gown. He tipped back in his chair, leaning on just the two back legs in the most cavalier display she'd ever seen.

And wasn't that depressing. That a gentleman balanced on a chair was untoward. It just proved how boring her own life was. Perhaps she should take up some of those druidic ceremonies.

Or the activities depicted on the pages of the book, a sly and incredibly brazen voice whispered inside her head.

"That is why ladies get married, isn't it?" Eleanor said, keeping her voice as light as possible. Not as though she was entertaining images of him and her doing some of that. Another thing that married ladies could do, not always necessarily with their husbands in Lady Vale's case. "So we can be freer than we were before? There is certainly no other advantage," she continued, only to stop short as she realized that her jest rang true for her.

There was no advantage beyond helping her family out of a scandal. Ensuring that her younger sisters could also settle into marriage so they could wear non-white colors. Though if just one of her sisters fell desperately in love, and was able to marry the gentleman of her dreams because of Eleanor's own sacrifice, it'd be worth it—wouldn't it?

It would, a voice that was far less compelling than that earlier one said inside her head. *It would have to be*, the voice continued, more firmly than before.

"I should finish up here and then be on my way. My maid is likely fretting," Eleanor said, dropping her gaze back to the page she'd been working on. Knowing that no matter what was on the pages, however shocking it was, it was less shocking than what was happening in her own thoughts.

Keenly aware of him still watching her across the table.

*Lady Eleanor's Good
List for Being Bad:*

---

*Be open to new experiences,
no matter how shocking.*

Chapter 12

*W*here have you been?" Olivia demanded as soon as Eleanor and Cotswold walked inside. Ida rolled her eyes and crossed her arms over her chest.

Well, she couldn't very well answer that, could she?

"At the bookshop," she said. She could partially answer it, at least.

Cotswold removed her wrap and walked upstairs, folding it as she went. Eleanor glanced up as her maid ascended to the second floor, wishing she had the freedom to just walk away whenever she wanted.

Then again, Cotswold also had to stay up to help Eleanor out of her gowns after parties, meaning she was often up until two or three o'clock in the morning. And then up again at ten o'clock to bring Eleanor her chocolate.

So there was something to be said for being a duke's dowered daughter—she would have to marry someone she didn't know, but she wouldn't have to lose sleep or bring hot beverages to anyone.

Unless her husband demanded she do so.

And there she was, back again in her conundrum. At least a maid wouldn't have to promise to honor and obey until death did them part.

"Lord Carson was here. He was surprised to learn you were out. He left you flowers—look!" And Olivia pointed grandly to where Eleanor could see a large bouquet of flowers—lovely yellow roses with a few random white flowers joining the group sat in a vase on one of the hallway's side tables.

"He was here?" Eleanor said, withdrawing her spectacles from her purse. Because wasn't he too busy to be bothered trying to get to know her? Wasn't that why his brother had taken on the duties of courtship by proxy?

Did that mean he was no longer busy, and her adventure, her translation, and all of her frankly inappropriate feelings would be cut short?

Please don't let him be less busy, she thought selfishly.

"He was on his way to some business meeting or another, he said, and he just had time enough to stop by and ask after you and leave the flowers." Ida recited the facts as though they had come from one of her books. Flatly, without emotion.

Perhaps that was why Eleanor always found Ida's monologues—they couldn't be called conversations, there was no conversing—so trying. She didn't modulate her tone at all, unlike Olivia. Maybe she was overcompensating for their other sister's exuberant spirit?

But now wasn't the time to try to untangle the dynamics of sisters.

"Ah, so I was a convenient stop for him on the way to somewhere else," Eleanor said, knowing she was being unfair—after all, she didn't want him to stop going somewhere else, if possible, she'd like him to go far, far away—but unable to stop the piqued tone that crept into her voice.

"It is not as though you were here," Olivia pointed out. Correctly, if annoyingly. "And he wouldn't take tea, even though Mother asked." She grinned. "I wonder if Mother would get Lord Carson's tea correct? Perhaps we should have another bet."

"That presumes Lord Carson will return for tea at some point in the future," Eleanor replied. She walked over to the bouquet and leaned in close so she could smell the roses. They were beautiful up close, each bloom in the prime of its growth.

Only to be cut and placed in a vase, not allowed to continue to survive in nature.

And would she be seeing everything now through the lens of impending marital shackles? When even the sight of beautiful flowers made her throat close over and her eyes prickle?

Maybe she was just allergic.

Or maybe she was just lying to herself.

"Are you all right, Eleanor?"

She heard Ida's voice from a distance, muted through the rushing of thoughts in her head. She noted that Ida sounded, for once, as though she was concerned. She must look terrible if her pedantic sister was worried about her.

"Eleanor?"

Olivia's voice reached her through that same hum of emotion. Her sister stood directly in front of her, hands on her shoulders shaking her gently.

"It's fine. Thank you," she replied, looking at both Olivia and Ida. "Where is Pearl, anyway?"

Not that she was concerned that Pearl would follow Della's lead and elope, but since that time Eleanor had found herself constantly checking her sisters' whereabouts to make certain they were safe. That they hadn't done anything foolish, that they wouldn't bring even more scandal to the Howlett family.

That would take more than just Eleanor marrying Lord Carson. They'd have to find an unmarried royal personage or three just to right the balance.

"She is practicing playing cricket in the garden," Ida said with a sniff. A return to her normal condescending tone.

"Ah," Eleanor said. She took a deep breath, swallowing against the lump in her throat, then took Ida's and Olivia's arms. "Let's go find her."

Eleanor resisted the urge to squeeze her sisters' arms, to remind herself why she was going to do what she was going to do.

Because she was going to do it. It didn't matter that she'd rather be in prison, or a maid, or be forced to wear white for the rest of her life. Her family needed her, her sisters deserved their own chance at happiness, and it didn't matter how stifling Eleanor found the prospect of marriage. Even to Lord Carson, who seemed like an honorable man with a staunchly supportive brother, a man who'd taken time out of his very busy schedule to bring her flowers.

If she didn't anchor the family in respectability, there was no telling what would happen to her younger sisters. She didn't want to think about it, but her father could die at any moment, leaving the four unwed Howlett sisters with nowhere to go and nobody who wanted them.

So she would do it.

If she could just prolong the moment until she had finished the translation, gone to a gambling house, perhaps seen Lord Alexander play cricket again. If she could just do a few of those things, the things on her precious list, those memories would have to suffice for the rest of her life.

That was all there was to it. She was going to savor this time, jump into the moments—however few there were—with enthusiasm and interest.

She felt a half smile on her lips as she thought about it. The next time she saw Lord Alexander, she would tell him that not only was she going to continue, but that she wanted more.

More wasn't so much to ask, was it?

Damn it, he had never had to resist temptation so—so thoroughly before. He'd watched her from across the wooden table, her spectacles perched precariously on her nose, her tongue darting out to lick at the corner of her mouth as she was writing.

He wanted to lick at the corner of her mouth too.

He had returned home from the bookshop

and stalked immediately to his father's study—it wouldn't be occupied. His father left everything to Bennett, and Bennett conducted all his business in the library.

The study had become Alex's refuge, although what he was refuging from was something he shouldn't be thinking about.

But he was. He absolutely was. About her and the past few hours, watching her translate the poetry as he tried very hard not to stare at the accompanying illustrations and wish he could enact them with her.

But then she had made some comment or another about marriage, and being female, and her lost tone made him feel something he'd never felt before. Sympathy? Or even empathy? Far more than just lust. Which he had also, but she was an attractive female, after all. He wasn't the one with poor eyesight; he could see plenty of her and his vivid imagination could make up the rest.

Whatever the emotion was, he felt it, and he didn't like it. It was too complicated, and he didn't like complications. Simplicity was the best way to operate—one wanted something and one took it. Or took her.

This, this discovering that she was a person, a person with concerns and desires and a fierce intelligence he'd seriously doubted only days before—that was all bad. He was supposed to be persuading the lady to enter into marriage with his brother, a simple equation of one lady plus one gentleman equaled a beneficial relationship for both families. Perhaps even for the parties involved.

Not this wanting to learn more about her, to discover just how complicated she could be. That she was far more than the sum of her white dresses and her poor eyesight and her delight in puns.

"Alex?"

He heard Bennett's voice from far away, and he had to shake his head to clear his thoughts.

Bennett stood directly in front of where he was seated, his brother's clothing indicating he'd just come from some business meeting or another. As though he didn't know that already simply because Bennett was always coming from some business meeting or another.

Sacrificing his time, agreeing to make the ultimate sacrifice, joining his life with a person he didn't have the luxury of choosing for himself.

And then suddenly he had an inkling of how she must feel, moved about the marriage chessboard like a pawn. A pawn dressed in white, stepping where she was told to go.

"I hate chess," he muttered as he rose. "Were you saying something to me? I was thinking about—" *her*, he wanted to say, he very nearly did say, but he couldn't do that to Bennett, not when so much was riding on the union.

"Thinking about whatever you please, I daresay," Bennett replied, his tone envious as well as amused.

"Yes, that," Alex replied.

"I was. You must have been thinking very intently on something, I said your name a few times."

Complicated emotions could certainly clog up one's brain.

"What is it?"

Bennett's expression turned odd. Was he in the throes of complicated emotions as well?

"I stopped by the duke's house today."

Oh.

"Oh?"

"And Lady Eleanor was out. I was—that is, I was wondering if she was with you?"

Well, you did ask me to keep company with her in order to convince her to marry you. Where else did you think she was?

"Uh, well."

"Because I've been thinking about it, and I shouldn't have asked you to persuade her to marry me. I should be the one doing that." He let out a chuckle devoid of humor. "I mean, she is to be married to me, after all, if you are successful. How odd would it seem if you were the one she spent this time with?"

No odder than having her translate frankly obscene poetry in clandestine meetings.

"Of course." He should feel relieved. He did feel relieved. That was relief he felt, wasn't it?

Perhaps he shouldn't answer that, not even to himself.

"Only," he began, not sure he knew himself what he was going to say, just that he was going to say it, "I don't believe she is quite ready for you to approach her yet. I want more time"—*to spend with her*—"to persuade her as to your character."

"My character?" Bennett said, sounding surprised.

And of course he would, since nobody had ever seen fit to question Bennett's character before.

"Lady Eleanor is, well, there is more to her than meets the eye," Alex continued, knowing at this moment he was speaking the truth. "She requires delicate handling." And he nearly winced as he said that, hoping Bennett wouldn't get the right idea about what he was saying. "And I think she needs more time to adjust to the idea of you as a husband. And you said yourself," Alex said, spreading his hands out in explanation, "that I am the brother most accustomed to getting ladies to do what I want." And then he did wince, but turned his head away so his brother couldn't see.

"More time," Bennett repeated. He paused as Alex nearly held his breath. What if Bennett didn't believe him? What if he decided to forge ahead with his own courtship?

Then he'd have lied for nothing, and he wouldn't get to help her find her joy. Or overwhelm her.

Or kiss her again.

Bennett shrugged, his expression relieved. "That is fine, then. I've got enough to deal with now anyway. Of course I will continue to dance with her and such, but I will leave the convincing to you." He raised an eyebrow at Alex. "Unless you're going to be taking her to more cricket matches."

"No, of course not." *Yes, of course he would.* He

hadn't missed her expression when she'd seen him shirtless. He had replayed that look many times in his mind as he thought about what it might look like if she got to see even more of him.

"Thank you. I do appreciate what you've taken on," Bennett said in a sincere tone, nearly making Alex confess his lie. Nearly.

But the thought of her, of her expression, of how he felt when he was with her, made him bite his tongue.

What was the worst that would happen? He would spend more time with her, and eventually she would be married to his brother and all would be right with their respective families. Money, reputation, and honor, all assuaged.

It was perfectly fine, he assured himself.

Lady Eleanor's Good
List for Being Bad:

Wear a color other than white,
off-white, ecru, cream, or bone.

Chapter 13

*Y*ou will make certain you speak to Lord Carson and beg his pardon for being out when he paid a call."

Olivia rolled her eyes behind their mother's back as she spoke. The duchess was fussing with Eleanor's hair, which was making Cotswold nearly dance with anxiety.

They were in Eleanor's room, preparing to go to yet another party. Eleanor wanted to roll her eyes at herself now; when had going to parties become such an onerous chore?

Perhaps when she realized she was being sold off to the highest bidder? Or when she felt as though she was unremarkable except for her family name and the scandal attached to it?

Or when she had more questions than answers?

But it was her duty to attend the parties, no less a responsibility than Cotswold having to keep Eleanor's clothes tidy, or the scullery maid to light the fires.

At least she didn't have to iron or kneel in front of sooty fireplaces.

Pearl was still playing cricket, thank goodness, and Ida was off lecturing the mice on proper cheese etiquette or something, so at least two of the Howlett ladies (and their maids) weren't completely miserable.

Eleanor glanced down at her gown, wishing it were any other color.

Although that would mean she was married. Or had joined a convent, neither of which she particularly wanted to do.

She had enough female companionship now, thank you very much. She didn't want to squirrel herself away with even more women.

What she wanted sounded so simple, and yet was so complicated—she wanted to be able to wear colors other than white, she wanted to feel joy, and she wanted to know what it felt to be free to make her own decisions. Not even the important decisions. She just wanted to be able to decide on a lemon ice rather than a chocolate one. To take a stroll in the afternoon to the bookshop without having to clear it with anybody. Without having to have accompaniment at all times.

"Have you heard a word I've said?" her mother demanded as she undid a curl that had taken Cotswold ten minutes to arrange.

"Yes, Mother. I should tell Lord Carson I am sorry I wasn't here to greet him, even though he had given me no indication that he would be visiting, and it seemed as though he was just stopping by on his way to another appointment."

Olivia clapped her hand to her mouth and uttered a quickly stifled snort. Even Cotswold allowed herself to smile, but it was tight, since her focus was still on that dratted piece of hair.

"Precisely," her mother replied in satisfaction.

Eleanor should add another item to her list: *Have her mother actually listen to her when she was speaking.*

"Olivia, do go and tell your father Eleanor and I will be down in a minute," their mother said over her shoulder.

Olivia darted another amused glance at Eleanor, then left the room.

"I don't understand why you told Lord Carson you needed more time anyway," her mother continued. Eleanor tried to edge away from her mother's fingers, which were still creeping toward her hair, before Cotswold exploded in a fit of lady's maid frustration.

"We know it is going to happen. Why delay the inevitable?" she said, not waiting for an answer from her daughter. Which she never did. Hence the listening to her daughter unattainable goal she'd added.

Why *not* delay the inevitable? Eleanor wanted to respond. Not that her mother would listen to her, but that was the whole point of this, wasn't it? To experience something that wasn't bland and merely tolerable. To do something good in the world, even if the good she was doing was highly salacious and entirely inappropriate.

To spend more time with Lord Alexander, who had the same feelings of uselessness she had, but the freedom she lacked. But who could allow her to share in his freedom, at least for a little while. Taking her to a cricket match, driving with her in the park, maybe eventually allowing her to choose her own flavor of ice.

To escort her to a gambling den.

When he'd first said it, she had thought it was merely something he was dangling in front of her, like a shiny toy. Not anything to actually play with, mind you, but something to tempt her with.

But why not? Why not do these things, all of these things, since she would never get the chance again? Since it was all, as her mother said, entirely inevitable?

"We're all ready," her mother said, nodding to Cotswold to open the door for them. Eleanor swept ahead of her mother eagerly, knowing that when she saw Lord Carson at the ball tonight that she would also see Lord Alexander. And she was going to insist that he fulfill his promises to her.

Before the inevitable happened.

"ALEXANDER."

Alex paused as he was about to accept his hat from their butler. His father seldom addressed him, and when he did, it was always to convey how deeply disappointed he was in his second son. He turned to see the marquis standing at the doorway to his study, his face set into its normal dour lines.

He wondered if his father smiled when he was with his mistress. He did not wish to find out. It was bad enough his mother was usually too anxious or too ill to do her duties as the lady of the house; to see another woman performing some of the duties of his mother would make Alexander furious, and he'd no doubt end up saying something that he would regret.

Had Bennett told their father that Alex wanted the chance to continue his acquaintance with Lady Eleanor? He wouldn't have. Would he?

"Step in here for a moment, if you please," his father continued, not waiting for Alex's reply, just walking back into the confines of the study.

Alex shrugged at the waiting butler, then strode across the hallway to the study.

He seldom entered this room. Not because his father was often there, he wasn't. He was usually with his second family. Alex had only discovered he had half siblings a few years ago. They were ten and twelve years younger than he, and there were two of them, a boy and a girl. He did regret never getting the chance to meet them.

No, he never came in here because it reminded him too much of the promise his father had had that he had thrown away. He could have been the one to make the deals and support the family business. He could have done what he was supposed to so that Bennett wouldn't have to sacrifice himself.

But he hadn't. He was just as selfish and irresponsible as he'd accused Alex of being so many times, and Alex couldn't stand the hypocrisy.

"What do you want?" Alex said, adding "sir" after a few moments.

His father frowned. "I know you are aware of my efforts on your brother's behalf. To get him married to the Duke of Marymount's daughter, whatshername."

"Lady Eleanor," Alex replied through a clenched jaw. His father couldn't even remember the name of the woman he was planning to pair his eldest son with for the rest of his life?

"Yes, well," his father said in a tone that indicated the lady's name didn't matter in the least, "now that Bennett is on his way to being married—I expect to hear the news of the engagement any minute now—it is past time for you to consider marriage as well."

Alex opened his mouth to respond, but discovered that for once, he had nothing to say. Because there was so much to say.

Not only did his father not seem to know that Lady Eleanor was reluctant to enter into the engagement, he thought that his second son should also get married.

"You are handsome enough to look at, I suppose, even if you seem to have no other purpose in life." His father's normal tone of disapproving disappointment didn't rankle as much as usual. Perhaps because someone else had taken the time to get to know him? To know that he liked cricket and puns and—and other things?

Kissing her ranked at the top of his current list, not that she would mention it.

"And there are plenty of young ladies with handsome dowries out there for you," his father continued. As though the man hadn't spent his whole life being disappointed in Alex—was he so unfeeling that he would want another person to have the chance to be as disappointed as he was, with no recourse to get out of it?

Well, that he could answer.

"No."

Alex didn't even bother thinking about what he was saying, he just said it. He'd never said no so directly to his father, but then again, his father had never asked him anything to which that was a response. Normally the questions were, "Why can't you be more like your brother?" or "Why are you wasting your life?"

Things that didn't have such a simple answer as no.

"No?" his father replied, the color in his cheeks becoming a bristly red. Not quite chaise-longue-ish. More like an angry tomato.

"No." Alex punctuated his word by crossing his arms over his chest and nodding his head definitively.

"And why not?" his father demanded.

Because I don't want to be a pawn in your manipulations like Bennett. Because I am just beginning to realize I can be more than a rakish dilettante. I can do something. I can try to help people.

By selling them erotic literature? a sly voice said in his head.

Hush. It's early days yet.

But Alex didn't say any of that, not to his father, who wouldn't understand, much less listen in the first place.

"Because I will not. When or if I decide to marry, it will be because I wish to. I won't be—" How had she put it? "It just doesn't seem fair that external forces should dictate who I spend my life with. I want to make my own choices." It wasn't precisely what she'd said, but he didn't think his father would appreciate Alex's demurral of white gowns. So he left that part out.

"Not fair?"

Was it something everybody did, repeating the words of another person, and Alex had never noticed it? Had his reputation for blunt speaking only happened because he didn't parrot people's words back to them like a—well, like a parrot?

"What do you plan on doing instead?"

As though it was either/or. *Marry or go discover a cure for your mother's illness. Marry or jump out of a high tower to your death.*

Marry or never have the chance to find out on your own if there is someone in the world you can love who might love you back.

"As I always do." Alex raised his eyebrow in a move calculated to make his father even more furious. "Visit my clubs, indulge in a few indiscretions." Even though that thought held no appeal now for a shortsighted reason he chose not to admit to himself. "Go to parties. Help Bennett when he needs me."

His father's lip curled at the last words, as though

he couldn't possibly imagine what Alex could do to help his older brother.

"Fine," his father said at last, startling Alex so much he had to drop his eyebrow.

"Fine?" Alex repeated.

Dear lord, now he was doing it.

"But as soon as Bennett is married, I will expect you to get yourself engaged to a respectable young woman. I've drawn up a list," his father added, gesturing to a piece of paper on his desk.

How had he had time, what with never being home and neglecting all his familial obligations? Impressive.

Though he would not be sharing his admiration with his father.

A deadline. Like the one Lady Eleanor was chafing against. The same one, in fact. When she was married to his brother, he would have to at least consider marriage also. It wasn't as though he had a plan for his life, after all, beyond what he'd said to his father and thought about himself.

Maybe he could find satisfaction and solace in marriage, even if it were to a woman of his father's choosing.

But if he could just delay Bennett's marriage, he could figure out what it was he truly wanted in life. Even more motivation for spending time with Lady Eleanor. He wanted to talk it out with her as he did not want to talk it out with Bennett— Bennett was too invested in all of it. He would be biased about the eventuality of it all.

She would understand precisely what he was

feeling. His frustration, his anger, his fury at being told what to do.

"Am I allowed to leave now?" he said after a few moments.

His father's color was still high, and he looked as though he wanted to say more.

"Yes. Go."

Alex didn't speak in response. He turned on his heel and stalked out of the room, knowing that while his father might be disappointed in him, he was not disappointed in himself. For once.

And he was very much looking forward to seeing Lady Eleanor at the party that evening.

Lady Eleanor's Good
List for Being Bad:

Ask the questions you want to.
Not the ones you think
you should.

Chapter 14

"Lord Carson is just over there," the duchess said, nodding toward the right. As though she believed Eleanor could actually see anything that far away.

Although she probably did believe that, if she thought about it at all. Which she did not.

Eleanor dutifully glanced in the direction of her mother's head nod, her breath hitching as she saw the fuzzy form of a very tall gentleman.

A gentleman who was even more impressive on the inside, she was beginning to discover, than the outside. Which was certainly impressive.

"He is walking toward us," her mother said in a low tone, her fingers squeezing Eleanor's arm.

Was *he* walking toward them as well? Eleanor squinted, wishing she could just see properly, or at the very least, wear her spectacles in public. It was remarkably difficult to pay attention to anything when it was all murky.

"Your Grace, Lady Eleanor." Lord Carson stood in front of them, close enough that Eleanor was able to see him clearly.

Lord Alexander must have remained back in the corner, she thought in disappointment. *Perhaps he is bored with having to keep company with me.*

But even she knew that wasn't the case. She'd seen the glint in his eyes, the way his gaze traveled to her mouth when they were speaking. How, when he hadn't known she was looking, his expression had turned almost feral as he looked at places other than her face. His look had felt almost tangible, as though it was his hand that was on her shoulders, her breasts, her skin.

She had to admit she wished it were. The book she was translating was adding a lot of details to her very active imagination, not to mention giving her plenty of list material.

"It is a pleasure to see you, my lord," her mother was saying. "Thank you for stopping by this afternoon. Lady Eleanor wishes to say something about that. Don't you, Eleanor?" her mother added, punctuating her words with an elbow to Eleanor's rib.

"Yes, my lord," Eleanor replied. She glanced at her mother, whose expression already looked impatient. "I am sorry I was not at home this afternoon. The flowers are lovely."

"Of course. I hadn't let you know I would be visiting. I just—well, I saw the flowers as I was on my way to a meeting, and I thought you would like them."

"She does, my lord," Eleanor's mother reassured him. As though Eleanor was about to declare her hatred of all yellow roses.

"I do." Eleanor smiled ruefully at Lord Carson. Could she help it that she preferred the more dangerous, taller, less respectable brother?

"Could I entreat you to dance with me, Lady Eleanor?" Lord Carson accompanied his words with a gesture toward the dance floor, which was just beginning to fill with other guests. Of course, Eleanor couldn't make out who was out there, but she could see the dark colors on the gentlemen and the lighter colors on all the ladies.

"Yes, thank you," Eleanor said, holding her hand out for him to take.

"I am sorry I did not see you this afternoon, but I am hoping you would care for a drive tomorrow? Say around three o'clock?"

She had thought she'd be going to the bookshop again for more translation work at that time, but she certainly couldn't claim a prior commitment.

"Eleanor would enjoy that very much," her mother answered for her.

Besides which, if she just hesitated, her mother would answer for her anyway.

"Excellent," he replied. He didn't look to her for confirmation; he just spoke directly to her mother.

Then he did look at her, holding his arms out for her to step into just as the music began. It was a waltz, which meant they would have to—that is, be able to speak together, rather than getting separated by the dance.

"I've been thinking about our conversation of a few weeks ago."

The one where she refused him, at least temporarily? Wonderful. This wasn't going to be a polite exchange about the weather.

"Yes?"

"And I agree. About needing time. I realized after that I don't know you at all. I know that you are"—and he paused, as though searching for the right word—"pleasant," he said at last, making Eleanor's heart sink. "And that you are devoted to your sisters."

Because I am willing to marry someone to save them?

"That is all true," she said. "I know very little of you as well, my lord."

"What do you know about me, Lady Eleanor?"

He was—well, it sounded as though he was flirting with her. His gaze was intent on her face, he held her a fraction closer than was absolutely necessary, and there was a searching look in his eyes that indicated his interest.

How could she help but feel flattered, even as she felt manipulated?

"I know that you are a busy man. You seem to be working very hard on—something," she finished at last. "I know that your brother admires you, and it seems as though he would not hide his feelings if he did not, so I am presuming you are a true gentleman."

"There is more to me than that," he replied, deepening his words with the addition of a warm smile.

She wanted to say the same thing back to him, but that wouldn't be polite. And she wasn't Lord Alexander—she couldn't just say whatever she wanted to.

"What do you want me to know about you, my lord?" It felt odd, but not unpleasant, to flirt in response. *Not unpleasant.* She couldn't be not average even inside her own mind.

"I love to dance," he said, his eyes crinkling up at the corners. He was attractive, she had noticed that, but until this moment she hadn't found him attractive. But now? Now she could say he was.

Had she made a terrible, tall mistake? Even if she did find him attractive, he didn't make her heart race. Or her skin tingle. Or anything close to overwhelming her.

"That is surprising to hear," she said. "Although less surprising than if you'd told me you did not like to dance while in the midst of dancing."

He let out a bark of laughter, one that made her feel more than average. He thought she was amusing, apparently. That felt good.

"That would be incredibly rude," he replied. "Something my brother might say aloud, but nothing I would ever say."

Right. He had to mention his brother also.

"And what else do you like?"

If he said foreign languages, particularly Italian, she was going to have a difficult time keeping her composure. Whether that meant shrieking with laughter or sobbing in despair, she couldn't guess.

He shrugged. "I haven't really thought too much about it before. I suppose I like strong tea, riding my horse, and solving problems." The last was said with a slight frown, as though solving problems had become more unlikeable. Or perhaps she was reading into it, since she knew something about what he was busy with, thanks to his brother.

"But you likely don't share those likes," he continued. "Besides tea. I haven't found very many ladies who like to solve problems."

She bristled. "Mostly because nobody has asked us to," she retorted, wondering if Lord Alexander's blunt speaking had rubbed off on her. Because she had never been quite so direct before meeting him.

Perhaps there was something to being that way. It certainly meant she had to worry a lot less about her choice of words.

"Of course," he replied hastily. "I was not meaning to—anyway, I apologize."

His words were said so sincerely she couldn't help but believe them.

"Thank you for that," Eleanor said, a smile accompanying her words.

"Of course." He sounded relieved. Probably because she wasn't prickly any longer.

The music stopped, and he bowed to her as she curtseyed. He wasn't as tall or as troublesome as Lord Alexander, but he was far more suitable, what with being the gentleman her parents wished her to marry.

But he wasn't the gentleman who still had to take her to a gambling den. Whom she was translating things for, a project that would do good, albeit in a decidedly scandalous way.

ALEX PLANTED HIMSELF in the corner, watching as Bennett danced with her. As he should. He had the strong urge to pop Bennett in the nose when he saw her expression tighten, as though his brother had said something with which she didn't agree. And then wanted to pop him in the nose again, but for a different reason, when he saw her smile.

Really, what was it about her that made him so different from usual?

She had a lovely, curvaceous figure he knew would be soft and lush under his hands. She was intelligent, amusing, and brave. He didn't know of any other women who would have taken on any of the challenges he'd presented her, from cricket matches to self-discovery to inappropriate translations, so easily and with so much courage.

Her face was pretty, but what made it breathtaking was when she smiled, or when she discovered some previously unknown truth. As though she was on an adventure all the time, and it was a pleasure to watch her learn.

He was not doing a very good job at making her seem just like every other woman he'd ever met. In fact, he could say with some confidence that he seemed to have fallen under her spell, and he didn't know what he could do about it.

Besides nothing. She was supposed to marry his brother. Their father would not take it well if Alex was the one to bring the Howlett dowry into the family—it was up to Bennett to lead the way, to solidify the relationship between the duke and

Alex's family. If Alex was the one to do it, it would be seen as a failure on Bennett's part for not being able to secure her.

"What are you doing over here, Lord Alexander?"

The woman's voice startled him from his reverie. It belonged to Lady Vale, a lady he'd spent some intimate time with the previous year. Her husband was much older, and Dorothea enjoyed Alex's vigor. As he did hers.

"Waiting for you, of course," Alex replied easily.

Even though he felt himself glancing over Lady Vale's head to see his brother and Lady Eleanor continue their dance.

"I was hoping you would say that." She looked around the room, her delicate nose wrinkling in apparent disdain. "This is a dull affair. I am certain there are other things that would be far more enjoyable, aren't you?" And then she swept her gaze pointedly down his body, the sly curl of her lips indicating just what she meant.

He experienced the frisson of attraction as he felt her gaze. Why not? Why not try to forget all of his incomprehensible attraction to Lady Eleanor in Lady Vale's arms?

"Perhaps I could escort you home and we could discover those more enjoyable things?" he said, deepening his voice.

Her eyes gleamed. "That would be lovely. My husband is out of town, you see, and I would appreciate an escort."

Alexander took Lady Vale's hand and tucked it into his arm, walking with her toward the entrance determinedly not looking in her direction any longer.

IT WAS DIFFICULT, even for someone with as poor eyesight as herself, not to notice when a particularly tall gentleman left the room.

And it was even more difficult when that tall gentleman was the only one who'd ever kissed her properly and who was also the brother of her future betrothed. And seeing him leave in the company of a woman who, a quick conversation confirmed, was Lady Vale, made it the most difficult of all.

She had never felt so—so heated before. As though she wished she could march up to both of them and demand what they were doing together.

As though she couldn't guess. She'd seen the pictures, after all.

"Are you all right, dear?" The question came from the Countess of Hartsdown, one of her mother's friends, since goodness knows her mother would never ask such a question.

"Yes, my lady, I am. I am just a bit tired." And angry, and jealous, and frustrated. She knew it wasn't fair, but she wished he was smitten with her as much as it seemed she was smitten with him. Or at least smitten enough not to escort another woman home.

But what claim did she have on him? None. Two kisses and a few inappropriate pictures was probably just a usual day for him, at least from the gossip she'd overheard.

"Actually, I think I should go home soon." Eleanor didn't see her mother anywhere about, but that was because she couldn't see. She presumed her mother was somewhere, no doubt sharing all the details of how her daughter had asked for more time when Lord Carson proposed. Or just sharing the details of the last trifle she'd eaten; either topic would be pursued with as much alacrity as the other.

"Can you tell my mother I have gone?" Eleanor said. Now that she'd said it, there was nothing she wanted more in the world—to go home, to lie in her own bed by herself, and try to talk herself out of this madness that seemed to have overtaken her mind. A single madness not shared by him.

"Are you certain that is wise?" It wasn't, of course. "Going home alone? Shouldn't you find your mother and tell her you wish to depart?"

Eleanor hesitated before replying, and the marchioness laughed. "Ah, of course. I understand completely." She was friends with Eleanor's mother, after all. "Let me send you home in my carriage."

"Thank you," Eleanor said, relieved that the lady understood.

She curtseyed and walked swiftly toward the entrance, hoping nobody would stop her, and she could just go home where she could be herself. Even though it seemed nobody else wanted her that way.

"You've changed your mind?" Lady Vale said, frowning.

Alex released his hold on the frame of the carriage and stepped back, putting his hand on the door in preparation for closing it.

"I have. Thank you, but I just cannot."

She shrugged, her beautiful face in a pout, as he swung the door shut, leaving him on the pavement.

He raised his hand to gesture to one of the servants to call the carriage. As he turned, a spot of white caught his eye, and he felt something inside of him—not *that* part, although that part was certainly intrigued—leap as he realized who it was.

Had he been waiting to see her again? Had he known he'd be seeing her?

"Lady Eleanor," he said, walking toward her. She held her cloak in one hand, the other holding a small purse, one so tiny it probably only fit a handkerchief. Or her spectacles. But not both.

"Lord Alexander," she said in a surprised voice, and then that part did indeed make itself known.

"Are you leaving? Where is your mother?" he asked, glancing behind her. The only people he saw, however, were the various servants running for carriages.

"I left on my own. I am tired," she said, emphasizing the last word as though it had more than just that meaning. "My mother's friend offered to have her carriage take me home." She glanced to the servants waiting, as if about to summon the carriage. "And I thought you had already left?"

So she had seen him. Had she known what he was about to do? What did she think?

But he couldn't ask questions, not standing out here where anybody could see them. He took her wrist in his hand and stepped close to her, so close nobody could overhear their conversation. "Can I escort you home? I was just about to call for my carriage." Though even he knew that an unmarried lady getting escorted home by an unmarried gentleman was the height of impropriety.

Well, perhaps not the height—he could think of more improper things—but it was close to the top of the list.

"Are you certain?" she paused, and he saw a swath of emotions cross her face, and he wanted to know about each one. "Because I thought you were already—?"

"No," he answered in a firm tone. "I am not. I am here, with you. Right now. So I'll repeat myself. Can I escort you home?"

"That would be lovely," she said, her mouth widening into a smile that made all the parts of him feel as though they'd been caressed by the sun.

Caressed by the sun? That turn of phrase was even more egregious than some of what that poet had come up with. Though far less scandalous.

They stood in silence as they waited for his carriage, her glancing up at him every so often as though to check he was still there. It didn't feel like an awkward silence, however; it felt fraught with emotion, but not the unpleasant kind. More like an anticipation of what might happen. What should not happen as well, but what might happen.

He glanced over at her as they heard the hubbub of conversation behind them. Some other guests leaving the party, apparently. She stepped in front of him, making him into a shield from the eyes that might be looking their way, and he had to swallow against the swell of emotion that brought up in him. To protect her, to be her actual shield against something that might harm her—the feelings that summoned up in him were entirely new, overwhelming, even. Feelings he knew he would be reluctant to let go of, once the time came for him to do so.

"There you are, my lord," the carriage boy said as Alex's coachman brought the carriage up. He was grateful he'd chosen to ride in his own carriage this evening; Bennett's curricle was too flimsy to bring to an evening such as this one. There were too many other vehicles that might crash into it, and the curricle was made for speed, not for sturdiness. He'd given Bennett a lift over, but he'd already told his brother he'd have to find his own way home.

Not sharing that he would be escorting Bennett's potential betrothed home, scandalously alone in an enclosed carriage. And not just because he hadn't known at that time.

He spoke in a low tone to his coachman, giving him the address as discreetly as possible, placing Eleanor between his body and the carriage so nobody would see her. He paid his coachman's wages, and he'd had past interludes that required discretion, so he had no doubt the man would stay silent about tonight's adventure.

He held the door open for her as she stepped in, her hand on his arm for assistance. The spot where she'd touched him felt as though he'd been burned—more time in the sun, he could only presume with a wry twist of his lips—and he vaulted up after her, closing the door quickly after them.

Leaving them alone in the dark together. He felt his pulse quicken, and his cock harden, and he had to slow his breathing. Had he ever been so responsive to a female before? He didn't think so.

"I've given the coachman your address," he said, sitting down beside her and immediately stretching his legs out. This coach had been especially constructed to accommodate his height, and there was a greater than usual space between the front and back seats.

She looked at him with an amused expression, then stretched her legs out as well, uttering a sigh of satisfaction as she got herself into a position no respectable young lady would be seen doing in public.

That made him oddly pleased, that she felt so at ease around him that she would forgo convention in order to feel comfort.

Although he was anything but comfortable in her presence, he had to admit.

The lights from the street lamps cast sporadic yellow gleams onto her face and body, highlighting the curve of her smile or her breasts.

She wore an evening gown, of course, which

made her less covered up than he'd seen her on their outings or at the bookshop. Her skin glowed in the darkness of the carriage, and her scent—something light and floral—tickled his nostrils.

"Why are you leaving so soon, and without your mother?"

"Why aren't you with Lady Vale?" she said in what he recognized as a jealous tone. He wished that didn't delight him.

But it did.

"I wanted to dance with you, and I knew that people might talk if I did so." He avoided talking about Lady Vale; perhaps now wasn't the time to admit what he was planning with her. As though she didn't know already.

"And you didn't think to ask me yourself?" she replied in a short, brittle tone. "Why do gentlemen defer to other gentlemen when they could just ask the lady in question what she thinks?" She uttered a snort. "I know the answer to that—because most gentlemen, most *people*, in fact, believe that ladies can't possibly know their own minds." He felt her turn toward him in the darkness, and then she caught his hand in her own. "I wanted to leave because I wanted to spend time with you, not your brother, pleasant though he might be." She paused, and then spoke in a slower tone of voice. "And then I saw you leave with her, and it hurt. It hurt, and it wasn't fair to anyone. Not your brother, at the very least." She exhaled. "I didn't want to compromise, so I decided to just go home. Only now you're here."

"What are we going to do about that? About us being together now?" he asked, squeezing her fingers. Feeling as though he was doing something he'd never done before, felt things he'd never felt before.

Which was true. He hadn't ever dallied with an unmarried woman—he'd kept himself to widows and wives such as Lady Vale. Nor had he ever felt as though he cared just as much about her brain as her body.

"What aren't we going to do about it?" she said in a tart tone, and then she pulled on his hand so he was forced to follow it, getting closer to her. "Your brother has made it clear he sees me as nothing more than a transaction to be ticked off. But you—you see me as something else. As someone else." And she tightened her hold on him. "That is important to me."

He felt her warmth, her softness, and he knew he was on the verge of making the biggest mistake he'd ever made.

But then again, so was she.

"Kiss me," she demanded, placing his hand at her waist.

Lady Eleanor's Good List for Being Bad:

Be bad. It's as simple as that.

Chapter 15

She didn't think, for once. She just *did*.

She plunged her fingers into his hair, drew his head down to hers, and lifted her face. His fingers tightened on her waist as he stared down at her.

"Are you certain about this?" he asked, his gaze on her mouth.

No. "Yes," she replied, craning her neck up even more to reach him.

She did admire his height, but she had to admit it was an impediment to carriage-kissing.

But the strain of it paled in comparison to how it actually felt when his mouth met hers—his lips were warm and firm, and his hand slid to the small of her back, tugging her up so she found herself half on his lap, one hand holding on to his hair, the other sliding up and down his arm.

His very strong, muscular arm, she couldn't help but notice.

She clutched onto that arm, onto his bicep in particular, her eyes closed, her head tilted back against his other arm. He kissed her, yes, but what was most enthralling to her was that she was kissing him back.

She licked at his mouth, and he opened for her, his tongue finding hers in what should be something entirely unpleasant but what was absolutely and totally not.

No wonder that Italian poet had so much to say about all this. She had to admire his skill; if she had to write some sort of poetry it would be:

> *Oh*
> *Oh!*
> *My goodness!*
> *Heavens!*
> *More, please*

So perhaps she shouldn't be so quick to castigate the poor poet who had to figure out a way to describe all of this—this feeling.

And now it seemed she had moved herself entirely onto his lap, her legs twisted to one side and dangling off the seat, her bottom resting right there.

And that feeling would require an entirely different poem, one consisting only of various moans, sighs, and exclamations.

He pulled her closer, and her breasts—somewhat bared because of her evening gown—pressed up against his chest, the fabric of his coat and shirt rubbing against her skin. She felt a tingling all over her body, both hot and cold as their tongues tangled, his large hand splayed against her back, holding her tight against him.

She was most definitely overwhelmed.

And now his hand was moving, sliding lower, along her hip to caress her bottom, a place she didn't know was quite so sensitive. Until now.

Her breasts ached, and she squirmed even closer into him, causing him to utter some sort of noise, she couldn't tell if it was dismay or delight, as she wriggled on his lap.

He drew back, breathing hard, leaning his forehead against hers. He slid his hand back up her back, resting it at her waist again.

The rest of her body immediately missed his touch.

She heard him swallow. "I didn't mean for this," he began.

She shook her head, removing her fingers from his hair and placing them on his mouth.

"I know you didn't." A pause as she discovered it was difficult to speak, what with how tight her chest felt, how her whole body wanted something she couldn't put into words. "But I did."

"You don't know what you're doing," he said. If he truly meant not to continue any of this, he would have pushed her back onto the seat. Instead, his grip tightened, and she felt the strength of his fingers on her arm, holding her to him. *Aha!* a triumphant voice shouted inside her head.

"I don't," she agreed. She took a deep breath. "But that doesn't mean I don't want to."

"You don't know what you're saying."

She felt an oddly welcome surge of anger bubble up through her body, and she moved herself over to her side of the seat, looking at him in the dim light. "You can't continue to think I am stupid," she said, keeping her gaze locked on him. "First you say I don't know what I am doing, then that I don't know what I am saying." Not that she did necessarily know what she was saying; for once, she hadn't thought it out, she was just speaking, letting the words flow as she felt them.

It was entirely freeing, and she wished she had adopted his mode of blunt speaking long before this. But if she had, she would have been ostracized by society and her parents wouldn't have wanted to marry her off to Lord Carson, and she would never have met Lord Alexander in the first place.

It was an equation of time and roads not taken she didn't think even Ida could unravel.

"But I do know that right now I feel entirely and absolutely alive." She lifted her chin as she regarded him. "I left the party this evening because it was dull. Everything seems more muted now. Now that I know what it is to attend a cricket match, of all things, or do something productive and useful with my education, even if it is translating scandalous poems," she added in an aside. "Or kissing you. I asked you to overwhelm me, and you have. But I can tell—I *know*, that there is so much more you can show me. Or that I can show myself," she continued, reasoning it out as she spoke.

"But I want you to be there as I do it. I want to find out more about this." And she gestured at the space between them, as though he didn't know just what she was referring to. "I don't want to end up average and pleasant."

"Average and pleasant?" he repeated, then shook his head as though annoyed at himself. "I'm doing it too," he said.

"Wha—?"

"Fine," he interrupted. He reached forward to take her hand, laying both their hands on his thigh. *His thigh.* "I don't want you to end up average and pleasant either." He uttered a rueful noise. "You're far from average, Eleanor."

"What about pleasant?" she heard herself say, then brought her hand up to her mouth to suppress her giggle. Although—why? And so she dropped her hand, letting herself laugh as she thought about how bizarre this whole situation was, and how she could never explain it to anybody.

He stared at her for a moment, then began to laugh also, until they were both curled in on each other, laughing so hard she was surprised she could breathe.

It wasn't that it was so humorous, because it wasn't. It was just—it just felt free, and open, and overwhelming in an entirely good way.

Their laughter subsided as the carriage began to slow, indicating they were approaching her house.

He straightened, raising his hand to push the stray lock of hair that had fallen onto his face.

"What adventure do you wish to go on next?" he asked, his tone low and intimate.

And now she just wanted to launch herself onto his lap again and kiss him for a few more minutes. Days. A *lifetime*.

She was in more trouble than even she suspected.

"A gambling den, I think," she replied instead, sitting upright in her seat as well, placing her hands in her lap as though she were paying a social call, not alone with a rakish gentleman in his custom-fitted carriage.

"You don't do things by half, do you?" he mused, and she could hear the admiration in his tone. Had she ever heard that before? She'd heard gentlemen admire her dowry when they didn't know she could hear. She'd also heard them admire the fact that she wasn't as hideous as her dowry could allow her to be. But she had never heard that kind of frank, unadulterated admiration.

"A gambling den, then. What about more cricket matches? Or are those too tame for her ladyship?" he teased.

The image of him shirtless, his muscles shifting in the sun, made her all squirmy again. "More cricket matches too, please," she said in a breathy voice.

He laughed again, only this time it wasn't as though it was in humor, but as in some shared secret.

The secret that she wished she could do nothing else but kiss him? That she very much enjoyed seeing his unclothed form?

That he knew just how to overwhelm her?

There was no time to even consider all of that as the coachman swung open the door. It seemed the carriage had stopped without her noticing, too immersed in her thoughts of gambling houses and naked skin to pay attention.

Lord Alexander—although perhaps she should refer to him as just "Alexander," given that she had sat on his lap, for goodness' sake—leapt out of the carriage and held his hand out for her to dismount.

She took it, smoothing the skirts of her gown as she did so, feeling her cheeks heat as she pondered whether or not anybody would be able to tell.

And by "anybody," she meant Olivia, the most curious sister it was possible to have.

Hopefully she could divert Olivia's attention when she mentioned she had danced the waltz with Lord Carson. Why couldn't Olivia be the Howlett sister to marry the eldest brother?

But no, it had to be the eldest sister who was chosen for the honor. Not least because Olivia couldn't even come out into society until Eleanor was safely married off.

Not a fair situation at all. No wonder Della had left. Although there would have been less drastic ways to combat that.

"Shall I take you for a drive tomorrow?" Lord Alexander asked as he walked her up the stairs.

"Tomorrow will not be possible," she replied, thinking of the promise her mother had made to Lord Carson. Who couldn't do anything other than pale in comparison with the improved version standing next to her now.

"Oh." He sounded disappointed and faintly piqued, and she wanted to laugh aloud all over again that this incredibly handsome, charming, and fascinating gentleman seemed to be jealous of time she spent elsewhere. Had not escorted the alluring Lady Vale home for some reason of his own, a reason she couldn't help but know had something to do with her.

"The next day," she said, patting his arm. His muscles tensed where she touched him, and once again, she had the urge to laugh.

Honestly, if she had known being this scandalous was also this enjoyable, she might have done it years ago. But she didn't think she would find scandal quite so entertaining if he was not accompanying her on the journey.

"I will see you the day after tomorrow, then," he said, bowing low over her hand as the door to the house opened.

"*Bene*," she replied in a mischievous tone.

ALEX SLAMMED THE door of the carriage, stretching his legs out to rest on the opposite seat.

If only he could slam the door to his emotions so easily.

Dear God. What had he done? More importantly, what had she done?

He could still feel where her body had touched his. Her fingers in his hair, her hand on his arm.

Her round bottom resting snugly on his cock.

The thought of which immediately made his cock stiffen, and he groaned, putting his palm on his forehead and raking his fingers back through his hair.

Why her? The one woman in the world he should not be interested in at all. There were dozens of equally lovely young ladies in London. Hundreds in England. Thousands and thousands in the world.

Why did it have to be her?

He hadn't thought about any of that while he was kissing her, of course. He hadn't been able to think of anything but the soft warmth of her mouth, her tongue sliding against his, her breasts pressed against his chest.

He regretted not sliding his fingers up to touch her breasts, cup the warm fullness in his hand.

No, he did not regret it. Touching her breasts would be wrong, and he would absolutely be in the wrong toward his brother if he did so.

Only he knew he was lying to himself. He did regret it, and what's more, he wasn't certain he would be able to resist if they were to find themselves in a similar position again.

Thinking of her voice when she'd said, "Yes," made his throat get thick. Would she say yes with as much want if he were to ask her if he could undress her?

Would she say yes when he asked if he could bury his cock inside her welcoming warmth?

God damn it. He would have to make himself say no—no to the temptation of her, the allure of her wit, the infectious way she laughed, how right and utterly appealing it felt to have her body close to his.

He had gone from being merely lackadaisical to a person who was actively engaged in thwarting his brother's plans.

"LORD CARSON IS arriving this afternoon?" the duchess said as Eleanor nodded to the footman holding up the teapot.

"As though you hadn't arranged it." Eleanor smiled at the footman and put milk and sugar in her tea.

"You do know that the season is over in a few weeks," her mother continued, gesturing to the footman to replenish her own cup. Ignoring her daughter's pointed comment. Like she always did.

"Yes, and you have to be engaged, at least, before the end of it or we will be even more delayed," Olivia said from the other side of the table.

As though Eleanor weren't acutely aware that her sisters' futures were resting squarely on her white-clad shoulders.

"And you don't want to lose him," her mother said, staring pointedly at Eleanor.

Don't I? she thought.

I do.

And if she'd thought it, perhaps she ought to say it, as Lord Alexander would.

"I know I said I needed more time, but I am beginning to wonder if there is that much time in the world." She spoke in a tone that tried to indicate she had just thought of the idea. Not that she had become fully persuaded of it over the past month or so. "I am not certain that Lord Carson and I will suit one another."

Mostly because she knew she was falling in love with his brother. But that she wouldn't share.

She couldn't believe she was speaking so boldly to her mother. To anyone, honestly.

Neither, at least according to their expressions, could her mother and Olivia.

"What do you mean?"

For once, her mother was actually asking her a question that didn't presuppose the answer.

"I mean," Eleanor said slowly, feeling how her chest was tightening at even the thought of saying something so undebutante-like, "that I do not wish to go driving with Lord Carson this afternoon. I mean that I would like to be unhampered by an engagement for just a bit more. That how you all are bearing down on me makes it feel as though I am a thing to be manipulated, not a person who could live her own life."

Her mother's mouth dropped open, while Olivia looked as though she didn't know whether to cheer or to slap her sister.

"Live your own life?" her mother said, her voice rising into a screech. Eleanor winced at the sound. "Your sister made it impossible for any of the rest of you to live your own lives, unless you plan on living your lives in penury and disgrace."

"It isn't that horrible," Olivia pointed out in a reasonable tone. "The worst that could happen is that we settle for gentlemen we actually like rather than gentlemen you and Father decide on for us."

Now Eleanor wished she could cheer for her sister.

"Lord Carson could be the man I am destined to marry, Mama," Eleanor said in a soft tone. "Or he might not turn out to be that man at all. I need to—to"—*be overwhelmed. To find my joy. To kiss a tall, blunt gentleman a few more times*—"make my own decision."

"Well," her mother said, getting to her feet, "I will have to go speak to your father about this. And you will not be allowed to go driving with Lord Carson this afternoon because goodness knows what you might say!" she said, as though that wasn't precisely what Eleanor wanted all along.

She left with as much fury as a scattered duchess could, while the footman glanced between Eleanor and Olivia and made his own way out of the room, leaving them alone.

"I'm sorry, Eleanor," Olivia said, stretching her hand across the table to pat the back of her sister's hand. "We haven't considered your feelings. We've all been selfish. Della worst of all," she said, an angry scowl on her face.

"Don't blame Della," Eleanor replied. "How can any of us know why she ran off with Mr. Baxter? I wish she had said something. Did she feel trapped into doing what our parents wanted? Was she so miserable?" The thought made her ache, that her sister, her closest friend, hadn't been able to confide in her until it was too late.

"She should have told us," Olivia replied, her tone implacable.

"She should have. But she didn't." *Just as I am not telling you everything*, Eleanor thought guiltily to herself. But what was there to tell? "She probably just wanted more." *Like me*, Eleanor wished she could say.

"What more could she want?" Olivia asked.

Eleanor couldn't answer that, but her thoughts could. When she imagined what more looked like, all she could see was a very tall man at her side, making her laugh, making her feel things she hadn't known she could feel before.

Making her feel special.

"You should do what you have to, Eleanor," Olivia said, nodding as she spoke. "If I were in your situation, being forced into something I didn't want to do—well, I don't know what I'd do. Just that I wouldn't do whatever it was that someone wanted me to," she continued in perfect seventeen-year-old logic.

"Thank you," Eleanor replied softly.

*Lady Eleanor's Good
List for Being Bad:*

Kiss him again.

Chapter 16

*E*leanor was first to arrive this time, Cotswold accompanying her, as was proper, and she insisted on staying at the bookshop at least until Lord Alexander arrived, to make sure her charge was safe.

Even though there was nothing safe about it.

Just being in this building made her feel a warm, illicit thrill that had nothing to do with books and translation.

Eleanor made her way to the back of the bookshop, keeping her gaze on the floor—not as though she could make it out clearly, but still—so that she wouldn't accidentally spot someone who knew her. Who would report back on her whereabouts to her mother. Or worse yet, her father.

You are visiting a bookshop instead of rescuing your family's reputation? Ensuring that your sisters can be properly and respectably wed?

The horror.

The night before, the duke looked displeased as her mother reported that she'd not allowed Eleanor to go driving with Lord Carson because of what she termed her "high spirits." He had glowered, but hadn't said anything more than "It's past time you resolve this business," as he'd skewered another piece of meat with his fork.

Eleanor felt herself wanting to retort, to tell him how "this business" was the business of her life.

But he wouldn't care. Neither of her parents seemed to even notice that Eleanor was away from the house for hours at a time. As long as she had Cotswold with her, and some sort of reasonable answer, he just didn't bother with finding out what was happening with her. He never had cared, or bothered, and she had no reason to think he would now, not when the rest of his daughters' futures were at stake. She wished she could ask him why he was concerned about who she married now, but she couldn't.

Because when had any of his daughters ever questioned him?

Except for Della, who had questioned everything, but hadn't spoken up when she'd gone and fallen in love, or whatever it was she was doing, with their dancing master. The dancing master who had taught the eldest Howlett sister how to waltz, how to curtsey, and how to properly behave in a ballroom.

Until the day he, along with her sister, had disappeared, quite improperly.

And here she was, courting scandal of her own, spending time with a gentleman who was not only the man who should not be courting her, but was the brother of the man who was. It was nearly a farce, only it was her life. She shook her head as she withdrew her spectacles from her purse and put them on.

The book was on the table, and she sat down in front of it, preparing to begin. Even though the sooner she began, the sooner she'd be finished, and then she'd have no excuse—flimsy or otherwise—to continue to come here, to meet with him in secret.

"Good afternoon," the man in her thoughts said as he ducked his head to walk into the room. He held a package in his arms and he met her gaze, smiling almost abashedly.

Goodness, what was in the package if he was embarrassed? She felt her cheeks flame at the thought.

His smile turned to a grin as he regarded her, and he placed the package on the table in front of her. "Open it," he said, gesturing to it.

"What is it?"

He sat down opposite her, shaking his head mockingly. "How will you know that until you open it?" he asked, crossing his arms over his chest.

She reached for the string holding the paper on the package, undoing it slowly, glancing up at him every so often. His gaze was fixed on where her fingers worked, and she pulled the string off, dropping it onto the table as she turned the package over to find the edges of its wrapping.

It felt like a book.

He hadn't seemed embarrassed at all about showing her that book, the one with the words and the pictures and all the things that made her squirm. So what kind of book was he offering her now that was making him behave so oddly?

If she were the woman she was just a few weeks earlier, she'd be turning fiery red and refusing to open the thing at all. As it was, she could feel her cheeks heat, but she also kept going, drawing the paper back to reveal—

"*Lemprière's Bibliotecha Classica*?" she said, reading the title. She looked up at him, her eyes wide. "How did you know?"

He shrugged, and that lock of hair fell down over his brow at the movement. "I wasn't certain, but you said you liked mythology, and so I asked Mr. Woodson what the most likely book would be for a person who had those interests."

He had gotten her a book. Not only that, but it was a book that meant something to her, a fact he couldn't possibly have known.

And yet he knew her.

"This is the same book I had when I was young."

His smile was one of relief, and she felt oddly honored that he cared so much that his gift be a good one. He cared for her. And what she wanted, not what he thought she should want.

"Mr. Woodson said it was the most popular of those type of books. I thought you might already have it, but he said this is a pristine copy, so I thought if you already had it, you wouldn't mind."

He spoke faster and faster as he explained, and her heart felt as though it was swelling inside her chest. With the exception of Della, nobody had ever considered what she might like when giving her a gift. Her other sisters tried, and she did have to admit to liking ribbons and candy and such, but those gifts weren't specific to her.

This one was.

"Thank you," she said, picking the book up and holding it to her chest. "This is so thoughtful." She couldn't help the sting of tears in her eyes as she spoke, and she saw when he noticed them; his expression got startled, and he appeared to wish to leap out of his chair, likely to run away.

But he didn't.

Instead, he rose, shoving that lock of hair back with an impatient hand. He strode over to her side of the table and touched her on the shoulder, gesturing to her to stand as well.

She did, still clutching the book.

He drew her into his arms, as though he wanted only to touch her as a friend would. A friend who had just given her the most thoughtful gift of her life.

She turned into his chest, the book an awkward impediment between them. She felt the tears fall down her face, and she tucked herself under his arm, fitting perfectly, even though he towered over her.

"Shh," he said, sliding his hands up and down her back in a soothing gesture.

Until it wasn't.

She felt it when the moment changed, and she withdrew just enough to place the book on the table, then returned to him, wrapping her arms around him to clasp her hands at the small of his back.

She lifted her face to his, only she couldn't reach him, and he lowered himself down at an odd angle, his hands at her waist holding her up. She stood on her tiptoes, and then their lips touched. Just barely, not nearly enough.

And then he hoisted her up and put her on the table, then placed his palms flat on its surface on either side of her. Effectively caging her in, not that she wanted to go anywhere.

"I have to kiss you," he said in a low, rough tone. Her insides felt all trembly at how desperate he sounded, and she gave a vigorous nod, tilting her face up in unspoken agreement.

His mouth crashed down on hers, his tongue demanding entrance to her mouth, access she granted eagerly.

And then his tongue was in her mouth, searching, licking, sucking, and she felt her knees weaken and was grateful she was sitting down.

His hands went from the table to her waist, holding her up, his thumbs stroking her waist, moving up her body to—

"Ohh," she gasped into his mouth as his fingers brushed the underside of her breast, that trembly feeling now turned to a torment of wanting something—she didn't know what.

Except she did know what. She'd seen those pictures, the one in the book; she knew just what she wanted. The satyr and the nymph, Ovid and Corinna, Alcibiades and Glycera. Him, her, them, together, wrapped around each other in whatever carnal way felt right.

No wonder that poet had tried to capture this moment in words, but there were no words—no articulate ones, at least—that could properly describe what she was feeling.

He raised his mouth and stared down at her, a triumphant expression on his face. "You like that, do you?" he asked, his thumb flicking at where her nipple poked up from her gown.

"You know I do," she replied honestly. Because he knew she would want the Lemprière, what kind of adventure she craved, how she wanted to be touched. That she wanted to be touched, not just tolerated from afar in a white gown.

His smile deepened as he lowered his mouth to her neck, kissing the area where her shoulder began. Biting the tender skin, then soothing the bite with a swipe of his tongue.

She held onto his shoulders, her head leaning back. Her breasts ached, and she suppressed a moan as his mouth moved from her neck to the upper area of her chest, pushing aside the fabric of her gown.

His fingers moved up to the top of her breasts, the palms of his hands finding her skin and stroking it.

Then he straightened, and she let out a soft noise of disappointment, only to exhale in surprise as he leaned her back on the table. Remarkably like Polyenos and Chriseis, if she was recalling it properly.

Her knees dropped over the edge, her whole back resting on the hard wooden surface. She was acutely aware that she was laid out in front of him, her chest rising and falling with her rapid breath, her feet dangling toward the floor.

He didn't move for a moment, his gaze traveling over her face and body with a ferocity that made her breathless. As though what he'd been doing hadn't been enough to rob her of breath in the first place.

"You are so lovely," he said, his voice a low rumble.

She couldn't doubt his sincerity, even though she didn't think many would agree with him. Now was not the time to point out that she had brown hair, blue eyes that didn't work so well, and a figure that was rather more than fashion would like.

"Thank you," she replied. "You're rather stunning yourself."

And he was, of course. She was grateful she had put her spectacles on, because it meant she could see him in all his glory, from that sun-streaked hair to the intent green eyes, to his long arms and lean, rangy frame.

His legs were likely as long as her entire self, or so it seemed to her.

But she couldn't do the calculations on that, not now, not when he was bending over her again, his legs nudging hers apart so he could stand between her thighs, leaning over her, his hands sliding over her breasts, his fingers finding her taut, aching nipple.

"I want—" she began, then bit her lip as she thought about what she wanted to say.

"I do too," he replied with a grin. He did, didn't he? That she could answer, thankfully.

He lowered his mouth to her skin, his fingers pushing the fabric of her gown free. It felt as though the fabric might tear, but at this moment, Eleanor did not care. She wanted his hands on her, wanted his mouth to kiss her, not just on her lips, but wherever they could reach.

And then the fabric didn't tear, it eased down and he let out a groan as he saw her breast pop out from the gown.

He licked his lips as he regarded her, and it felt almost—almost—as though he'd actually put his mouth on her.

But then he did do precisely that, and the truth of how it felt was so much more than just a look.

His lips closed around her nipple and he sucked, gently, his hand on her other breast, rubbing and plucking as he tormented the hard, aching flesh.

She heard herself moan, and she squirmed up against him, feeling his hardness against her, imagining what it would look like if someone were to draw a picture of them at this moment. As erotic and delicious as one of the pictures in that book. Alexander and Eleanor joining Hercules and Dejanire and all the other illicit lovers.

Her lying on the table, her legs wide, his body

planted between them, his head buried in her chest, his hands touching her skin, his hair falling forward to tickle her.

Her hands were in his hair, holding him to her, not as though he seemed reluctant to leave. He took his mouth off her and blew air onto her nipple, and she moaned again, only to swallow the noise as he took her breast in his mouth again. His tongue licking and sucking, making trails of heat all along her skin.

And then he drew back and looked at her, his gaze heavy-lidded and so filled with want, and he leaned forward again to kiss her, his hands now sliding down her body, pulling up the skirts of her gown to rest on her thighs.

His hands were on her bared skin now, his palms rubbing up and down her legs as he kissed her, his tongue a welcome assault in her mouth.

And then she heard him groan, and her whole body felt as though it was quivering, and she wanted all of it, everything she'd seen and read in that book, and she wrapped her arms around his shoulders and pulled his chest onto hers, the weight of his body a satisfying pressure.

But not satisfying enough, not for right where she could feel him lying against her.

"Please," she said, hoping he'd know what she was asking for when she wasn't even certain.

"It would be my pleasure," he murmured, sliding down her body, his hands trailing over her skin. He got off her, and the table, making her utter a low noise of dissatisfaction which turned to a sigh as he put his hands on her legs, his fingers moving up, pushing the skirts of her gown up to her hips. Lying wantonly on the table, not caring in the least. Because he had her where he wanted her, and she was where she wanted to be as well.

She was exposed, all of her, in front of him, and she could feel how she was wet down there, and wished she was ladylike enough to be embarrassed about it, but she wasn't. Not when she was so interested in what was going to happen next.

"I need to," he began, only to stop speaking as he placed his mouth on the inside of her thigh, his fingers holding her open to him. Every part of her was open to him now, her emotions, her wants, her desires, her whole self.

And he licked her, dragging his mouth on her skin to the juncture of her legs, sliding over so she could feel his warm breath right there, right where she was moist and wet and longing for him. Well. She hadn't seen this happening in that book, but she couldn't deny it was what she wanted.

"Please," she said again, putting her hands in his hair, twisting on the table as she waited for whatever it was he was planning on doing.

And then she cried out as he placed his mouth on her right there, greedily licking and sucking on her until she didn't know if she could stand the pleasure.

Could one die of pleasure? And why hadn't the book covered that, if it were possible?

He raised his mouth and blew on her, making

her shiver. He chuckled at her reaction, raising his head to look in her direction.

"I want to see you come apart for me, Eleanor," he said, his fingers digging into the soft skin of her thighs. Her whole body shrieking for him to stop talking and resume doing what he was doing, only she didn't know the words for what it was he was doing, nor was she entirely certain she could speak words in the first place. "Will you come for me, Eleanor?" he asked as he slid his thumb over to that sensitive spot he'd been kissing before. His thumb began to move, rubbing in an erotic circle that made her moan.

She could see his satisfied smile, and then she couldn't see his face anymore because he'd buried it once more between her legs, his mouth and thumb working together now, heightening the pleasure.

Every part of her was focused on that spot right there, the spot he was touching, and kissing, the spot that made all other thoughts fall away.

Her fingers were clutched in his hair, and she had to bite her lip from screaming her pleasure. Until—until it felt as though she were about to reach the top of a hill, and then his tongue did something, she wasn't sure what, and she reached the summit, a wash of pleasure coursing through her.

"Aaah," she moaned, bucking under his hands, which were smoothing her skin. Touching her there, only more gently now, as though knowing how she felt.

Her entire body felt suffused in it, in the joy of

what he'd done to her, and she lay on the table boneless. Knowing that if anyone should happen to walk in she would be completely and entirely ruined, far worse than Della, even, but not having the energy to care. More than that—it was worth it, to feel this kind of overwhelming feeling. This was what she'd wanted, even though she hadn't known it. But he had.

"Eleanor," he said at last, sliding up to lean over her body, dropping his mouth to kiss the sensitive spot under her ear—not that she'd known it was sensitive until just this moment—licking her neck, his hands gently putting her back into place.

"Oh," she sighed. "That was—that—oh," she said again.

She heard him chuckle as he dropped a final kiss to her mouth, a soft, sweet reckoning, then straightened, his chest rising and falling with his heavy breaths.

And she couldn't help notice there, there where the fabric of his trousers stuck out, where that thing was that seemed to be the focal point of so many of those pictures.

Was it as large as the rest of him?

That was not a question she should be having, she thought hastily, even as her mind was calculating just how big it was, given the angle of the fabric. And it was most definitely not a question she should ever find the answer to.

He put his hand on his chest, directly on his heart, and he reached forward with his other hand to pull her upright.

"I hadn't imagined," he began, then shook his head as though he couldn't finish. His cheeks were flushed, his eyes ablaze with what she knew was want. Desire. Passion.

"Me neither," Eleanor said with a smile, her fingers reaching up to smooth back that lock of hair. Her body tingled with awareness of what he had done, and where he had touched, and it didn't feel wrong, even though it absolutely should, given everything. "But what about—?" And she gestured vaguely toward him, feeling her face heat. As though now was the time she got embarrassed, which was ridiculous given everything that had just happened.

He shook his head. "I'll be fine. It was worth it to see you. You are gorgeous when you climax, Eleanor." He reached up to touch his mouth, licking his fingers. "You taste gorgeous too."

Oh, goodness. That was nearly as erotic as all the rest of it, watching him slide his fingers into his mouth to savor her taste.

Her breath caught, and she couldn't take her eyes off him, off his mouth, off his fingers that had done such wicked things to her.

And then he smiled and reached forward to slide the fabric of her gown back down over her legs, and she could breathe again.

"Thank you for the present," she said with a wry smile.

He grinned back at her. "I'll make certain to give you presents every time we meet, if that is the reaction."

And then they both laughed, entirely comfortable together, even though they shouldn't be. Couldn't be, if their respective family's plans were to remain intact.

"Well, that was intriguing. Overwhelming, almost," Eleanor said, reaching out to take Alexander's hand and scooting herself off the table to stand in front of him. Her skirts fell back down to a respectable height, and she regretted she wasn't still lying on that table while he continued doing what he had been to her. Perhaps if it had continued she could have done something to him as well.

Not as though she didn't know what those things were, thanks to the book.

Now that she knew more of what the poet was talking about, firsthand, she discovered she was looking forward to the translation.

Plus it meant she could spend more time with him.

Until it all ended.

*Lady Eleanor's Good
List for Being Bad:*

Explore.

Chapter 17

*A*lex sat back down in the chair opposite her, wishing he were less of a cad—which would mean he wouldn't have touched her in the first place—or more of one, which would mean he'd be continuing what they started to the inevitable end.

Anything but this in-between area, guilt warring with desire inside his head.

His cock was hard, throbbing with the need to thrust into her wet warmth. Perhaps he should have accepted Lady Vale's offer, although he already knew there was only one lady he wanted to fuck. And she was seated opposite him at this table, a lady clad in the white of her virginity, not to mention she wasn't supposed to be his at all in the first place.

He would just have to suffer.

"It's not your fault," she said, suddenly. As though she were reading his mind.

"Isn't it?" He spread his hands to indicate the two of them, alone in this room. "It is not as though you have a reputation as a powerful seductress."

"Hardly," she said ruefully.

"I didn't mean," he began, only to stop speaking when she chuckled without humor.

"I know you didn't. I know that somehow you believe me to be lovely, as you said earlier." And then her cheeks started to turn pink, only now he didn't find the color appalling in a chaise-longue way. Because it only made her prettier.

"You are. Anybody who says you aren't is lying," he said in a fierce tone, forgetting he shouldn't be speaking to her this way. Touching her that way.

"Then why does your brother have to have you woo me? If he cared at all, he would do the job himself."

He wanted to, but he didn't, really. He doesn't know you. He doesn't want to get to know you. He sees you as an obligation. But he couldn't say any of that, not without betraying everyone in the situation.

She shook her head, speaking before he could come up with some sort of reply. "That part doesn't matter, really. Because all of this"—and then she gestured between them, and he knew just what she meant—"keeps happening, and somehow I don't want it to stop. Even though I know it's wrong."

"I don't either," he said, admitting it to himself as much as to her.

"So what do we do about it?" She regarded him from behind her spectacles, the glass of the lens making her large eyes seem even more enormous.

He'd like to see her wearing only her spectacles. So she could see all of him.

"I haven't fulfilled all the parts of our bargain," he said. Watching as her cheeks turned even pinker.

"You haven't?" She sounded breathless again, and he felt his cock twitch in response.

"There is more," he said, raising his eyebrow, "and there will be no guilt. On either side." Even though there was, on his side. Because he did love his brother, but his brother—didn't love her.

And Alex was nearly certain he did. He nearly stumbled at the thought.

Dear god, he'd done the worst possible thing he could have: fallen in love with the woman his brother was supposed to marry.

His beloved brother who was only trying to do what was right; when all the time Alex was doing what was wrong.

But it wasn't wrong. It felt right, even if nobody but he and Lady Eleanor thought so. And he was as blunt in action as he was in speech. Which left him no choice, given how he felt about her.

"What do I get out of it?" she asked, tilting her head and giving him a sly smile.

"More of this," he said with a grin.

"Oh," she said, her tongue darting out to lick her bottom lip. "Oh," she said again, her chest rising more rapidly.

"And the gambling den too?" she added, a mischievous expression on her face.

"Absolutely. I promised to help you find your joy, Eleanor. I am going to do just that. All of it." And he didn't dare think of the future. He wouldn't allow himself to.

He hadn't thought this through, hadn't thought any of it through, but from the expression on her face, it didn't matter. It felt right.

He was doing what he'd promised to do, and she would continue knowing what joy and pleasure there was to be had in life. It would be enough. It would have to be enough. For both of them.

He stretched his hand across the table, holding it out for her to shake.

She laughed, then stuck her hand out as well. "To our bargain, then," she said. "When do we continue?"

That was a much better question than, "When do we end?" This question he could answer.

"Tonight."

"BUT WHY AREN'T you wearing white?" Pearl asked in a soft voice.

Olivia glanced at her twin, then at Eleanor. "Perhaps she needs a change," she replied in a knowing voice.

The chances of Olivia keeping Eleanor's rebellion quiet were slim. So slim she doubted anyone at the gambling den she'd be visiting later that evening would take her up on the wager.

"Needs a change from what?" Pearl asked, looking confused.

Cotswold glared at Eleanor, daring her to answer her sister's question. Cotswold hadn't known all the details, of course—if she had, she'd currently be sitting on top of Eleanor refusing to let her out of her sight—but she had agreed to let Eleanor have her adventure, since she knew as well as Eleanor did that it would be only temporary. That it wouldn't cause a permanent scandal.

But that didn't mean Cotswold had to like it.

"A *change*." Olivia emphasized the word with all the enthusiasm she could muster.

"I might have told our mother that I wanted to make my own choices in life," Eleanor said in a deliberately low tone. "And tonight I am going to a place that young ladies usually do not. It isn't entirely respectable, but it's not unrespectable."

And that was the most prevaricating she thought she'd ever done.

"Huzzah!" Pearl yelped, making all three of the other ladies in the room stare at her. She blinked at them in confusion. "It is just that—well, if you can't do what you want, then what are the chances we will be able to?" Pearl continued in a much-softer voice. "What would happen if Olivia or I fell in love with someone our parents said was unsuitable? Would we have to just walk away from love?"

"I didn't know you had such strong opinions about it," Eleanor said, reaching out to stroke her sister's cheek. "And it's not as though I am going to cause more scandal. I promise that." He had promised as well. Even though he had also—well, she couldn't think about that, or her sisters would wonder what was setting her ablaze. "It is just that I want to see more of the world than a few ballrooms and museums."

She wouldn't tell her sisters—nor Cotswold, for that matter—that Lord Alexander was taking her to a gambling house that evening. There was only so much honesty she could muster.

"And it's not as though Eleanor is tromping around in a red dress or anything," Olivia said, sounding as though she wished she could tromp around in a red dress.

Eleanor looked down at what she was wearing. It wasn't scandalously red, but then again, it wasn't demurely white either. It fit her figure perfectly, making her admire Cotswold's skill with a needle—it had been a discard from their mother, who thought it made her look "like a blueberry."

The gown was made of printed blue satin, discreet roses making the relatively plain gown seem sumptuous. White lace edged the neckline and the sleeves, while darker blue ribbons encircled Eleanor's waist. Cotswold had dressed her hair in a more mature style and had found dark blue gloves that went past Eleanor's elbows.

She looked at herself in the glass, her sisters' admiring faces behind her, and smiled at the reflection.

The woman she saw looking back at her wasn't nondescript. She was . . . *descript*, if such a word existed. She looked as though she was fully capable of making her own decisions, would live a joyous and wonderful life, and could wear colored gowns anytime she felt like it.

She looked, in short, as though she had made a

delicious bargain with an altogether too-tall and too-handsome man.

Olivia and Pearl both got up to stand behind her, one on either side.

"You look marvelous," Olivia said in an admiring tone.

"You do," Pearl echoed.

"You be careful," Cotswold warned, the pleased expression on her face showing the Howlett sisters' admiration had been appreciated.

"I will," Eleanor promised, hugging her sisters and taking her purse from Cotswold's outstretched hand.

"And you'll have to tell us all about it," Olivia said. "Because how else will we know what we have to live up to if you don't share the details?"

Eleanor laughed as she walked out the door, glancing up and down the hallway to make sure nobody—meaning her parents—was about.

She stepped down the stairs feeling as full of emotion as she ever had.

This was life. This was what she wanted.

Would she be able to turn it away when it was time?

She couldn't answer that now. Wouldn't answer it either.

What she could answer was that yes, she was going on a clandestine journey to a place no young lady should go with the entirely wrong gentleman.

And she had never been happier.

ALEX HEARD THE quick knock on the carriage door and swung it open, reaching his arm out to help her inside, quickly, before anyone saw her.

And then felt his throat thicken as he caught a glimpse of her.

She looked—radiant. Her gown was some sort of dark color, and her hair was piled on top of her head, making her look like a queen.

The gown was cut low in front, giving him a view of her breasts, and suddenly it wasn't just his throat that was growing thick.

"You look . . ." he began, then shook his head.

"What?"

He heard the anxiety in her tone, and rushed to reassure her. "Beautiful," he said, rapping on the roof of the carriage so the coachman would know to get moving. He crossed over to sit on her side as the coach began to move.

"Do you think that is a good idea?" she asked pointedly. "For you to sit next to me? We can't just—" And then she stopped, as though even saying the words was too shocking for her.

Even though she was alone in a carriage with him heading to a gambling den, a place no decent young lady would know about, much less frequent.

"We can't just what?" He leaned over and grazed her lips with his. "Kiss like this?" And then he grasped her upper arm and kissed her again, deeper this time.

He heard her make some sort of approving

noise, and she curled her fingers in his hair, her tongue darting out to lick his mouth.

She broke the kiss and placed her palm on his chest, her fingers sliding under his jacket in what he thought must be an unconscious caress. "We should not start all this again," she said, "or we will never reach our destination."

"I suppose that depends on what destination you want to reach, Eleanor," he replied. He didn't press the matter, however, removing his hand from her arm and clasping his fingers together to prevent himself from touching her.

From finding out just what destinations they could reach together. From bringing her to that place where she broke apart, her soft sighs of pleasure the most delicious thing he'd ever heard.

"I brought money so I could gamble," she said, turning her head to gaze out the window. He noticed her fingers were knotted together too. He wasn't the only one affected by what they had been doing, or more importantly, were on their way to doing.

Not that he didn't know that already; he could tell, not just because she'd asked him for more, but also because of how her chest rose and fell more rapidly, her cheeks turning pink, the desperate need of her fingers on him.

Fuck, and now his cock was throbbing inside his trousers and the last thing he wanted to do was— was anything that wasn't removing all of her clothing and making her scream with pleasure.

What would it sound like if they were in a bed with no one around to hear? If he could bring her to climax with his mouth and then again by thoroughly fucking her?

What was he doing?

Oh, of course. Fantasizing about the last woman in the world he could possibly have. And here his father had always said Alex didn't aspire to anything.

"Do you know how to play?"

That did not come out the way he wanted.

"Cards, that is," he said, before he accidentally asked her if she wanted to fuck right in the carriage or something. Or perhaps not so accidentally.

She turned back to him, a forced smile on her face. The polite one she used in company when she couldn't truly see. "I have played *vingt-et-un* with my sisters. Ida is a sharp." Her smile widened, a real one now, and he settled back against the cushions, content to watch her, watch the play of expressions on her face. "She fleeced us when she was only eight years old. She won the twins' favorite ribbons, and she got a shell I had picked up in Brighton." She smiled more broadly. "But I was able to win it back, although I have to admit I peeked."

"How could you see? What with your eyesight?"

She looked startled, as though surprised he would remember. As though he could forget anything about her.

"Well, I used that to my advantage. I was wearing my spectacles, but then I said I had a bit of dust on them, and asked to borrow Ida's handkerchief. While I was cleaning them, I was able to glance at her cards." Her smile was mischievous. "I confessed later, of course, but it was wonderful when I won."

"There will be no cheating this evening," he said sternly, folding his arms over his chest and giving her an exaggerated look of disapproval.

"Of course not, my lord," she replied. Then stuck her tongue out at him so quickly he thought he might have imagined it, only to realize he hadn't when her eyes widened and she clapped her hand over her mouth.

"Oh my goodness," she said. "I didn't—that is, I . . ."

He unfolded his arms and touched her arm. "It's fine. It's more than fine. I want you to be who you are, Eleanor, even if that means you stick your tongue out at me. I want you to be as honest as you can be."

At his words, her face grew thoughtful. "I don't even know who I am myself," she replied. Her mouth tightened. "I suppose that is what this is truly about," she said, gesturing between them. "I mean, it is lovely to—" And then she stopped, and he could see the color flooding her cheeks. "To have this bargain, but it isn't about that." She paused, and one corner of her mouth lifted. "I just realized that." She met his gaze. "Thank you. I want to find out who I am."

As do I, he wanted to reply, but that was too close

to the truth. He'd never not just blurted things out before, but he couldn't now. Not with her, not with this situation as it was.

"I am glad to join you on the journey, Eleanor," he said instead.

Lady Eleanor's Good
List for Being Bad:

Visit a gambling ~~house~~ ~~place~~ den.

Chapter 18

$\mathcal{E}$leanor wanted to do everything all at once: throw herself into his arms, kiss him everywhere, drink champagne from a shoe or some other ridiculous drinking vessel, gamble all night, sing loudly without caring what anyone thought.

It felt as though she had drunk champagne, actually; she had a fizzy sort of feeling bubbling up inside her, making it seem as though all the colors were brighter, her skin was more sensitive, her hearing more acute.

"Thank you," she blurted out, her words sounding sharp and clear in the darkness.

"It is I who should be thanking you," he replied, that low voice sending a shivery feeling through her body. As though his proximity in the carriage wasn't doing that already.

"Why?" She tilted her head and regarded him, her eyebrows drawing together. "We will not be doing anything you haven't done before," she said, then heard the words and gasped, making him chuckle in response.

"You never know, Eleanor," he said, his words a dark promise that made her throat grow dry.

"I mean," she continued in a firmer tone, "that you have gone to this gambling place before."

"It's a gambling *den*," he corrected. "A gambling place would be far too dull."

"Fine. Gambling den," she repeated grouchily. And here she thought she'd left correctional pedantry behind with Ida.

"But I have never gone there with you," he said in a softer tone. A tone that made all of her definitely want to throw herself into his arms. "I want to see it through your eyes. It can be quite wonderful, these late-night excursions to places people don't discuss in polite society. Or it can be depressing." He smiled. "I am guessing it will be wonderful because of you."

Because of you. The words hung in the air, a challenge and a compliment all at once. She had never been so singled out before, not in society, not even in her family.

Della was the adventurous one, Olivia and Pearl were the twins—one talkative, one not—while Ida was the intelligent one.

Eleanor was just . . . Eleanor. The oldest daughter, the one whose only attribute was that she had been born first.

Nobody had ever thought something would be different, would be *special*, because of her presence.

Until him.

"I did not bring a mask or anything. What if someone recognizes me?"

He shook his head. "Nobody will recognize you. You don't look like yourself. You'll be wearing your spectacles, so you can take it all in, plus you are wearing a colored gown. Anybody who sees you will think you are someone entirely different than Lady Eleanor Howlett, the demure debutante."

His description sounded so dull. And accurate.

"People see what they want to see," she mused. "Except when they can't see at all," she continued in a rueful tone. "Are you certain you wish to be seen with me in my spectacles?" He'd said she was beautiful, that she was gorgeous, but she had been told far more often than that that a lady wearing spectacles was not an attractive lady.

He slid closer to her and placed his fingers on her jaw, turning her face to his. She would have been able to see him clearly even if she hadn't been wearing them, he was that close.

"I want you to be able to see clearly." He paused, and she saw his jaw tighten. "Everything."

What did that mean? Perhaps more importantly, why did that make her body prickle in awareness?

"Well, then," she said, pushing her spectacles farther up her nose, "we should go inside so you can overwhelm me."

And she couldn't resist giving him a smile that she hoped was as alluring as one of the ancient seductresses she'd read about in her books—strong, fearless females like Helen of Troy or Venus (who had the added benefit of being a goddess). Not

Lady Eleanor Howlett, nondescript eldest daughter of the Duke of Marymount.

She heard his sharp intake of breath when he looked at her, and a new sensation, one of feminine satisfaction, coursed through her.

"Shall we?" she asked, gesturing for him to leave the coach. He brushed by her, his fingers trailing over her bare skin as he stepped down onto the pavement.

She shivered, taking his hand to help her down. He drew her to him as her feet touched the ground, his hands at her waist. He leaned down, and down, and down some more, until he could reach her mouth.

She did appreciate how tall he was, but she did wish it wasn't so difficult to make this kissing thing happen.

And he brushed his lips over hers, his tongue darting out to lick at the corner of her mouth. She sighed, and he withdrew, his expression one of teasing triumph.

"Let's show you an adventure, Lady Eleanor," he said, turning so he was at her side, holding his arm out for her to take.

"Let's," she echoed, walking with him up the stairs to where a servant in an old-fashioned powdered wig waited, his hand on the door.

IF HE HADN'T promised her, if he wasn't so keenly aware that this was temporary, a temporary madness that had overtaken them both, he would have told his coachman to keep driving so he could explore every inch of her. Kneel in front of her as she sat on the carriage seat, her knees wide, her skirts pushed up so he could see her legs. And more. Taking advantage of the additional length of the carriage to place her as he wished he could see her, her breasts undone from that pretty gown, her legs wrapped around his as he thrust inside.

Alex shook his head, knowing that it might be too shocking even for a gambling den if he walked in with an obvious erection.

He had to gain control of himself before—well, damn it, there was no before. There was only this, and they were knee-deep in it together. In their madness, in this desire to discover who they were and how they could be important before things were resolved. Her marriage, his marriage, and the rescuing of their respective families' fortunes—both literal and figurative.

Think of unexciting things, he thought to himself. Things like all the bills Bennett had to juggle, how horrible his friend Charles looked after a particularly vigorous cricket match, and what it would be like when he had to watch his brother marry this woman, a woman he was fast coming to believe was exceptional, and possibly too good for even his very good brother.

And definitely far too good for him.

"I can't call you by your name," he blurted out as the thought struck him. At least he hadn't lost the ability to completely speak his mind.

"Oh, you can't. I hadn't thought of that," she replied. She turned her face up to look at him, her eyes mischievous behind the glass of her lenses. "Can I choose the name? How about Cordelia, King Lear's daughter?" She paused, and then her expression brightened further, if such a thing were possible. "Or Zenobia. She was a queen who challenged Roman authority. Ida was telling me about her," she explained.

"Or Dejanire?" he replied.

Her cheeks began to flush. "Dejanire. You remembered."

How could he forget?

"And so, of course, you will have to refer to me as Hercules," he continued, cocking a brow at her.

"But everyone there will know you already!"

"I didn't say you had to call me that in public. Just in private." He watched as the meaning of his words settled over her, making her rosy cheeks turn that flame-red he used to dislike.

Not anymore. He didn't dislike anything about her anymore. Except that she was supposed to marry his brother.

"Fine. *Hercules.*" She tossed him a playful smirk, practically skipping up the stairs, him following behind.

ELEANOR HAD TO force herself not to gasp and drop her mouth open like the most naïve young lady—which she was, actually, until a few days ago—when they walked into the gambling house. *Den*, she corrected to herself.

It was more opulent than anything she'd ever seen, and that included a party where the servants were handing out drinks from gold-plated trays.

The first impression she had was of red, from the dark red flocked wallpaper, to the red velvet upholstery on the chairs, to the red baize covering the tables. The people who appeared to be working there were also all wearing red, with only a few touches of gold accents to relieve the redness. Olivia would likely love it.

The guests were red-faced as well, matching the room, the noise a clamor that indicated that most of the guests had been drinking copious amounts of (likely) red wine.

A thick haze of smoke hung over the tables, while the mixed odors of perfume, tobacco, and sweat mingled in Eleanor's nose, making it tickle.

It probably wasn't customary for gambling den habitués to start sneezing, was it?

She felt his hand at her back, steering her to an empty chair. Nobody was looking at her, which was a relief, if also something that happened to her when she was not in a gambling den.

She might have eschewed a white gown for something more colorful, but that didn't mean she was any more noteworthy. A lowering thought, but also somewhat freeing—if nobody noticed her, she could do what she wanted. To whom she wanted, she thought wickedly, feeling herself blush at her own thoughts.

"I'll get you some chips," Alexander said, brushing her on the shoulder.

A balding older man was to her left, his attire indicating he had likely been at one of the parties she would have attended if she weren't here. He didn't pay her any attention, just kept picking up his chips and dropping them into a stack, over and over. *Click, click, click.* The woman to her right was someone she did recognize, although she had never been introduced. At least ten years older than Eleanor, and likely many more years wiser, she was wearing a gown that would be risqué at a society party but fit perfectly here. It was a brilliant purple color, cut low at the bosom, with only the barest suggestion of sleeves. The woman's hair was jet-black, coiled and curled on top of her head with purple luminescent feathers sticking out from various sections of her head.

Cotswold would be very impressed.

The woman, Purplehead, didn't look over at Eleanor either. She was staring at the table in front of her, a look of complete and utter concentration on her face.

Eleanor glanced to the spot as well, wondering what Purplehead was looking at. Nothing; just the red baize of the table.

The dealer tapped two fingers in front of Eleanor. "Are you in? You'll have to place your stakes."

Resting on the table was a board with a sequence of cards, all in the spades suit.

"Bet on what you think the winning card will be." It was Alexander, who was leaning over her shoulder to place chips in front of her. "You can bet on a few cards to have a better chance of winning, but that means, of course, that you stand to lose more."

"Of your money," she retorted, picking up four chips and dropping each one on a different card.

"Excellent point," he said in an amused tone. She was acutely aware of him behind her, his breath on her shoulder, his presence making her body tingle.

She and the other players watched as the dealer removed a card from a box and placed it to the left, then repeated the action, placing the card on the right.

"I don't know how to play this game," she whispered.

"There's not much to it," he whispered back, his words tickling her ear.

"So that's why you chose it for me?"

She could practically hear him roll his eyes. "I don't think you're stupid, if that's what you're implying. Just watch."

She uttered a *hmph*, but did as he said, watching as the dealer gestured toward the cards with chips on them and paying out the bets. It seemed that each player had to bet on which card the dealer would turn up, which did seem rather easy, so perhaps she shouldn't mock Alexander's judgment.

"You can move your chips around, if you want," he said as the dealer completed the payouts.

She shrugged. "I might as well keep going the way I am." The dealer hadn't paid her any money, but she supposed that might just mean that she had better odds in the future.

"You should." His voice, low and resonant, made her think about all the things she could keep going with, and she shivered with awareness.

If she had to bet on what would happen later that evening, she was sure to win if she said "kissing" and "potentially other things."

A gambling den was certainly exciting, but not nearly as exciting as the prospect of being held in his long arms. Not to mention those other things.

The dealer drew another card, and then some chips ended up in front of her. "I won!" she exclaimed, making the man on the left and Purplehead both turn to her, identical scowls on their faces.

It was exciting, not nearly as exciting as the other activities, but she would have to move it up the excitement queue. It was definitely more exciting than standing against the wall at yet another ball, clearly more exciting than listening to Ida discuss some mathematical formula, and possibly more exciting than having her mother get her tea correct.

But she had no real-life circumstances to test that last one out.

She waited as the dealer did another round of dealing and paying out, and then she turned to look at Alexander, who stood behind her, his expression amused. "This is fun! No wonder people—"

And then his expression changed, and he clapped

his hand over her mouth, grasping her elbow and making her stand with the other. "Shh. Do you want everyone to know you're not supposed to be here?"

She shook her head vigorously until he removed his hand from her mouth. She wanted to laugh at his expression, but kept herself quiet, merely grinning up at him.

"What game should we play next?" she asked, her eyes darting around the rest of the room. There really was an awful lot of red.

"We should try Hazard. Or, more specifically, you can watch as I play Hazard. It's a very complicated game."

"So you're saying I'm stupid again?" She surprised herself—and probably him—by winking as she spoke.

He responded as though he was going to lean down and kiss her, at which her whole self yelled an internal cheer, but then stopped himself. Leaving herself quite disappointed. And nearly cheerless.

"Fine, let us go so I can marvel at you playing another game. At least this time you won't be removing your shirt," she muttered.

He glanced at her, his eyebrows drawn up as though knowing precisely how much she'd like to see him without his shirt.

She had to admit he and his eyebrows were right.

Lady Eleanor's Good
List for Being Bad:

Bet on what you want.

Chapter 19

 $\mathcal{Y}$ ou were the caster?" she asked. "And why do they call it 'Hazard' anyway?"

They'd spent another hour or so after he'd won at Hazard wandering from table to table, her stream of interested observation amusing him more than anything else. More than winning, even.

Nobody had recognized her, and in fact, he'd caught a few glances of appreciation from some of the other gentlemen present, something that made him want to growl at them and claim her as his own.

Which she most definitely was not.

They returned to the carriage, her still peppering him with questions, all about what she'd seen and who she'd spied and why people spent all their time staring at cards, anyway?

He couldn't seem to keep himself from staring at her, honestly. She was bright, and lovely, and he couldn't believe nobody else had seen it before this evening. It was as though she was something only he could see, and he couldn't stop looking at her.

"I was," he said. "And the other players were the bank, and they were betting on what the rolls of the dice would show. Although actually the rules are more complicated than that. It took me a while to learn them."

"So I might have to return then, hmm?" she asked. She had an enormous grin on her face.

"Did I manage to overwhelm you, then, Eleanor?" Her given name slipped out without his being aware of it, although to call her Lady Eleanor when his mouth had been on her breast seemed unduly stuffy.

And he was not unduly stuffy.

"You did, Hercules," she replied, accompanying her words with a happy sigh. "Do you know," she began, now crossing over the carriage to sit next to him, "it wasn't the fact of being at the gambling *den*," she said, emphasizing the last word, "that was so exciting. It was that I was anonymous, yes, but that I *chose* to be anonymous. And that I could see everything! You can't imagine what it's like to wander around with everything being fuzzy. Having clear vision to see what's around you is something I didn't realize was so important."

She stopped speaking abruptly, uttering a surprised, "Oh!" as she heard herself.

"Yes, it is." He took her hand in his and raised it to kiss her knuckles. "Thank you for making that clear to me as well."

She turned to look at him, her expression fierce. "You don't see yourself clearly, not at all. I see that." And then she uttered a rueful laugh. "Imagine me telling someone I can see. But the thing is," she continued, her earnest tone making him pay attention, as though he wouldn't otherwise, "is that you are far more than what you think."

"How do you mean?" He was genuinely curious; he'd never been accused of being more of anything, unless it was in height. And sexual expertise. But the first wasn't under his control, while the second wasn't something that would be widely discussed, even if it was widely known.

"I mean that you are a good brother—you agreed to my demands because you were concerned for your brother's future. Even though you thought I might be dim-witted." She paused. "That is what you thought, correct?"

Not until the second time they met. But that didn't matter. He swallowed. "It was. Only—" he began, stopping when she held her hand up and kept speaking.

"I certainly don't think you think that now, not after all of this," she said, gesturing between them. "Because if you did, you would not be the man I know you are."

The kind of man who kisses—and more—the woman his brother is supposed to marry? That kind of man?

"I know you don't believe me," she said in a matter-of-fact voice. "Because you're thinking you betrayed your brother or something. But the truth is, your brother hasn't exactly been clamoring to get to know me."

Not clamoring, precisely, no.

He really was a terrible person. Only—only she was so lovely, and fun, and witty, and he liked spending time with her, liked seeing her tongue dart out to the corner of her mouth as she worked on translating erotic poetry. He couldn't deny liking, also, the way she looked at him, that sly but innocent look of desire.

"Can you come to the bookshop tomorrow?"

He had not meant to ask that. He should have been telling her he couldn't see her like this any longer, that he could find someone else to do the translation, that they shouldn't be spending time together so intimately.

Instead he'd asked her about the translation. Which meant spending more time alone with her. Just thinking about it made him want to smack himself in the head.

"I would." Her reply was immediate and enthusiastic. So perhaps she spoke without thinking as well? "I have to be home for calls, but I am free for some hours around lunch. If that is when you are going," she added in a hesitant tone.

He strongly disliked that she ever felt hesitant. That she felt she couldn't see, either in front of her, or who she was. He wished she could just be Lady Eleanor, not someone to be bartered for funds, or salvaged in pursuit of reputation. That she was seen only as what she could do, not who she was.

"I'll bring something for lunch." He spoke in a gruffer tone than usual, his words tinged by the emotion he couldn't—or wouldn't—acknowledge.

"That sounds lovely, thank you." She beamed

up at him, her smile nearly blinding him, even though it was relatively dark inside the carriage. "I think I should be able to finish tomorrow," she added, her tone not seeming to indicate that that meant they would no longer be spending time with one another. That then Bennett would propose, and she would be his sister-in-law. Not his translator, not the woman he'd come to value, but something much, much less.

But meaning so much more.

"WELL? How was it? Wherever you went?"

Eleanor blinked as she entered her room. Cotswold was nowhere in sight, but her three sisters were, all three perched on her bed in various states of relaxation. Olivia was sprawled diagonally, while Ida was seated at the end of the bed, and Pearl was tucked between the two of them.

All three had expressions ranging from curious to condescending. No surprise at Ida's expression, though Eleanor could detect a hint of curiosity there also. Or else why would she have waited up?

She turned her back to her sisters and gestured for one of them to start undoing her gown. "It was wonderful."

"How disrespectable was it? Was it a house of ill repute?" Olivia said the final words in a voice that indicated she should not be knowing about such a thing, much less saying it aloud.

"Of course not!" Even though Eleanor was not entirely certain herself what a house of ill repute was. Eleanor pushed her sleeves off her shoulders and wriggled out of her gown, immediately picking it up and folding it over the chair at her dressing table. She gestured for the girls to make room, and climbed up into the middle of the bed.

"If I tell you, you're not going to accidentally tell Mother, are you?"

"You mean behave exactly like Mother would?" Ida said drily. "No, not on your life. I cannot speak for the twins."

"No, we won't." As usual, Olivia answered for both of them, Pearl nodding her agreement.

"I went to a gambling den."

Ida's eyes widened, and Eleanor congratulated herself on being able to shock her usually dismissive sister.

"And did you gamble?" Pearl asked, her voice rising to a squeak on the last word.

"I did." Eleanor paused for dramatic effect. "And I won."

Olivia clapped her hands together. "That is wonderful! And nobody recognized you, of course, since it's not as though people truly pay attention to you anyway, at least from what you've said."

Eleanor winced at the truth, but she couldn't deny it.

"You were accompanied by Lord Alexander, weren't you?" Ida asked.

"Mmm."

Eleanor tried to keep her tone noncommittal, but she should have guessed her sisters would see through her.

"You like him, don't you?" Olivia said in an accusing tone. "More than Lord Carson?"

"Well," Eleanor began.

"Eleanor, do you want to marry Lord Carson?" Ida turned her shrewd gaze on Eleanor, who wanted to squirm under the scrutiny.

She took a deep breath. She had to be as direct—as blunt—as Lord Alexander himself now. She couldn't tolerate it any longer. "No, I don't." And it wasn't as though it was just because of Lord Alexander. It was that whenever she thought about marriage with Lord Carson, it was as though someone had clapped her in irons and thrown her into that matrimonial cell she'd been dreading.

"Then you shouldn't."

All of the sisters gawked at Pearl, who had spoken with such firmness.

"Why should she?" Pearl spread her hands out in explanation. "It is not as though we are on the verge of total scandalous collapse."

"Even though we are," Eleanor muttered.

"But if she doesn't, we won't get our chance!" Olivia wailed. Even though the other day she had urged Eleanor to do what she wanted. The perversity of a younger sister, Eleanor supposed. "And then we'll be stuck here, never being allowed to go anywhere, and Mother will complain and complain and Father will be furious and grunt more than usual." She paused for breath, speaking again before any of her sisters could interject. "But it doesn't matter, does it, if Eleanor finds herself more enamored of the feckless brother. Not that he has asked to marry her, has he?"

"No," Eleanor said. "But—" she began, only to have Olivia speak some more, flinging herself dramatically on the bed in emphasis.

"And we will never get our chances to fall in love, even Ida!"

"You leave me out of this," Ida warned. "I have no intention of getting married, much less falling in love," she added dismissively.

"But, Olivia," Pearl said in a firm tone of voice, "the whole point is that if Eleanor does what she wants to do we might be allowed to do what we want to do. And what is it you wish to do most in the world?" she asked, with a significant nod.

Which Eleanor didn't entirely understand, but she could guess, judging by Olivia's blush, that it involved Lord Carson. "We will be fine," Pearl continued. "There is nothing more important than your happiness, Eleanor. Aren't we all in agreement?" And she looked around at her twin and Ida, both of whom eventually nodded their heads.

"But if I decline Lord Carson's suit, I'll still be unmarried as of next season." *Unless something happens.* Which wasn't going to happen—that wasn't part of the bargain. Not that she wanted it to be. Not to mention, if she didn't marry Lord Carson, his family wouldn't get her dowry. And she had no idea what that might mean. Maybe she would end up doing substantial harm to people she had never met.

Pearl shrugged, apparently having taken on the role of Spokesperson for the Howlett Sisters. "Della ran off. We can't change that. We can't make people not talk about it. We can't change Mother, even though we might want to."

"Nothing in my tea, thank you," Ida muttered ruefully.

"We can only do what we can do," Olivia said, sounding as though she were inciting a riot. A riot of debutantes, but a riot nonetheless. "If you don't want to get married to Lord Carson—though goodness knows I can't understand that—then you shouldn't have to. What kind of sisters would we be if we wanted you to sacrifice yourself just so we could have a chance at marriage?"

Sometimes Eleanor forgot how mercurial and young Olivia could be. Usually until she spoke.

"The usual kind?" Ida answered, her eyebrow raised in clear disdain.

Eleanor laughed and poked Ida on the shoulder. Ida looked startled to be treated so casually, but then her face brightened in a smile, one that didn't appear to be conscious of possible judgment. It was a night of firsts, it seemed.

"I don't know what I might end up doing." It wasn't that she wanted to warn her sisters as much as be clear about what might—or might not—happen. "I will tell them I do not wish to marry Lord Carson after all." It felt like the right thing to admit aloud to her sisters, after all this time of just thinking it. "I will speak to Mother, and ask her and Father to allow you all to come out, no matter what marital state I am in. It's not fair to keep you from all the fun simply because I don't yet have the perfect husband."

Images of what a perfect husband would look like flashed across her mind, looking dangerously like a very tall man who teased her, admired her, and kissed her breathless.

Followed by a man who thought too little of himself, who wanted to do something that would help the world rather than just float through it. He should be free to live up to the potential he couldn't seem to recognize in himself. Not that he had even brought up the possibility of their finding a way to be together forever.

It would be enough that she could and would say no to his brother.

Lady Eleanor's Good
List for Being Bad:

Re-enact some of that
erotic poetry in real life.

Chapter 20

*I*t's all here," Alex said as soon as she entered the room, removing the wrap from her shoulders. He gestured to the table, which normally held the book—or That Book, as she had come to think of it—and was now filled with all manner of food arranged on mismatched plates.

There was cheese, and bread, and sausage, and grapes, and little tarts that appeared to hold bits of strawberry, blueberry, and cream.

"Oh!" Eleanor said, surveying the food. She looked up at Alex, who had the same anxious and proud expression he'd worn when he'd given her the Lemprière. "You brought all the delicious things," she continued, snatching up a piece of cheese and popping it in her mouth. The rich flavor made her utter a contented sigh, and she closed her eyes in satisfaction.

Her eyes snapped open as she heard him clear his throat; he was regarding her now with a timely hungry look, only she didn't think he was craving cheese.

"You don't know what you do to me, Eleanor," he said, sliding his finger between his neck and his cravat as though to loosen his clothing.

She smirked, picking up another piece of cheese and stepping forward, holding it up—and up some more—to his mouth. "Taste it," she urged. "It's delicious."

He reached up to clasp her wrist, encircling it with his long fingers so they met, with her effectively trapped in front of him. He drew her hand to his mouth and opened his lips, keeping his gaze on hers as he ate the bit of cheese.

She froze, her entire body reacting to how he looked as he chewed, how his strong throat worked, how his eyes blazed.

She definitely knew he wasn't craving cheese.

"I—I am hungry," she began, stumbling backward to go seat herself at the table, picking up one of the small plates and putting food on it with a shaky hand.

"As am I," he said. She heard the humor in his voice and met his gaze squarely.

"I don't believe we are discussing food at this moment, Lord Alexander," she said in a mischievous tone.

"Oh, Lady Eleanor? What are we discussing then?" he replied, grinning.

She raised a brow and looked him up and down, letting herself admire the view. He was truly gorgeous, all tall, godlike self of him.

His grin twisted into a smirk as he watched her looking at him. She liked that he didn't pretend not to know what she was doing, that his attitude and smile appeared to encourage it.

She just wished he were wearing fewer bits of clothing. So she could admire him more.

Her gaze returned to his face, and she smiled at him. It was incredible how powerful she felt at this moment. How she knew that whatever she did, it would be her choice.

She licked her lips and his eyes tracked the movement as he inhaled quickly.

"Let's eat and finish up this translation," he said, leaning past her to grab some of the food from a plate. She laughed and took a few more bits of the food, then helped him clear the table so he could lay the book out again.

She found her place, one of the last plates, a picture depicting Mars and Venus.

She'd gotten almost inured to what the couples (and sometimes more) in the pictures were doing, but she allowed herself to look at the drawing more thoroughly than she had before.

Mars was lying on a bed, while Venus knelt over him, her legs tangled up with his. Between them was his male member, upright and almost urgent in the depiction. Mars's expression was one of intensity, a look she thought she'd seen on Alexander's face when they'd last been in this room.

When he'd—well, yes, when he'd done that.

She couldn't say what it was even within the confines of her own head. How would she describe it, anyway?

Lord Alexander kissed me down there, in a place I

wasn't aware was at all conducive for kissing. And then he touched me and made me practically see stars, it felt that good. Not only that, it felt as though he were worshipping me, at the altar of my body, and I felt desirable, and beautiful, and wanted.

That went somewhat to it, but not entirely.

How about:

I wanted to be overwhelmed, and Lord Alexander has done just that in so many ways. Ways I cannot possibly describe.

That was better.

Satisfied, she picked up her pen and tried to ignore how the picture of Mars and Venus in their private rapture made her feel.

"It's DONE," SHE said after about an hour. Alex had been too keenly aware of her to do anything but watch her, intrigued by her change of expressions, as fluid and delightful as she was.

She glanced at the clock, frowning. "My maid will be here soon."

His heart sank. For a reason he couldn't examine too closely, not now; that would be wasting time he could be spending with her.

"But I will just go tell her there are some unexpected complications," she continued, shooting him a knowing smile as she spoke.

And then something else on his body rose, and he suddenly very much wanted to examine things more closely—namely her in this room when they were by themselves.

Did she mean what he thought she meant?

"Just give me a minute." She raised her eyebrow. "And you might want to get started, I am not certain I can remove your jacket myself—you're so much taller than I am."

She did.

He was out of his chair, shrugging out of his jacket before she'd left the room. She looked back, a mischievous expression on her face, and shut the door behind her.

Meanwhile, Alex placed his jacket on the corner of one of the bookshelves, not worrying about whether or not it would fall off. He undid his cravat then, putting it on a bookshelf. He was starting in on the buttons of his shirt when she returned, slipping into the room and closing the door softly behind her. "Hold on," she said, gesturing toward him. "I want to help with that. It was just your jacket, and perhaps your boots, that are problematic."

His fingers stilled, and he jerked his chin toward her. "Come over here and take care of it, then," he said. He could already feel how aroused he was, and she hadn't even touched him yet.

She stepped over to him, raising her fingers as she did, walking to stand directly in front of him, her hands at his chest. She placed her palms flat on him, sliding them up and down, an intrigued look on her face. "Your chest feels so different from mine," she mused, making him laugh.

"I imagine that is because I don't have your gorgeous breasts," he replied, looking down at the items in question. She had been wearing a shawl, but had removed it earlier while working at the table. He could see the soft mounds of her bosom rising up from her gown. He knew just how she tasted there—and elsewhere—and he felt his mouth water at the thought of tasting her again.

He might not make it beyond her removing his shirt—he was that excited. He should think about something boring, about some of the poetry he'd read with his tutor, not the erotic literature she'd been translating. Boring things about wars, and flowers, and feelings.

"I want to see what's underneath," she said, her pretty face twisting up in concentration.

"You did already. At the cricket match."

She raised exasperated eyes to his. "It wasn't close up, and I couldn't touch. It's entirely different." And then she returned to the work, undoing the buttons of his shirt and yanking the hem out from his trousers.

He bent down so she could draw the shirt up and over his head, amused as she folded it neatly and placed it on the chair opposite.

And then she regarded him, an admiring expression on her face, and he felt his breath quicken. And his already-hard cock get even harder.

"You are even more beautiful than I remembered," she said, stepping forward to put her hands on him. The shock of her skin touching his made him gasp, and she paused. "Am I hurting you?" she asked, looking up at him.

"No, Dejanire." Except in the most deliciously agonizing way.

"Well, Hercules," she replied, the corner of her mouth curling up into a smirk, "let us see what feats you can accomplish."

ELEANOR HAD NEVER felt better in her life. Nor as terrified, nervous, and excited. *This was what life was.* This—this joy at spending time with another person, sharing an intimacy that couldn't be described.

She smoothed her hands over his chest, feeling the warm, strong muscles underneath her fingers. She drew her fingers over his nipples, and she heard his breath hitch in response. That had to be a good thing, right?

A quick glance down his body told her it was.

Goodness, that was a lot of whatever it was. His Herculean member.

But she couldn't get distracted, or she would never know what it was like to touch him. Everywhere.

This was definitely an overwhelming experience. She would have to thank him, when she could speak properly.

"I want to kiss you," he said, his words making his chest rumble.

She tilted her head up at him and smiled. "I want you to kiss me too," she replied, stretching her hands up to the back of his neck, raising herself up on her tiptoes as much as she could. "So we are in agreement."

He shook his head gently, undoing her arms and pushing her backward so her bottom hit the table. Without breaking eye contact, he swept everything off the table, the book, her papers, the pen, everything, and it fell to the floor with a crash. She glanced to the door.

"Nobody will hear, Eleanor," he said in a whisper. "Mr. Woodson is the only one who might care, and he will ignore whatever occurs here."

"Oh," she said, licking her lips.

He eased her onto the table, her legs dangling over the edge as they were before, when he—when they—and she couldn't stop the low moan that emerged from her mouth.

He smiled, a confident, knowing smile that told her he knew precisely how she was feeling, and he had every intention of making her feel more.

"Oh," he echoed before lowering his mouth to hers.

His kiss was possessive, plundering, his tongue sweeping into her mouth with an authority she couldn't deny. And yet she had learned a few things since starting to kiss him, so she kissed him back, her tongue tangling with his, her mouth widening, their lips moving over one another.

She had her hands on his back, and was running her palms up and down his body. So strong, so smooth, so powerful. So much.

He really was supremely tall, which made her grateful that this sort of thing could occur when they were lying down, to lessen the discrepancy between them.

His hair had fallen forward, that delicious lock she'd noticed since the first time they met one another, and the strands tickled her forehead, adding to all the sensations—his mouth on hers, his chest lying on hers, his fingers tugging on the pins in her hair, drawing them out, undoing the locks so they fell around her face.

And then his hands were at the bodice of her gown, tugging, and she raised up slightly, not breaking the kiss, and his fingers went around to the back of her gown and she felt him begin to undo the buttons.

She widened her legs to better accommodate his body, and he nudged forward, that hard part of him right there, right where he'd kissed her before. Right where the sensation was the most intense.

How could she bear it? She knew there was more to this, more than just kissing—he'd done more to her before this, and yet she already felt as though she were at the peak of something, as though if there was more she just might die from the pleasure.

But then that would mean she couldn't experience the rest of it.

He broke the kiss to raise her up farther, sliding the sleeves of her gown off her arms, his gaze intent on what the fabric was revealing. She looked down as well, seeing his fingers on her skin, making her shiver everywhere.

He cocked a brow and nodded to her gown. "We should get that off you. I don't want it to wrinkle." As though he were truly concerned about her gown, of all things.

She grinned and hopped off the table, the gown sliding down to pool at her feet. She stepped out of it, now clad in her corset and shift, and picked it up, laying it on another chair.

His gaze narrowed, and she caught her breath at his expression. As though he was preparing to strike, only not in an unpleasant way. Not even just pleasant, but absolutely deliciously.

She couldn't wait.

His fingers went to the laces of her corset, and he was so close she could feel his heat. She wanted to curl into it, to entwine herself up in it and luxuriate.

Her corset removed, tossed to the floor, he knelt down in front of her, taking the hem of her shift in his hands. He looked up at her, as though asking her a question. She nodded, and he began to draw the fabric up, up over her shins, her knees, her thighs, and he stood up, continuing to draw the fabric up, now over her waist, her breasts, her shoulders, until she was completely revealed.

And she felt far, far more than average now.

He stared at her, his eyes blazing, his chest heaving, and she had to suppress a smile at seeing him so undone.

Only he wasn't undone enough, was he?

"And now you," she said, reaching forward to grab hold of the waistband of his trousers. He smiled and stepped forward so she could undo his buttons. Her fingers trembled.

This was truly about to happen, and she already knew she would not regret a thing. This was an experience the likes of which she had never had, nor would she have in the future.

A future that was appearing less and less certain the more she thought of it.

She placed her hands at his hips and shoved the fabric of his trousers down over his long, long legs, pulling them down when they clung to his leg muscles.

At last he stepped out of them, and she picked them up and folded them as carefully as he had her gown, sharing a smile with him as she did so.

Then she took a deep breath and looked at him. He was long and lean, muscles in places she didn't know humans had muscles, his solid self making her long to touch him everywhere.

And she could, couldn't she? He was giving her permission to do whatever she wanted, and she would. She placed her right palm on his upper chest, sliding her hand down the middle of his body, to his waist, then lower still, to where his member thrust out, proud and erect and gravity-defying.

She took another breath and put her hand on him, wrapping her fingers around the length, still covered by his smallclothes. He hissed, and she paused, but he shook his head. "No, please," he said. "Touch me, Eleanor."

She swallowed, tucking her fingers in between the fabric of his smallclothes and his skin, drawing the fabric off him, sliding it down until it, too, fell to the ground.

It should have been ridiculous—two people

naked in the back room of a bookshop, discarded clothing piled and folded around them like some bizarre laundry day adventure—only it wasn't. It was beautiful. It was glorious.

It was . . . "Overwhelming," she declared as she looked there at where he was so clearly excited.

He uttered a soft snort, stepping forward to draw her into his arms and lay her back down on the table.

"You overwhelm *me*," he said softly, his lips sliding over the skin at her neck, at her collarbone, to her breasts. His fingers played with her nipple, making her shiver, and she felt how it stiffened and lengthened, and how her whole body reacted to his touch.

That place *there* was particularly reactive, especially since now he was pressed against her, his member hard and throbbing.

His mouth was moving lower now, his lips closing over her nipple, sucking gently, his fingers at her other breast, holding the weight of it in his hand.

"Ohh," she moaned, gripping him on the arms, wanting all of it, all of him, before she died from it.

"Please," she said as she wriggled her body closer to his, pushing that part of her right against that part of him. It felt wonderful, only she knew there was more, more to him, and them, and this.

He lifted his head, her nipple released from his lips with a soft pop. "Are you certain?"

She smiled at him, allowing all of what she felt to be seen in her eyes. "I have never been more

certain of anything in my life," she said, punctuating her words with a slide of her body to him,
rubbing there against him, making him hiss in
reaction. "Just like Alcibiades and Glycera," she
said in a mischievous voice.

"Hold on then," he said, and he put his strong
hands on her thighs, holding them apart as he
stood in front of her, her god come to life, her adventure made physical.

She felt him nudge at where she most wanted
him, only she rather doubted he'd fit. But then
again, he had done this before, presumably he'd
have said something if she wasn't like the other
women he'd been with. That would be a far less
awkward conversation to have than now telling
her it just couldn't be done after all.

And then she felt stretched as he pushed into
her, his hands keeping her legs apart, his bottom
lip in his teeth, his expression one of concentration.

"Is there anything I should be doing?" she asked,
unable to keep herself from speaking.

He looked up, his pained expression lightening
for a minute. "Just relax, love," he said, and then he
thrust all the way up inside her, and she gasped at
the feeling. He was too much, too there, too right.

"Are you comfortable?" he asked, his breathing
loud and quick in the small room.

"I think so," she replied, and then he reached
between them to put his fingers there, and he began to rub and touch and fondle her, and then she
knew she was really all right, she was more than

all right, she was wonderful, and he was making her feel that way. No, both of them were making her feel that way, she had just as much a part of it as he did.

As he touched her, he began a rhythmic motion of his hips, sliding in and out of her, making the tension build inside. Her whole body felt alive and tingly, and she held onto his arms, touched his chest, his hips where he was joined to her.

He kept up the movement of his fingers, and she groaned, flinging her head back as she felt that summiting peak feeling all over again, only this time it was even more intense.

As she hit that peak, he began to move faster and faster, and she could hear the thwack of their bodies hitting, another sensation adding to the entire erotic feeling.

He was pistoning in and out, and she had hold of his arms, she could see the lock of hair flying up and back down onto his forehead at his movement, could hear his breathing as he labored.

And then—"Aah," he said as he grabbed hold of himself and withdrew, his body shaking. She felt something warm and wet on her thigh, and then he collapsed onto her, his member still throbbing, but not as hard now.

She curled her fingers into his hair at the nape of his neck and kissed his head. A lovely languor stole over her, and she thought she would be just fine if she died of this feeling. This was what it was like to be alive, to feel things, to have an adventure that was not only overwhelming but exhilarating, marvelous, and spectacular.

Only she couldn't say anything at the moment, not with the rush of emotion flooding her brain. Not to mention his body on hers meant breathing was a bit more difficult.

She should be feeling guilty. At everything—at having let go of the one thing that defined her as a duke's daughter, at allowing this all to happen without the promise of something more. She should be. But instead she was overwhelmed.

She was happy.

And she was in love.

"Thank you," he said at last, his words muffled by his skin.

"Thank *you*," she replied, smiling.

This was far, far better than anything she'd put on her list.

YOU ARE FAR more than what you think.

Alex paced in his room, far too keyed up to contemplate sleep, no matter that it was closing in on four o'clock. Images of her face, laughing up at him, her eyes wide in delight when she won at the gambling den, how her expression had grown determined and serious when she had spoken to him about who she was—and who he was—running through his mind. How she had looked when she was undressing him. When she was lying underneath him on that table.

When she came as he was inside her.

Was he more than what he thought?

He knew he couldn't be much less, especially now that the memory of lying to his brother kept returning to him. What would happen if he were able to do something that meant anything? More than bringing pleasure to a woman, or being the decorative younger brother whose casual nonchalance was part of his charm?

What would it look like if he could be more? What would it look like if he could feel more? Feel as much as she did?

He couldn't deny that more also included having her in his life—permanently. He wanted to steal her away from Bennett, not that she was Bennett's in the first place. Not that she was his, either; she was her own person. She should be free to make her own choices, after all. But he couldn't deny he wanted to join his life to hers, bring her pleasure and let her know she was valued each and every day.

He knew what it would look like; he just didn't know how to go about it.

"Bennett, I have something to tell you. You recall how you asked me to persuade Lady Eleanor to marry you? Well, it seems I've gone and fallen in love with her, and I am hopeful that she returns the sentiment, so I'm going to have to ask you to step aside."

Bennett might do as Alex asked—he knew that—but his father wouldn't, no matter how much he explained. He would likely delight in thwarting his vastly disappointing second son. Nor did he think the Duke of Marymount would accept the said second son when the heir in line for the title and the gentleman with all the responsibility could be had.

Nor could he ask Eleanor to consider it in the first place, given the importance reputation was to her. She'd said as much when they were first discussing the arrangement. His family provided respectability, hers provided funds. The usual marital calculation conducted in every aristocrat's study.

For once, he couldn't just speak his mind and have it all work out. He couldn't tell Eleanor he had fallen in love with her, he couldn't tell Bennett either, and he couldn't allow his father to know any of it.

He wished he could return to those days of blunt speaking and cavalier affairs. Only he didn't. Now that he'd spent time with her, kissed her, touched her, had her, he didn't want to be the person he'd been before. He wanted to be more.

You are far more than what you think.

He'd prove that she was correct. Not to her, she already believed it. But to himself.

Lady Eleanor's Good List for Being Bad:

Do something you can't even possibly begin to think of writing down.

Chapter 21

*E*leanor took a deep breath before nodding to the footman to open the door to the breakfast room. She hadn't gotten much sleep the night before—staying up too late with your sisters and then staying up after that to relive the day's events didn't leave much time for sleeping—but she felt refreshed, alert. Alive.

And sore.

"There you are, dear," her mother said, lifting her gaze from her toast to welcome her oldest daughter. None of her sisters were in the room. "There's a letter for you. I wonder if it is from Lord Carson." And she waggled her eyebrows significantly. "Your father and I are most eager to see this betrothal become official. Not that it isn't official, since it is official within the family, of course, but I would like to be able to announce it to the world." She returned her attention to her toast, her daughter's future apparently less important than her breakfast.

A cold feeling of dread settled in Eleanor's stomach. Official within the family? She knew that it

was relatively settled, but having her mother pro-
claim it like that made it seem far too real. She'd
have to say something sooner rather than later in
spite of what she'd decided. What all the Howlett
sisters had decided.

The feeling of dread was replaced by a feeling of
wonder, at her sisters for supporting her so thoroughly. Even Olivia, who was not the most selfless
of sisters. She would never have imagined it, not
even two weeks ago. But it had happened, and she
was going to see it through.

She went and took her place at the table, picking
up the envelope next to her plate, tearing it open as
one of the other footmen poured tea into her cup.

She'd barely registered the handwriting on the
envelope when her vision clouded with tears, and
she stifled a cry, getting up so suddenly her chair
tipped over.

"What is it?" she heard her mother ask.

Eleanor shook her head fiercely, clasping the
envelope to her chest as she ran out, running upstairs up to her room, waving Cotswold out before
slamming the door shut, holding the envelope
close as though she were hugging her sister.

Della, Della, Della.

Her sister was in trouble. And Eleanor would
have to fix it.

Dear Eleanor,

*I miss you and our sisters. I have cherished all
the letters you've written me. Thank you. I am*

*writing to let you know that Mr. Baxter and I
have parted ways. I am still in England, north of
London. Thankfully we never made it across the
border to get married. I know you and the rest
of the world might see my not being married as
a bad thing, but I am relieved. I made a terrible
mistake, Eleanor.*

*I do, however, have a child. A little girl whom I've
named Nora, after you. She is just three months
old, and she is already as smart as Ida. I love her so
much. That is why I am writing.*

*I've run out of money—Mr. Baxter made cer-
tain of that—and Nora is hungry. Can you send
me something, anything, to help feed us?*

*Please don't try to find us. Just send the money
to Mrs. Howlett, care of the Golden Arms. I'll get
it. I don't want to bring any more shame onto the
family. I am so sorry to have done this to you all, it
was never my intention to cause this much trouble.*

*Lovingly,
Della*

Eleanor leaned against her bedroom door, reading the few lines over and over again. So much
was said there, and yet not enough—why weren't
she and Mr. Baxter married? Why had he left her?
How could he have left her when she was going
to bear his child? Would Father even give him
money? What would happen if word spread that
not only had Della run off, but she wasn't even
married to the man?

More questions. So many questions. One question she could answer, however, was the hardest: Yes, she would marry Lord Carson if it meant that it kept Della safe and her sisters' reputations unscathed. If it meant she could go and fetch her sister home, bringing her to Eleanor's respectable home, daring anyone to face the combined force of the Duke of Marymount and the Marquis of Wheatley.

That was a reason to get married, surely.

What did her wishes matter in the greater scheme of things? Lord Carson was perfectly nice. He wasn't his brother, true, but then again, only his brother was his brother.

Which didn't make sense, but she couldn't care about that now. No matter what she had done the day before. No matter what she felt about him.

Not when her whole life seemed to rest on one roll of the die; listen to what her heart said and gamble with her sisters' futures, or listen to what her head said and compromise her own wants for everyone else's.

The choice was clear.

Armed with her purpose, she focused again on the now, starting as she felt a repetitive thumping underneath her back. She turned, the letter still in her grasp, twisting the doorknob with the other hand.

Her sisters spilled into the room, all of them with the same wide-eyed, curious expressions.

Olivia snagged the letter from her hand before

Eleanor could realize what she was doing. She held it out so Ida and Pearl could read as well.

"Oh my," Pearl said on an indrawn breath. "Oh my," she repeated, meeting Eleanor's eyes. "We have a niece? And Della is—oh my," she said again.

"We have to find her," Ida announced. "I will fetch my atlas and plot out the general area she might be in." She flew out of the room, a determined set to her mouth.

Olivia narrowed her gaze at Eleanor, who tried to return her sister's look without flinching.

"Don't you even th—" she began, only to whirl around as their mother propelled herself into the room, breathing heavily.

Their mother didn't wait either before snatching the letter, yanking it out of Olivia's hand and holding it right up to her nose.

Eleanor knew where her poor eyesight had come from.

"Oh no," she moaned. "Duke! Duke!" she called, leaving the room with the letter still in her hand, waving it in the air like a flag of surrender.

"Now what?" Pearl said in a quiet voice.

Both sisters looked at Eleanor, who felt her chest tighten. "Now I suppose I'll have to marry Lord Carson if it means there's a chance we could get Della and Nora back into the family again." She held her hand up as Olivia opened her mouth. "The thing is, I know that possibility is remote. I know that. But I also know the possibility doesn't exist if the reputation of our family remains in jeopardy. There is simply no way for Della to return to London, return to us, if we aren't better situated." She exhaled. "And the quickest way to make that happen is for me to get married."

Olivia snapped her mouth closed and glared at Eleanor, Pearl doing the same but adding folded arms to the picture of furious sisters.

It was only a dream, the chance of being free of marriage. The chance of exploring what other adventures Lord Alexander could show her.

"But, Eleanor," Pearl started to say, only to turn her head as they heard the unmistakable footsteps of their father coming up the stairs. Their mother was talking, as usual, and it didn't take a genius like Ida to know what she was saying.

The duke appeared at Eleanor's door, something he hadn't done since she was young. He glanced at all the sisters in turn, his gaze alighting on Eleanor. "I want to speak to Eleanor alone," he said, his eyebrows lowering.

Olivia and Pearl looked as though they wanted to stand their ground, but they left after a nod from Eleanor.

The duchess was behind her husband. He held the letter in his hand and shook it at Eleanor as though it were a weapon. "Do you see what has happened?"

Well, yes, it is my letter, she wished she were brave enough to reply.

"I do, sir," she said instead.

"I allowed you some leniency because you are so

sensible." *I am?* Eleanor thought. Followed quickly by, *That was leniency?*

"But we must settle this business now. You must announce your betrothal to Lord Carson." He glared down at the letter again. "I am going to have to raise the amount of your dowry as well to ensure the matter is taken care of."

Eleanor blinked as the meaning of his words settled in her brain. So not only was she going to have to marry someone she didn't wish to, but her father was going to have to pay more for the privilege of her doing so?

Well, thank goodness she was already aware of her value in this family or she would be suffering from a strong lack of confidence. She knew her sisters loved her, and that was the most important thing.

No, that was wrong. The most important thing was that Della and her daughter would be safe. And Eleanor could do that. As her father paid through the nose.

She allowed herself a moment to roll her eyes, and then she nodded at her parents. "Fine. We should go now to settle it all. We need to take care of this before there is any more talk." Before ladies like Lady Vale spread their malicious truths. Not that she cared about the scandal. She just needed to make sure her sisters, all of them, were taken care of.

"We cannot go now, it is too early!" Her mother sounded horrified at the prospect. Because it was one thing to go exchange your daughter and a hefty sum to another family for respectability, but it was another thing to arrive before lunchtime.

"I'll just send a note around to the viscount to let him know we will be paying him a call." Her father held Della's letter to Eleanor as though it was something too distasteful to touch, then left without another word.

Thankfully, or not, her mother had plenty of them.

"I told you to accept Lord Carson straightaway. Now who knows if he will have you?"

He would. He was as honorable as his brother, she knew that. She also knew how important his family was to him, so he would do this, even if it wasn't something he wanted either.

And Lord Alexander would let him, since he thought so little of himself he wouldn't believe he should have a say in the matter.

"We'll have the wedding in a month. That will be enough time for the planning, and everyone will still be in town."

Her mother was still talking, even though Eleanor hadn't heard a quarter of what she said.

None of this would matter, would it? In twenty years, or even less, when she was unhappily married to a perfectly fine, perfectly average gentleman who wasn't the one she wanted?

"Milk and sugar." She spoke in an assertive tone, one loud enough to make her mother stop talking and stare at her, mouth still open.

"Pardon?"

Eleanor took a deep breath. "I like my tea with milk and sugar. A healthy splash of milk and two teaspoons of sugar."

"Why are you telling me this?" Her mother's expression was affronted, as though Eleanor had said something with which she didn't agree. Something like, "I will not marry someone just to suit your plans." Because she'd tried that, and it wasn't going to work out.

"Because you don't know. You've never known." Eleanor thought for a moment, her mother still struck dumb. "You say you want these things to happen for the family's respectability, so that the girls and I can marry well. But that's not what it is about, is it? It's all about you. You can't bear the thought of being less than the highly venerated Duchess of Marymount. God forbid one of your daughters makes a mistake, runs off with the wrong man. Marries the wrong man," she added, her brain whirling. "The thing is, before anything else happens, I want you to know that I take my tea with milk and sugar." She could cross that item off her list, at least. It was cold comfort, but she had to settle for what she could possibly achieve.

She walked out of her bedroom leaving her mother alone, still speechless.

ALEX STRAIGHTENED TO his full height before tapping on Bennett's door.

"Enter," his brother replied.

Alex opened the door and went in. Bennett's valet was standing facing Bennett, his back to Alex, adjusting Bennett's cravat. Bennett took one look at Alex and frowned. "You can go, Saunders," he said.

Bennett's valet stepped back, bowed to Alex, and left the room.

"What is it?"

Alex took a deep breath. "I need to tell you someth—" he began, stopping as they heard a commotion on the stairs.

Bennett walked to the door and flung it open, stepping out into the hall, Alex following on his heels.

"What is it? What's happened?" Bennett called. Alex saw his father storming down the hallway, a piece of paper in his hand.

"It will all be settled today," the viscount declared.

"What? What will be settled?"

Alex felt a knot start to twist itself in his throat. There was only one thing that remained undone. And clearly there was something making it imperative, so now was not the time to tell his brother he'd gone and fallen in love with his brother's soon-to-be betrothed. If not already betrothed.

Oh, and relieved her of her virginity on a table in the back room of a bookstore.

"The duke is on his way here to make arrangements. It has gone on far too long. You should have taken care of this already." Their father glared at

Bennett, making Alex wish he could speak up and defend his brother, and Eleanor, for that matter:

He was too busy taking care of the family business you fouled up and then ignored to court her properly. Plus she is her own woman—dear lord, is she her own woman—and she is smart enough and valuable enough not to just say yes because someone asks her.

But he didn't.

"What should I have taken care of, Father?" Bennett spoke in a tone Alex had never heard from him before—low, measured, but also menacing.

"The wedding to the duke's eldest daughter, whatever-her-name-is."

"Eleanor," Alex and Bennett said simultaneously.

"Fine, Eleanor. The duke sent word he is on his way to discuss it." Their father waved the letter in the air. "What if they wish to withdraw the possibility of it? What if some other gentleman has been making up to her while you've been neglecting your duties?"

Alex felt a twinge—fine, far more than a twinge—at their father's words.

Bennett shook his head. "I don't believe that to be the case," he said, punctuating his words with a quick glance toward Alex. "I am guessing something else has happened that perhaps makes the matter more urgent from the duke's side of things. We should go downstairs and wait for the duke's arrival." He gestured to the stairs, their father's mouth gaping open at being told what to do by his eldest son.

The three men walked downstairs, the confession still poised on Alex's lips, but now wasn't the time—definitely not the time—to admit his feelings for Eleanor.

He didn't know what was at stake, and that was why he had to restrain his normal blunt speaking. Because if he said the wrong thing, it might affect her, and he couldn't have that.

Even if he never got to say what he wished to.

"THAT SEEMS TO be settled, then." Bennett held the door open for Alex, who shut it behind them.

They were once again in their father's study, their father having apparently decided he'd spent enough time with this family and returned to his other one.

Bennett walked over to the table that held whisky and glasses, not asking if Alex wanted anything before pouring two healthy servings. He almost downed his glass before handing Alex his.

"Have you ever not done something Father wished you to?" Alex said, not taking a sip, staring intently at Bennett, who shrugged.

"I suppose I always do. It's easier than arguing with him," Bennett said, pouring more whisky into his glass.

"I told you I needed to speak with you before the duke arrived." Alex set his glass down on Bennett's desk. "And I need you to hear me out." It burned, the urge to tell him. He'd tried to resist it, but hearing why the duke was pushing on the marriage didn't give him a good enough reason not to speak.

If he and Eleanor were married, they could hare off in search of her sister. It wouldn't matter to anyone which brother she married.

Would it?

"What is it?" Bennett said as he finished his second glass of whisky. Alex shot his hand out to grip Bennett's wrist when he was on his way toward pouring a third.

"What?" Bennett said in an aggravated tone. "Are you telling me how you want me to behave too?"

"No. I need to tell you something entirely different. Sit down."

Bennett sat, his normally reserved expression giving way to something approaching belligerence. Good. Maybe this would resolve itself as Alex was hoping it would.

"It's about Lady Eleanor." Alex took a deep breath, not sure how to proceed.

"My betrothed?"

"Yes." As though there were any other Lady Eleanor they might possibly be discussing. "You can't marry her."

Bennett raised his eyebrow. "It's been arranged. It will happen."

"No," Alex replied slowly, shaking his head. "It won't. Because I won't let you."

"Why not? Is she not good enough for me?" Bennett's tone sounded weary, as though he were tired of being the perfect son. Alex was damned tired of it too.

"That's not it. I don't think you're good enough for her."

There was a moment of stunned silence, and then Bennett rose, placing his knuckles on the surface of the desk. "I'm not good enough for her?" He exhaled, and his jaw tightened. "Do you mind telling me what you mean by that?"

"Just what I say. Listen, Bennett, you don't want to marry her either." Alex heard the stark honesty in his tone. He just hoped Bennett heard it too. "You're only agreeing because our father insisted. Because he's desperate to rescue the estates, and you're the sacrificial husband. Neither one of you deserves one another. Neither one of you. I agreed to persuade her to marry you because I wanted to be certain she was worthy of you. She's not. She's more than worthy of you, and the two of you would be fine together but you wouldn't be happy. Both of you deserve happiness. I know because I—" And he stopped short, nearly admitting that he loved both of them.

"Because you what, Alex?" Bennett spoke in a soft tone. One that knew what Alex was going to say.

"Because I love her."

"Well. That is an excellent reason, brother."

*Lady Eleanor's Good
List for Being Bad:*

---

*And then think about
doing it again.*

Chapter 22

"You're not actually going to agree, are you?" Ida had walked in and slammed the door shut behind her before Eleanor even realized she was there. Eleanor was seated at the small desk she used for correspondence, rereading the letter even though it had already imprinted itself on her brain.

She rose, dropping the letter on the table.

"I'm not." She couldn't. For a moment there, an admittedly panicked moment, she had thought she should, had resigned herself to being the sacrifice to her sisters' respectability. But her sisters wouldn't allow that, for one, and more importantly, Eleanor wouldn't allow it for herself. She deserved more than an average husband and an average life and an average marriage.

She deserved to be overwhelmed. She deserved to tick off more things on her list.

"Thank goodness," Ida replied, stepping forward to enfold Eleanor in a hug. Eleanor didn't recall the last time her sister had touched her; it felt—odd.

She drew back, still grasping Eleanor's shoulders. "Della made her own choices. You have to make yours as well. That Della is in need of our help doesn't mean it has to be the marrying the wrong person kind of help. I am intelligent—*we* are intelligent—surely we can figure out a way to help Della without you having to sacrifice yourself. None of us want that for you, no matter what our parents might say."

"Our parents," Eleanor echoed. "Father is on his way to the viscount's right now to settle things. And then Lord Carson is going to ask again, and I'll have to have some sort of reply."

Ida shrugged. "It is not so difficult to maneuver out of these things if you just know how."

"You've had a lot of experience turning down proposals, then?" Eleanor asked, her tone amused.

"No, of course not." Ida blushed as she spoke, making Eleanor wonder just what her studious sister had been getting up to.

"Let's get thinking, then," Eleanor said determinedly. "Because I want all of us to be happy and safe. All of us," she repeated, her heart sore as she thought about Della.

"Did you figure anything out?" Olivia said as she and Pearl walked into Eleanor's bedroom.

Ida and Eleanor both shook their heads.

"Drat," Pearl said in a soft voice.

Olivia clambered up onto the bed, a determined look on her face. "We will manage it somehow. We have to. Eleanor's happiness is in the balance!"

Eleanor's heart twinged, to know her sisters cared so much for her. She'd felt it before, certainly, but she'd never known it so thoroughly as now.

"Eleanor! Where is that girl?" Her mother's voice carried up the stairs, making the sisters jump.

Eleanor glanced at Olivia, Pearl, and Ida. They'd spent the past hour while their parents were away strategizing on how to make things work so Eleanor wouldn't have to marry Lord Carson, Della and Nora could return, and the rest of the girls could make their debuts without scandal.

So far Ida had suggested running off to America, while Olivia had said she would marry Lord Carson instead, so as to save Eleanor from it.

The other sisters just looked pointedly at Olivia, who blushed.

So they didn't have a solution, not yet. And it seemed as though a solution would be more difficult to think of than the sisters had originally thought.

How did those mythological figures manage to get romantically involved with so many people and marry so many of them also? It probably helped that they were gods, and the gossip about them tended to diminish with the threat of some godlike action occurring if someone spoke disparagingly about them.

"Eleanor!" her mother called again.

She took a deep breath and walked downstairs.

"Let me understand this properly," Bennett said, squinting at Alex. He'd gone ahead and poured his third drink, and then his fourth, after threatening to punch Alex in the nose for, as he put it, "having my best interests at heart." Alex stepped aside as Bennett swung wildly, and then made him sit down on the sofa, putting the whisky safely out of reach.

"You are suggesting we sell erotic literature to prop up the estates?"

Put that way, it—"Well, yes," Alex said.

"And you have had this idea since meeting the Duke of Lasham?"

"Yes." Alex's lips twisted up into a half smile. "I know that it is not the most usual of plans, but I couldn't think of anything else." He paused. "I'm not you, Bennett. I'm not the type of person who can manage things, and be responsible, and do all the things you do."

"You are, you know," Bennett said in a soft voice, peering intently—if somewhat drunkenly—at his brother. "You have never given yourself any credit. You've accepted what our father thinks of you, just because you were rash when you were younger."

"Rash doesn't really cover losing a house at the gambling table." The memory of it made him wince, as it always did. His father never allowed him to forget it either. It wasn't that horrible in the grand scheme of things, but the grand scheme of things didn't fit into his father's vision.

"But why did you do it in the first place? It was to help, wasn't it? It was right after our mother had her first illness, and Father was always off doing business, he said."

"Only now we know where he really was," Alex said in a bitter voice. The second family nobody was supposed to know about, but existed.

Bennett pointed an accusing finger at Alex. Accusing him of having the family's best interests at heart, but still. Accusing. "And you thought if you could just make some money, just return triumphantly with enough to stave off the creditors that Father would finally give you the respect you deserve. But he never would have, not even if you returned with seven brides and their respective dowries. He's never seen you as you are. You haven't seen yourself either," Bennett added.

You are far more than what you think.

"Perhaps I haven't," Alex replied, feeling his chest grow tight. "But neither have you. Why should you have to shoulder all the burdens of what our father has done? Why not let me help?"

Bennett shrugged, holding his hands up in confusion. "I don't know. I've always assumed it was just for me to handle. Which is why I accepted this engagement so quickly. It's just another thing that I have to do in order to keep us going. It isn't just for us—there are people depending on Father's lands for their livings. If we can't keep them up, those people will lose their livelihoods. Their lives."

"I believe we can make nearly as much as Lady Eleanor's dowry, provided we handle the thing properly. Mr. Woodson already has several buyers placing orders. And I can find more, I just have to find out who our prospective customers are and convince them to pay our price. Which I can do."

Bennett shook his head in disbelief. "And how can I help you in this disreputable venture? Besides not marrying Lady Eleanor?"

"You can keep the accounts and handle the inventory. I don't think Mr. Woodson is capable of dealing with the amounts I am expecting. And you should show me some of what you do so I can assist there, too, in the more reputable areas. I want to, brother. I need to."

Bennett looked at Alex for a long moment, then nodded. "Fine. I'll go in on this with you, provided you tell the lady how you feel."

"I will," Alex promised. "I will."

"WE'RE ALL GOING for a walk in the park," Eleanor said, with more insistence than usual. Her sisters nodded vehemently, making their mother shrug in acceptance.

"Fine, but you'll need to return to visit the dressmaker's to discuss your wedding gown."

Eleanor swallowed all of her replies—she had strategies to discuss, after all—and merely nodded.

"And make sure Ida stays out of the sun," her mother continued, even though she meant Pearl, who burned anytime she strayed from beyond a shady tree into the light.

"Yes, Mother," Eleanor replied.

"We're meeting them out in the park?" Olivia asked for perhaps the hundredth time.

Dejanire,

Please meet my brother and me in the park to-morrow afternoon at four o'clock to discuss the situation.

I want you to know you can do whatever you want to. I see you. I support you. I know you.

Love,
Hercules

There was no possibility of replying to him, not without causing comment, so he didn't know that she was going to be accompanied by her sisters. But her sisters were why she had even entertained the possibility in the first place, and they were the ones in staunchest support of her current decision (even though Olivia continued to grouse about missing all the parties).

Eleanor was guiding her sisters to the same lake where she and Alexander had seen the family that first time when the Carson brothers arrived, making a grand show of just happening upon them.

"Ladies," Lord Carson said. "How wonderful to find you here."

"All of you," Alexander said, sounding a bit . . . overwhelmed.

The sisters all turned at the sound of voices. Ida reached over and took Eleanor's hand, squeezing it tight. On her other side, Pearl looked fierce, at least as fierce as she could, while Olivia just looked dreamy-eyed.

Seeing him made her lose her breath. Had she really gone and fallen in love with the blunt-speaking tree who enjoyed erotic literature?

The brother of the man she was supposed to marry, if not fall in love with?

She was ridiculous. But she was her own ridiculous person, and it seemed that yes, she had fallen in love with him.

She wished she could regret it, but seeing him standing there, just behind Lord Carson, his whole self as charming and direct and wonderful as she now knew, she couldn't. Even though it might mean repercussions for the rest of her family, but they—the ones she cared about, at least—were with her in whatever decision she made.

She couldn't marry anyone besides him, never mind that Lord Carson was perfectly pleasant. She'd always known that, of course, but now she knew that she deserved more than pleasant. Alexander had taught her that by overwhelming her. What she hadn't expected was just how overwhelmed she would get. How in love she would get.

And then he stepped out from behind Lord Carson and walked directly to her, lowering his gaze to her face.

"I didn't know all of you ladies would be here this afternoon. If I may," he said, looking ruefully at Eleanor's sisters, "I would appreciate a moment to speak to you alone."

It was like that first time, when he had asked her what she required in order to marry his brother.

Her sisters had been there as well, and he had asked her, and she had told him, nearly as blunt as he, that she wanted to be overwhelmed.

And he had shown her that.

"Yes, of course. Excuse us?" she said to her sisters and Lord Carson. That gentleman looked more than a little knowing, and she wondered just what his brother had told him. Surely he hadn't—no, he wouldn't. He might speak directly, but he wouldn't jeopardize her reputation with his words, even though he had done plenty of that with his actions.

They stepped to the side, and he positioned her so his back was to the group, so he was the only thing she could see. Literally as well as figuratively.

He took her hands in his. "The thing is, I need to persuade you not to do this. I love my brother, and I love—" And then he stopped. Now was when he decided he needed to be discreet? She wanted to punch him.

"Bennett is a good man. He would be a good husband," he continued. "But you can't marry him. That is why I asked you to meet us. I told Bennett you shouldn't marry him. You are not for him, and he is not for you."

"My sisters have already persuaded me of that," Eleanor replied in a fond voice. She peeked over his arm and saw all three of them pretending not to be trying to listen, and she laughed. "I won't marry him. I cannot. Because I love you, you enormous lummox."

"Oh." His eyes were wide. Had she really said that aloud? "Enormous lummox?"

She had.

He stepped forward and cupped her face in his hands. "And I love you, Eleanor. My Dejanire."

"Excuse me?"

They both turned as Lord Carson stepped toward them, followed quickly by Olivia, Pearl and Ida. Alexander dropped her hand, and she felt the lack immediately.

"Well, it appears we are all discussing this after all." Alexander gestured to Eleanor. "Lady Eleanor has just said that she and my brother are in agreement. They cannot marry, at least not one another."

"We know that already," Olivia announced in a superior tone. "We do not wish our sister to marry without love."

"And you are a fine gentleman, we suppose," Ida stated, "but Eleanor does not love *you*." At which point Eleanor winced, since Ida's tone was her usual condescending one.

"So have you thought of a way to extricate yourself from the situation?" Lord Carson didn't sound piqued, which made Eleanor contrarily irritated. If a gentleman discovered he was not the person a young lady wished to marry he should at least be a little disheartened by it. He sounded matter-of-fact. As though all of his business dealings had made him far too . . . *businesslike*.

"No, we haven't," Olivia replied.

All the sisters looked downcast.

"Well, she can't jilt me," Lord Carson said, tilting his head to look at Eleanor. "That would be as scandalous as your sister's behavior. Especially if you jilt me for my brother."

Oh, so he did know already. That made her feel somewhat better about his matter-of-factness at discovering she didn't want to marry him.

"What should we do then?" Ida asked. As though she were truly asking, and not just assuming she had the answer and no one else did.

Lord Carson shrugged, looking at each of the sisters in turn.

"We should discuss it." Alexander took Eleanor's hand again, and four pairs of eyes tracked the movement. "All of us. I know, for example, that Ida is extremely intelligent, and my own brother is very good at negotiation. If we all put our heads together, perhaps we can figure something out."

"We can't discuss it here, however," Eleanor replied. "We have to be back to—" But she couldn't say she had to go to the dressmaker's to see about her wedding gown since she'd just announced she would not be getting married. At least not to Lord Carson.

"The bookshop," Alexander said suddenly. Eleanor started guiltily. Was he about to announce just where they'd realized how they felt about one another—and what they had done?

"What bookshop?" Olivia asked.

"Mr. Woodson's shop. We can meet there to discuss it tomorrow," Alexander said.

Oh. Of course. That would be a good place to have a discreet meeting. As she well knew.

"Good idea," Lord Carson replied. "How about

we meet there in the afternoon? Say around three o'clock?"

Eleanor's sisters all murmured their assent, making her heart swell with love. She was so lucky to have these people in her life, people who could be annoying (Olivia), pedantic (Ida), and quiet (Pearl), but who ultimately loved her and wanted her to be happy, no matter how it might affect them.

And him. He was still looking at her. It felt as though he hadn't taken his eyes off her since he'd walked her out here. He loved her. He'd said it, even after she'd called him a lummox.

She was well and truly overwhelmed. By love. By *him*.

*Lady Eleanor's Good
List for Being Bad:*

Stand up for yourself.

Chapter 23

*A*re we all here, then?" Eleanor nodded to Ida, who shut the door.

It was ten minutes past three, and the four sisters plus the two Carson brothers were packed into the small room where—well, she couldn't think of it without blushing, so she wouldn't, but it was the same place she and Alexander had worked on the translations.

And done other things.

"What are we going to do?" Olivia said in a plaintive voice. Sometimes—though not very often—Eleanor forgot how young she was. Not now, however. Now she sounded as though she was complaining about not getting any dessert.

As opposed to complaining she was going to have to accept the very pleasant gentleman as a husband.

"There's nothing for any of you to do," Alex said. He looked at Eleanor as he spoke, and she couldn't repress a shiver. He was just so—so tall, and authoritative, and she couldn't see anybody but him when he was in the room. Not just because he towered over everyone else.

Although yes, partially that.

"I am going to speak to our father," he continued. He crossed his arms over his chest, looking nearly ferocious. "I have a few ideas of how I can convince him to dissolve the agreement between our families so that Eleanor—and Bennett, of course—are free to make their own choices." He met her gaze. "And hear some other options." Oh, well now she was going to melt all over again.

"What are you going to say? Are you certain you don't wish me—" Bennett began, only to stop as Alex shook his head decisively.

"Remember how all of this began?" he asked, shooting Eleanor a conspiratorial look. "You wanted me to persuade Lady Eleanor that you would be a good husband."

"And look how well that turned out," Lord Carson said, grinning.

"Yes, well." Alexander's tone held a hint of embarrassment. "The thing is, you asked me to speak to Lady Eleanor because I can convince anyone of anything, usually."

"You can convince *ladies* of anything," Lord Carson corrected. "Not necessarily our father."

"Is he as—as father-like as our father?" Olivia asked.

Lord Carson chuckled, making Olivia blush and look down at the floor. Eleanor hoped she would grow out of this infatuation. Lord Carson was far too serious, and too busy, to indulge Olivia's fancies.

"I don't have the pleasure of being very well-acquainted with the duke, but yes, he is father-like."

"If father-like means being set in his opinions, convinced he is always right, and belligerent when you argue with him," Alexander added.

"Oh, like Ida!" Pearl exclaimed, then clapped her hand over her mouth.

Eleanor had to stifle a snort. Ida glowered at her sister.

"But even so, I have a plan for what I can say to convince him. And if I can't? Then we'll have to cause a scandal of some sort."

"Hold on, now," Bennett said, holding his hand up. "There was no mention of scandal."

"And hopefully there won't be. But nothing is more important than this engagement, this marriage, not happening as planned. Is there?" And Alexander stared his brother down, making Eleanor wish she could applaud and cheer "Bravo!" As though she didn't want to do that most times when she was in his company.

"And I will speak to Mother," Eleanor announced. The sisters all turned and looked at her. "I want her to know she can't just manipulate her daughters into doing what she wants, just because one of us did something she most definitely did not want. This is for the greater sisterly good, I promise," she said, holding her hand up to forestall objections.

Ida's mouth snapped shut, and Olivia heaved an exasperated sigh, whereas Pearl just nodded solemnly. "And then I will tell Father."

That would be even more difficult than speaking with her mother, but it had to be done as well.

Which made her think, of course, of Della. Della, who she had to figure out how to rescue, but she couldn't do any of that until she'd rescued herself.

"So we have our marching orders?" Alexander glanced around the room. "I'll speak to our father, and Lady Eleanor will speak to your parents. And then we will all be free to make our own choices." And he met Eleanor's gaze again, a dark promise in his eyes.

Everyone in the room nodded, beginning to move to the door.

"Lady Eleanor." She snapped her head around at his voice. "May I see you home in my carriage? I wish to—to strategize with you."

At which point everyone else in the room pointedly looked away, as though aware that was just an excuse, and a lame one at that, but none of them was willing to point it out.

"Yes, thank you, my lord. That would be lovely," Eleanor replied.

Strategize. Is that what he called it? She smiled as her sisters and Lord Carson left the room, leaving them alone. In their room, right near the table where they'd—

"I am going to take you home," he said, raising a brow as he looked at her. Was she that obvious?

Well, she supposed she was when it came to him.

"In your large carriage?" she asked, curling her lips up into a smile.

"In my very large carriage," he repeated knowingly.

"Excellent."

"WHAT ARE YOU going to say?" she asked after he'd gotten her settled in the carriage and told his coachman how to drive home.

Not the most efficient way, his coachman had pointed out.

Exactly, Alex wanted to say.

He picked her hand up where it lay on the seat between them, bringing it up to his mouth. He placed his lips on the back of her hand and kissed it, then turned her palm around so he could kiss her wrist. He allowed himself to linger there, to lick the soft skin, feeling how her pulse sped up.

"I have a plan," he replied. He didn't want to spend this time, this precious time, going over how he might speak to his father. He wanted to savor every minute he could with her. He had no idea what would happen after this. After snatching back her and Bennett's freedom. Would she listen to what he wanted for them? Would she agree to relinquish her independence just when she had won it back for herself?

"A plan," she repeated, sounding doubtful.

"Yes," he replied, "but I have another plan as well. One involving both of us now, in this carriage, with nothing but this moment. Do you prefer that idea?"

He could almost hear her smile. "I do."

"Good. Let us just be, just for this moment. Knowing that I love you, and that you love me."

"Oh," she said in a soft voice. "Oh, that sounds wonderful." He could hear the desire in her tone, feel how her fingers tightened on his wrist where he held her.

"And then? What happens then?"

Of course she asked. She wouldn't be Eleanor, determined to make her own way Eleanor, without wondering what the future might hold.

"Then, when we have done what we have to, both of us, then I will ask you something that you are free to answer however you wish. But until then," he continued, licking her index finger, hearing how she sharply inhaled, "I don't think we should speak." Because if he did continue to talk, all he thought he could manage were a few more "I love you"s. And he could show her so much better than he could say it.

"Oh," she said on a sigh as he drew her finger into his mouth and sucked gently. She moved restlessly, as though she wanted to move, and he chuckled and drew her onto his lap. Directly on top of his cock, which welcomed the pressure.

"What do you want at this very moment, Eleanor?" he whispered in her ear, the rocking of the carriage making for a delicious friction.

"I want you to—" she began, only to shake her head and bury her face in his neck. "I want you," she whispered in his ear, her breath sending skitters of sensation through his whole body.

"Excellent. I want just the same thing." And he

twisted her so they were both facing the back of the carriage, her bottom snugly on his erection, her hands on the outside of his thighs holding herself steady.

He placed his hands at her waist and drew her in closer, her whole back leaning against his chest, her head nestled on his shoulder. He kissed the juncture of her neck and tightened his hold on her, sliding his fingers around to her front to just under her breasts. He could feel how she was breathing faster, and he let his fingers tease her just there, just where he could feel the swell and curve of her.

"Please," she said in a moan, and he chuckled as he licked her skin.

"Please what?" He wanted her to say it, to admit her desires. To say what would overwhelm her.

"Please touch me," she said, and she drew her hands up to place them on top of his, moving his palms directly on top of her breasts. "Please," she continued, arching her back so her breasts were firmly in his grip. "Like Angelique and Medor."

Oh, he recalled that particular picture. Medor holding his lady in front of him as he penetrated her. That she had paid attention, that she wanted the same thing—well, that was more proof that she was for him. That she wanted to explore, and investigate, and be overwhelmed. And find her joy, as he had found joy with her.

He had said he wouldn't speak, not now. But he could show her how he felt. "As you wish, Angelique," he said, beginning to move his fingers. He could feel the sharp stab of her nipples, already erect and begging for his touch, which he was more than glad to offer.

He drew his fingers up to the edge of her gown, sliding his index finger down between the fabrics of her layers and her skin. She moaned, and he put his other hand to her back, nudging her forward so he could undo her buttons.

He worked swiftly, glad he was dexterous enough to undress her while not stopping his caressing of her breasts. Dear lord, they felt wonderful in his hand, and he heard his breathing quicken as he ran his fingertips over her tight little bud and felt the heft and swell of her breast in his palm.

He got the buttons undone and removed his hand from her bodice, making her utter a disappointed noise. He slid the sleeves of her gown down her arms, drawing the fabric down to her waist. She wore her corset and shift, and there was much more of her skin available to his mouth. He leaned forward, his hands going to her corset to untie the laces, his mouth moving over the skin on her upper back, licking her spine and feeling her shudder under his lips.

"You like that?" he asked, knowing the answer, but wanting to hear her pleasure.

"Oh yes," she replied, wriggling on his lap. She placed her palms back on his legs and slid them up and down, making him burn for her to touch him there. Put her delicate fingers on his cock, stroking his hard length, getting overwhelmed—in a good way—again.

"Take this off," she commanded, shrugging her shoulders to indicate the corset.

"With pleasure," he replied, removing the garment from her body and putting it on the seat next to them.

Now she was only in her shift, and it was easy to place his hands on her breasts again, his lips at the nape of her neck, his fingers kneading her nipples and caressing the soft fullness of her breasts.

"Touch me," she said, nearly in a growl, and he grinned against her skin. He put his long arms on her legs and began to draw her shift up to join where her gown was gathered at her waist.

"Are you wet for me, Eleanor?" he asked before putting his fingers just there on her mound, his index finger finding her sweet little nub and making her gasp, arching her back again, which caused another round of delicious friction on his cock.

"You are," he answered, sliding his finger inside her heat. He kept his thumb on that button of pleasure, setting a rhythm that made her moan.

His cock was impossibly hard now, thrusting against her soft bottom, throbbing as his fingers kept moving.

"Oh," she moaned, and she dropped her head down, her hair coming undone, her whole self lusciously disheveled. He increased the pressure and the speed of his hand, and he felt when she began to climax, the walls of her entrance tightening around his finger, her breathing coming faster and faster as she cried out in pleasure.

It felt as though she came forever, and he held

his breath as he felt how she moaned, her soft, breathy sighs going straight to his erection until at last she stilled, leaning back against his chest, her chest rising and falling with her still rapid breathing.

"That was . . . overwhelming," she said in an amused tone of voice.

"It was more than that," he said, unable to resist thrusting up against her body.

"And what about you?" she asked, twisting her head to look at him.

"Well, I have a few ideas, since my coachman seems to be taking the long way home," he replied with a smirk.

"Do tell," she said, wriggling on his lap.

"Let me show you," he said, grasping her waist.

Lady Eleanor's Good
List for Being Bad:

Definitely take the long way home.

Chapter 24

$\mathcal{S}$he felt glorious. There was no other word for it.

Well, perhaps overwhelmed also. In an entirely glorious way.

She allowed him to push her off his lap, his hand low across her belly holding her up. She bent forward and heard his grunts as he presumably removed his jacket. How had she not insisted he get undressed also?

Oh, because she was too busy feeling gloriously overwhelmed by his clever fingers and how the passion felt as though it was sizzling through her skin.

"Hold on to the opposite seat," he commanded, and she bent lower, grabbing the top of the seat and turning her head back to look at him.

There was enough light outside for her to make out that yes, his jacket was off, his cravat was off, and he had undone some of the buttons on his shirt. She could see the taut muscle of his chest. She wished she could turn around and put her mouth just there, right on his nipple, and lick it.

His hands were at the waistband of his trousers,

and as she watched, he shimmied them down so his pants were below there, right where he jutted hugely out.

That thing had been inside her already. She knew it fit—she just couldn't imagine how, even after it had actually happened.

His eyelids were heavy-lidded, looking at her bottom, and she shifted her hips, making his eyes widen.

"Vixen," he said, half standing in the carriage, putting one hand at her waist again and placing the other hand on top of hers.

"Hercules," she replied with a smirk.

He let go of her waist and he drew his hand back, and she felt him there, at her entrance.

It felt wonderfully sinful and wrong, to have him behind her like this, both of them half-clothed, the crucial parts exposed.

"Mmm," he said as she felt the head of him push inside just a bit. "Relax, Eleanor," he urged. "Think of how good it will feel when I am inside you. Filling you. Fucking you in this carriage as the world goes about its business without knowing you and I are in here doing this."

His words, his blunt, sexual words, made her nipples tighten all over again, warming her just there where she'd spasmed under his hand.

"Talk to me," she said in a throaty whisper, pushing back against him. Now she could see the appeal of his saying precisely what he felt at any moment. She relished his blunt speaking.

"Yes, I will," he said, now thrusting so he was

halfway in, the movement of the carriage making his body move back and forth, farther in with each lurch. "Do you want me to tell you how it felt as you came under my hand? Or how tight and welcoming you feel around my cock?"

"Oh!" she moaned, dropping her head down as she got a stronger grip on the carriage seat. "I want you to—to do that," she said, moving back against him so she could feel his strong thighs against the back of her legs, the carriage pushing them together. Her breasts swayed with each movement, still so sensitive from his touch. Every motion of the carriage made her body quiver. His hand was at her hip, his other clutching the carriage seat.

He took his hand away from her body, and then he pushed inside her, his fingers touching her as he guided himself in.

"You're so tight," he said as he thrust forward, so far in that his body touched her bottom, his hand now reaching around to touch her there, there where he'd touched her before, bringing her to such heights of pleasure.

"Tell me," she begged him, pushing back, hearing him grunt as their bodies made contact.

"Tell you what? How it feels to have my cock sheathed inside you? How I want to bury myself in you forever? How I wish we were traveling in this carriage for the rest of our lives so I could fuck and fuck and fuck you?"

"Yes," she moaned, his fingers moving again, bringing her to that brink of ecstasy again. So soon, and he hadn't even had the pleasure of whatever feeling this was once. He must have known what he was doing, since he eased his movement to concentrate on her, his fingers speeding up their rhythm. He was leaning over her, his mouth on her shoulder, and he bit her just as his fingers brought her to that edge and flung her over again.

She felt wrung out, but also as alive as she'd ever felt, and he was still inside her, a throbbing reminder of just what they were doing.

"God, Eleanor," he said, pushing himself faster and faster inside her, his motions faster than the carriage itself, his hand cupping her sex, the slap of his body against hers an erotic accompaniment to his heavy breathing.

And then he gave one final thrust and moaned, both hands coming to her hips to hold on as she felt something warm spill inside her.

"Mmm," she murmured, feeling sated and boneless and marveling at both herself and him. "That was wonderful."

He kissed her shoulder again as he eased out of her, and then he helped her sit down again, his fingers busily putting her back to rights. She allowed him to do up her various laces and smooth fabric, just watching him as he kept at his work.

"You're good at this." It felt odd, to know that he might have done this same thing with some other woman, but it wasn't as though she thought he was just as inexperienced as she—his previous actions in the back room of the bookshop were clear indications that not only had he done it, he was also quite skilled at it all.

He must have picked up on what she was thinking, since his fingers stilled and he brought them up to turn her face to his. "I have done this before, Eleanor, but it feels new with you. It feels . . . overwhelming. You overwhelm me." And then he leaned forward and kissed her, softly, so tenderly she felt her chest tighten with emotion.

"Oh," she replied, reaching up to push that lock of hair away from his forehead, feeling his fingers tighten on her jaw as they kept their gazes locked on one another.

The first thing she was going to do when she arrived home was to toss her list. She had adventures to embark on, not just to tabulate and hope for, and she didn't need anything to urge her to be bad. She just was. She was also brave, strong, stubborn, opinionated, and in love.

"IF YOU'D ONLY already told her," Ida whispered emphatically in Eleanor's ear.

They stood, all four of the Howlett sisters, in the Duke of Marymount's ballroom. It was an "intimate gathering," their mother had said. "No more than one hundred people," all of whom were members of either the Howlett or Carson families.

The purpose was to get the families acquainted before the official betrothal announcement. The party had been planned and the invitations sent while Eleanor and her sisters were meeting with the Carson brothers, and so here they were, all four of them in attendance since it was not a formal affair.

And if it continued, and her father said something, even though nothing was yet official—they were still working out the terms of the settlement—then it wouldn't matter when Eleanor said no, the word would be out that she had jilted Lord Carson and the Howlett sisters would be even less desirable.

"What are we going to do?" Olivia said in a frantic squeak.

Lord Carson and Alexander were walking toward them, no doubt with the same questions in their minds. But she knew Alexander hadn't been able to find time yet to speak to his father, who was conversing with her father at the edge of the room. Not yet announcing anything, but likely on the verge of it.

No, no, no, no, a voice chanted in Eleanor's mind. Not that the voice was any help, not at all, but it was there nonetheless. If only voices in minds did useful things like suggest ways to avoid having betrothals announced in public settings.

Pearl's eyes were enormous in her face, and she just stared at Eleanor, looking precisely the way Eleanor felt. Did she have the same voice in her head too?

And now she had more questions and no more answers.

"I don't know what we'll do," Eleanor said, glancing to where her mother appeared about to say something. *Please let it be about what she had for dinner, or how terrible it was that she had only been able to fit seven feathers into her hair instead of ten.*

Eleanor drew her spectacles out and put them on. If she was going to be publicly sacrificed, she at least wanted to see it occur.

Her mother began to speak. "I would like to welcome everyone to our home, all of our family and friends, to this very informal gathering." Informal even though the best gold plate was out, the champagne was circulating, and there had been no expense spared on the food, which Eleanor would have normally enjoyed, but not now, not when she couldn't eat.

"And I would like to discuss a few things that are of import at this critical time," Ida interrupted, stepping up to their mother's side. "Thank you for giving me this opportunity, Mother," she said with a regal nod in the duchess's direction. As though she were a queen herself, and the duchess was just another peon. "We all know that our modern society has made it possible to see in the nighttime, with gas lighting, but do you know the history of gaslight?" She took a moment to look at the guests, as though waiting for a response.

Some of them shook their heads, which Ida took as a sign to continue.

"The first man to explore the possibility of gas lighting was William Murdoch, who saw its potential, lighting his own house with gas in the previous century."

Where was she going with this?

The duchess was staring at Ida aghast, apparently too startled by her daughter's demonstration of knowledge to stop her.

Olivia and Pearl both joined their sister, one on either side of her, as she kept speaking. And speaking.

". . . And gas lighting has made it possible for us to read for longer"—a fact that would appeal to Ida, of course—"and for factories to have longer hours, and if we produce more, we can make more, and pay more wages."

By this time, nearly half an hour into Ida's monologue, the guests had mostly drifted away. The duke's face had flamed to a bright purple, but he hadn't stepped up to stop his daughter's talk. Probably thinking that his doing so might cause even more talk, talk he was paying a generous dowry to avoid.

As Ida continued, Eleanor couldn't help but look at Alexander, who was regarding her sister with a bemused look. And then he turned to look at her, a wide grin of complicity on his face. He nodded in satisfaction as Ida continued for at least another half an hour, by which time nearly everyone had made their escape.

"I COULDN'T THINK of what to do to stop things, so I just decided to talk." Ida shrugged, her expression showing her pleasure at having rescued the situation.

The sisters were all back in Eleanor's bedroom again, the evening having come to a precipitous (and gas-fueled) close, their father nearly recovering his color, but not his ability to speak, their mother speaking in her usual exclamatory fashion, but unable to make any sense whatsoever.

"You did wonderfully." Eleanor grinned at Ida, who looked abashed.

"It was so boring!" Olivia enthused, turning Ida's smile to a frown. "Nobody wanted to stay, and so Mother couldn't have her big moment, and our plans can proceed."

"Yes, that is what I was hoping for," Ida replied in a stiff voice.

"It was wonderful," Eleanor repeated, meeting her sister's eyes. "Truly."

"Thank you," Ida said in a soft voice.

"And you will speak to Mother tomorrow?" Pearl asked. "You cannot let it go any more than that, who knows what she will plan next?"

"Probably me in a wedding gown strapped to an elephant," Eleanor replied. "Lord Carson waiting in an elephant-tamer's hat prepared to accept me."

"Elephants don't have tamers," Ida pointed out.

"Or she'll just give you tea the way you like it, and when you're recovering from the shock, she'll ask you if you like it, and you'll say 'I do,' and then you'll be married."

Eleanor laughed at the thought, only partially rueful at the impossibility of her mother getting her tea correct.

"I'll speak to her tomorrow," she promised.

"You wanted to see me?" Alex's father said in an impatient tone.

Alex took a deep breath. "Yes. I need to discuss some business with you."

"Business, eh?" His father's tone revealed just how little he respected Alex's topic, at least since it came from Alex.

"Yes. Sit." Alex gestured to his father's chair, the one Bennett normally used when dealing with estate matters.

His father arched an eyebrow, but did as Alex commanded.

"What is it? What business can you possibly have to discuss with me?"

Alex placed his hand on the back of the other chair, but didn't seat himself. He wanted to loom over his father, make it clear he was leading this discussion.

"Bennett cannot marry Lady Eleanor." Well, that wasn't quite how he'd wanted to put it; he'd hoped to lead into it more gradually, but there he went, just saying things.

His father snorted. "Of course he can." He placed his palms flat on the table, preparing to rise.

"Sit." Alex imbued his voice with the assurance of knowing, finally, who he was, and that he could make a difference. It wasn't the usual method of doing things, but it was his method.

And hers. Once he resolved this, ensured that there would be no repercussions, he would ask her. He hoped she would say yes, but he would respect her decision either way.

Though he would try to cheat when he did ask, perhaps removing his shirt as he spoke. Or giving her more books of mythology, and not the kind with accompanying salacious pictures. Or perhaps he would offer her those; she did seem to enjoy re-enacting some of the scenes.

"Are you going to tell me why you are stating Bennett cannot marry Lady Eleanor, or are you just going to stand there?"

His father's sharp words shook him from his thoughts of the future.

"Fine. The thing is," he began, crossing his arms over his chest, "the duke is even more anxious to get Lady Eleanor married."

"Yes, I know that already."

His father really disliked him. But they were equal in that, as Alex returned the dislike, topped with a healthy portion of disdain.

"And you haven't thought to turn that to your advantage?" He spoke in a musing tone. "I would have thought a businessman such as yourself would have seen immediately what could be done."

"What do you mean?" Now his father sounded less dismissive, at least. Curious, but guarded. Of course. Always guarded when it came to his second son.

"Bennett is a fine matrimonial catch, isn't he? That is why you were able to secure Lady Eleanor, a duke's eldest daughter, for him. Her dowry is impressive, yes, but imagine how much more you could get if you just had time to negotiate." And here was where he gambled, again, on something that might not happen. "I have been busy working on a project that will bring in some funds. Cash in hand, enough"—or so he hoped—"to stave off the worst of the creditors and buy some time, so to speak. Time for you to go shopping for the best deal for Bennett." Even though Alex hoped it wouldn't come to that, again. But Bennett had insisted that Alex dangle the possibility of a higher dowry and Bennett's marriage when Alex spoke to their father—otherwise, the marquis would never agree, and either Bennett or Eleanor would have to call off the engagement, which would be ruinous both financially and in terms of reputation.

"Who else is out there?" his father demanded.

Here's where it got tricky. Even trickier. "You said yourself you made a list for me. What if you reviewed that list with an eye toward securing a bride for Bennett, one whose reputation is intact, one whose family has much more money than the duke?"

"You mean a family in business."

"It could be, yes," Alex replied, trying to ignore his father's condescension. "Or it could be a family that didn't have the disgrace of a runaway daughter. The thing is, there is no guarantee that this daughter won't follow in her sister's errant footsteps." Which might be truer than it would have been weeks ago, now that she'd spent time with Alex. But he wasn't going to tell his father that.

"And if she runs off, Bennett would still be married to her, so you couldn't just arrange another bride."

Alex waited as his father—not a stupid man, if he was an unpleasant one—turned the idea over in his head, his features tightening as he considered the fact that Eleanor might prove to be just as wayward as her sister. Bringing scandal to the Raybourns, as well as to the Howletts, if they were joined through marriage.

"How much do you have now?" his father demanded, glaring up at him.

"Enough," he said. His father didn't challenge him, since everyone knew Alex always told the truth.

"How about if you marry this Lady, then?"

I want to. Alex shrugged. "That would be up to her, of course." He sat down in the chair opposite, pretending to think about it. "But that would be a clever solution, wouldn't it? For your second son to secure the duke's daughter and the dowry, leaving the heir to find a better match somewhere?"

Unless she said no. But she wouldn't say no, would she?

No, she loved him. She'd told him so, even while calling him a lummox. If that wasn't true love, he wasn't sure what was.

"Very clever indeed," Alex's father said in satisfaction, drawing a piece of paper and a pen to him on the desk.

"Thank you, Father," Alex replied as he rose, nearly able to take a breath.

Now all that needed to happen was for her to inform her parents she refused to be bartered. He wished he could be there to see it, all firm resolve and fiery eyes and self-determination.

Because he wished he could be there to see her, to see the woman she had become. Forever and always.

He just had to ask her.

"I NEED TO speak to you, Mother." Eleanor stood at the doorway to her mother's sitting room.

"It is far too early," her mother replied. She glanced out the window. "And it's raining," she continued, as though that made it even more egregious.

It was raining. Eleanor knew how much Alex liked the rain. Something more she knew about him.

It was nearly eleven o'clock in the morning, which meant her mother had been awake for perhaps an hour. Long enough to have had her tea but not long enough to have gotten enough energy to speak nonstop all the time, which was why Eleanor had chosen this moment to say what she needed to say.

"I need to speak to you now, Mother." Eleanor walked into the room, gesturing to her mother's maid to leave. "Alone."

"It's not about gas, is it? I've had enough of that, thank you very much. You can go, Fletcher." Her mother waved her hand in dismissal to the maid who curtseyed, then left the room, shutting the door behind her.

Her mother sat at her dressing table, her hair undone, wearing her nightclothes and a wrapper. She looked older than she did when she was fully coiffed and done up as the Duchess of Marymount, and Eleanor felt a twinge of regret that she and her mother were not closer. Then again, her mother didn't appear to care, so it wasn't anything Eleanor could affect.

Her own future, however, she could.

"What is it?" her mother asked, drawing a brush through her hair. She didn't look at Eleanor, instead continuing to look at herself in the mirror.

Eleanor sat down on a small stool behind her mother, clasping her hands loosely in front of her. "I need to tell you something."

"Go on."

"I will not be marrying Lord Carson."

Silence. Blessed silence, then—"What?" her mother shrieked, slamming the brush down on the table. "Of course you are!"

"I won't." Eleanor rose, beginning to walk around the room. Her mother twisted on her seat to look at her, her mouth dropped open.

"But your father, and your sisters."

"My father barely remembers my name," Eleanor replied, "and my sisters support me. It is terrible that Della ran away, but I cannot sacrifice my life for her mistake."

Her mother turned back around, looking into her mirror. "It is not sacrificing your life—it is marriage." She made a harrumphing noise, as though Eleanor were ridiculous. According to her mother, she probably was. Who wouldn't want to be married to the perfectly pleasant Lord Carson?

That she did finally have an answer to. *Me. I don't want to marry him, I want to be happy. I want to be overwhelmed, I want to find my joy.*

I have found my joy. And he is going to ask me to marry him.

"We will see what your father says about this," her mother continued, speaking as though she were sputtering.

"I will tell him myself. Even though I don't actually care what Father has to say," Eleanor replied in a low, quiet voice. "Just as he didn't care what I had to say when he decided this."

She walked to the door and stepped outside without waiting for her mother's reply.

Hearing her mother's screech as she walked to her room.

"WHAT HAPPENED?" OLIVIA asked when Eleanor opened the door to find her sisters in her bedroom. Of course. Cotswold was there, too, giving Eleanor a worried look. All four of these women just—caring about her in a way her mother never had, and never would.

Eleanor took a deep breath, then smiled at all of them in turn. "I told her I wasn't going to marry Lord Carson."

Olivia bounced on the bed, making Pearl and Ida bounce as well. It made Eleanor dizzy to look at. "Does that mean you are going to marry Lord Alexander?"

"Well," Eleanor began, only to stop as Ida interrupted.

"She will marry him. Won't you? You love him, and he loves you. It is a simple equation really." And then Ida looked scornful, as though the math was far too easy for someone with her brain.

"It is," Eleanor agreed.

A knock on the door made all five ladies' heads turn.

"Yes?" Eleanor said.

The door opened to reveal the pursed lips and stern face of their butler. "Your father wishes to see you."

"Of course he does," Eleanor said.

"We are cheering for you!" Olivia said, punctuating her words with a wave of her hand.

Pearl and Ida echoed the gesture, while Cotswold nodded.

"Thank you," Eleanor said, taking a deep breath as she stepped out of the room to walk downstairs. To where her father waited, determined to make her do what he wished, while she was just as determined to do what she wished.

But she had the weight of the Howlett sisters on her side, and she would not be dissuaded.

THE DUKE WAS waiting for her at the entrance to his study. He didn't speak, just held his arm out to direct her into the room. She walked to the chair facing his desk and sat, crossing her ankles and clasping her hands in her lap.

She felt oddly calm. She was about to do something, say something, that was entirely unlike a duke's dutiful, dull, and duty-bound daughter. She was going to, in her own way, do something as scandalous as Della had, albeit more quietly.

She was going to make her own fate.

The duke closed the door and walked toward her. Not sitting himself behind the desk, as she'd expected, but planting himself a few feet away from her, standing with crossed arms.

"What is this I hear from your mother?"

She wanted to ask him if that was a rhetorical question—of course he knew what she'd said. He just wanted her to say it to his face, since he likely doubted she would.

"I will not marry Lord Carson." She spoke simply and directly, not allowing any kind of fear or concern change her tone.

His face purpled before her eyes, and then he spoke. But not spoke—thundered.

"You will do as I say." If words could flatten buildings, London had just been razed.

She shook her head.

"I will not," she replied. "And what is more, if only you could listen to us, if only you cared about us, any of us, we would not be having this conversation. My sister Della, the one who caused all the scandal you are currently trying to stave, was so unhappy with the choices presented to her that she ran off with a man she knew was a blackguard just so she could get away. I want her back. I want her safe. But more than that, I want all of us to be happy, and we cannot be happy when you are dictating our choices in life. We need to make our own choices, no matter how wrong," she said, thinking of Della, "or scandalous they might be."

She rose from her seat, tilting her head to look him directly in the eyes. "I will be making my own choices in life. I know you say you want the best for us, but the best isn't whether or not we are able to afford clothing that suits our position. The best is when you find someone you love, who loves you back, and you decide you want to spend your lives together." She stepped toward him, taking another deep breath. "I will not marry anyone whom I do not love."

"I can force you," he said in a low voice.

She shrugged. "You can try. But listen to this—I have been spending time alone with a gentleman, one to whom I am not engaged." At least not yet. "And not only that, I have been engaged in the vulgar pursuit of translating works of a scandalous nature with the even more vulgar intent of selling those prurient works. I will not hesitate to tell everyone who will listen what I have been doing, should you try to force me into something I do not want." She was trembling now, but she couldn't let him see it. "And I will have no compunction in announcing my part in that endeavor should you try to do anything like you did to me to my sisters."

He just stared at her, his eyes wide, as though he didn't recognize her.

Likely he didn't. He had long ago tagged her and put her in a box labeled "The Duke's Eldest

Daughter," and to see that the person in the box was a person, and not a puppet he could manipulate was likely something he'd never expected.

"I wish it had not come to this," she said, touching his sleeve. Wishing he had ever shown her more than just a tolerant disdain. "If you want to get to know me, to get to know my sisters, we would appreciate that." If he had, perhaps Della would still be home.

"I'm your daughter. I love you," she said in a soft voice. And she did, and she knew he loved her, but that he didn't know her. Because there had to be love there to get him to bestir himself to try to salvage the family's reputation. Even though she also knew that he was concerned for his own. But still. There was some love there; she just had to figure out how to get to it.

"I know you care about us. I know you don't want us to be unhappy. I know you never thought I would be unhappy being married to a perfectly fine gentleman. But he is not the right gentleman."

Finally, he spoke. "Have you—have you found the right one, then?"

He didn't sound furious. He didn't sound thundering. He just sounded—curious.

Maybe there was hope for him, and her sisters.

"I have." She smiled as she spoke, wondering if he was standing out there in the rain waiting for her even now. Wondering how her blunt lover would ask her to spend her life with him, nearly giggling as she thought about the myriad ways he might ask.

"You should find him and tell him, then," her father said slowly.

"I will." She drew up on her toes and kissed her father on the cheek, then walked swiftly out the door, ignoring the offer of an umbrella from the butler and stepping outside where he waited.

Standing outside in the rain, drops clinging to his face, his jacket, making his hair deliciously disheveled.

"IT'S RAINING," ELEANOR said as she descended the stairs to where he stood.

"It's perfect," Alex corrected. He took her fingers in his, holding her hand tightly, as though she were going to bolt or something. "It's perfect for what I want to do."

"Do what?" she replied, glancing up at him slyly.

"Not that, Dejanire." He took a deep breath then lowered himself onto one knee, directly into a puddle. He withdrew something from his jacket pocket and held it up to her before she could expostulate about his trousers or the damp or anything.

"Eleanor, I am overwhelmingly in love with you. I want to be with you each and every day of my life from now on. I want to be with you as you see things for the first time, to gamble on our happiness forever, knowing we will always win. I want to walk in the rain with you. I want to kiss you until you forget your own name, and mine."

He held the ring up a little higher. "Will you marry me?"

She nodded her head, lowering herself down into the puddle as well, her only thought one of *yes, yes, yes.*

"I love you too," she replied, holding her hand out for him to slide the ring on. "I want to marry you. You have shown me my joy." She paused as she considered it. "And many other things," she said with a grin. "I want to gamble on all of it with you. I want you to tell me whatever it is you're feeling each and every day. Especially if it is 'I love you.'"

"Thank goodness," he said, rising and taking her hand to rise also. "Now let's go confirm our betrothal in the carriage."

"And how do you propose we confirm—" she began, before he swept her into his arms and kissed her until she couldn't breathe, let alone speak.

Her last coherent thought was that now her sisters would be able to find their joy too.

Keep reading for a sneak peek at the
next sexy story in Megan Frampton's
Duke's Daughters series,

LADY BE RECKLESS

Coming in winter 2018.

Lady Olivia's Particular Guide to Decorum

It is not proper for a young lady to propose to a gentleman. Unless, of course, the gentleman has a deep and abiding (and silent) love for the lady, and he is not aware she reciprocates.

Chapter 1

"*O*livia!" The duchess's call could be heard from two floors away. And Olivia was seated in the same room, in full view of her mother.

"Yes, Mother?" she replied in an aggrieved tone. She had promised to deliver no fewer than ten shifts within a month's time to the society for Poor and Orphaned Children, and she was only on the second one, since her needle skills were not as good as her skills in promising things she might not be able to deliver, apparently.

Not for the first time, she wished that things were as she wished they should be so she wouldn't have to constantly be trying to improve things. Her needle-pricked fingers would no doubt wish that also.

"I cannot deal with Cook today. You will have to," her mother announced, not paying attention to what Olivia was already occupied with. As was usual.

Olivia merely nodded. Her mother had said the same thing, or a variation thereof, in the year or so since Olivia's eldest sister had married Lord Alexander Raybourn. The Duchess of Marymount hadn't always been so helpless; but once their sister Della had run off with the dancing master, and Eleanor had refused to marry the gentleman their parents had chosen for her, the duchess seemed to have given up all the duties she'd previously handled, leaving her remaining three daughters to handle everything. And since Olivia's twin, Pearl, was shy and preferred to be outdoors, and their sister Ida was too busy reading and looking down her nose at everyone else, it was all left up to Olivia.

Olivia did not flinch from doing what was necessary to make things right. Hence the shift-making.

"Olivia, are you listening to me?"

"Of course I am," Olivia replied, frowning at the knot in her sewing. She had to admit to being a terrible seamstress. "You want me to speak with Cook, and you probably also want me to review the guest list for next week's dinner party to be certain all the invitations went out properly. And to remind Cook that the Marquis of Wheatley does not like green beans."

"Hmph. Well, yes," her mother replied in a grudging tone.

The guest list for the dinner party included Lord Carson, the marquis's son, and the gentleman whom Eleanor had refused to marry.

Leaving him free to marry Olivia, something she had wanted since the first moment she saw him. She sighed as she thought about him. He was handsome, and kind, and very, very busy. Olivia wanted to help him, and she could tell, from how he spoke to her, that he wanted her to help him also. It would be a perfect match.

Not to mention it would mean she was able to run more things as she wished to. Including Lord Carson.

But it wouldn't be a match at all if the dinner party wasn't absolutely perfect, which meant she should go straightaway and speak to Cook.

Olivia dropped the fabric and thread on the table beside her as she prepared to take care of things. Again.

The door to the sitting room flung open and her twin, Pearl, launched herself inside, her eyes wide.

"Olivia, you have to come quickly!" Pearl said in an urgent tone.

"WHAT IS IT?" she asked as she rose to her feet.

"The gardener next door, he's—" And then Pearl stopped, shaking her head.

Olivia marched out of the sitting room, Cook and sewing forgotten, shoulders squared, as she went to right whatever wrong it was that made her twin so upset.

"He found some kittens in the shed and now he says he's going to—Oh, Livy, you have to save them!" Pearl said, her voice wavering in her emotion.

"Indeed I will," Olivia declared, brushing past a few startled servants to the back of the house.

She felt herself start to burn with the righteous fury that had become her constant companion over the past few years, since she'd realized that the world was not entirely just and that there were, indeed, terrible people who existed in it.

She hadn't been able to eradicate all the terrible people in the world, but she could acknowledge to herself—privately, not wishing to draw attention to her deeds—that she had made the world a slightly better place in the time since she'd come to her senses.

Only a few years ago she'd been equally consumed with parties, and balls, and pretty dresses. And Bennett, Lord Carson, whom she still had to admit to being consumed with.

She still enjoyed those things, of course, but they couldn't derail her from her purpose in life: to help people.

And, apparently, kittens.

"Sir!" she said as she stepped outside into the garden. She glanced around, Pearl on her heels, until she spotted the man in the Robinsons' garden, who was holding a small, wriggling thing in his hand.

"Sir!" she said again, louder, so that he turned and looked at her across the fence that separated their properties.

The two families had been neighbors for as long as Olivia could remember; the children had grown up together, but now the only Robinson left in this house was the matriarch of the family, a terrifyingly proper woman who had always looked at

Olivia as though she knew she was thinking of parties, and balls, and dresses when she should be thinking of better things.

I'm thinking of better things now, Olivia thought as she stomped toward the fence, swinging her arms furiously. *Namely saving small helpless animals from your ogre gardener.* "What are you doing?" she asked. Then she shook her head as she planted her fists on her hips. "Never mind, I know what you are doing. Although I can't fathom why you would want to harm such precious little creatures," she continued, her voice softening as she saw the tumble of kittens at the man's feet. There were three more down on the ground, all looking small enough to fit in her hand, all bumbling in and around each other in an adorably confusing way. Their mother was nowhere in sight, which likely meant these kittens would be dead if they weren't taken care of soon.

That furious anger heated.

"These precious creatures are living in the shed, making a mess everywhere," the man said, shaking the kitten in his hand for emphasis. The kitten in question was a grey tabby with, it seemed, one bent ear and whiskers that were nearly as long as the kitten itself was wide.

Olivia unlatched the gate separating the properties and launched herself through until she was able to remove the kitten from his hand.

The kitten promptly clawed her, but it was all part of the ongoing battle. *Every war has its wounds*, she'd told Pearl often enough. Usually when Pearl was complaining of a hand cramp after Olivia had wrangled her sister into helping her with her latest charity project. Pearl was a much better seamstress than Olivia, after all.

"I will inform Lady Robinson of your behavior today, and I will be removing these animals myself," she declared, holding the struggling kitten up to her chest.

The man shrugged. "The lady don't care. And as long as they aren't living in my shed, I don't care either."

Olivia opened her mouth to tell him just what she thought of his behavior, but decided it wasn't worth it to waste her breath. Not when she could be speaking out about injustice, or helping poor families find a better way in the world, or sharing her most fervent desire with Lord Carson. *Bennett.*

"Pearl," she said instead, turning her head back to address her twin. Pearl had already anticipated what she was going to say, and had retrieved a basket their own gardener used for roses, its handle slung over her arm.

"Good, take this one," Olivia said, putting the kitten into the basket, and then bending down to gather up the remainder in her arms. They were so tiny they all fit, their tiny claws shredding the fabric of her gown, not strong enough to draw blood, but stinging. The three looked similar enough to the first one to be siblings, and Olivia felt a swell in her heart as she thought about what would happen if she and her sisters were just as lost as these little mites, one of whom had just begun to bite her wrist.

Just another wound in service, Olivia thought as she placed each kitten in the basket, taking it from Pearl when all four were contained.

"If you find any other helpless creatures," she said as she marched back over to their property, "please send word so I can rescue them from your evil clutches."

The hero in *The Notorious Noose*, the latest penny dreadful she and Pearl had read, had used those same words. Olivia found it useful—not to mention entertaining—to read those books for language she could borrow to make her points. She had found people responded better to hyperbole rather than plain facts.

Besides which, wrongs were always righted, and misdeeds were suitably punished, which left her with a satisfied feeling after reading them. Not like in real life, where rights were often left unrighted, and people kept suffering.

But at least, she thought as she glanced into the basket, these four kittens wouldn't suffer any longer. Not if she had anything to say about it.

Which she did.

"DID YOU PAY no attention at all?" Bennett asked as he glared at Edward.

Edward couldn't help but smirk at his friend. Bennett was so outraged, as vehement as he was on the Parliamentary floor.

"You're asking if I paid attention during *dancing lessons*," Edward said, emphasizing the last two words to show his disdain.

Bennett flung his hands up, hands that had been trying to put Edward into the correct position for the waltz just a few moments ago.

"Yes. You do know that polite society deems it important to dance, don't you?"

"Ah, and that's the problem." Edward bent into a deep bow, spreading his arms wide. "Have you been introduced to Mr. Edward Wolcott, the most notable bastard of your acquaintance?"

Bennett rolled his eyes. "You don't have to constantly rub the fact into everyone's faces all the time, you know."

Oh, but I do, Edward thought. *Because if I don't make reference to it, remove the sting of its mention from anyone who might say something, they will think they've hurt me when they mention my dubious parentage.*

But he didn't tell his friend that. Bennett knew precisely why Edward did what he did; he just didn't understand how much it did hurt. The sidelong glances that had supplanted the outright fights his schoolmates had baited him into. Fights that Edward took pride in winning, even though winning meant he was called to the headmaster's office after each fracas.

Which is where he had met Bennett, and Bennett had stuck with Edward ever since, no matter how many times Edward pointed out that the son of a marquis should not be friends with the bastard son of a financier.

Which led him to now, and the dancing that Edward was making a mess of.

"Why can't I just speak with people about horses and hunting and the things I actually like to do rather than dance or make irritatingly banal conversation?"

Bennett did not deign to reply, instead holding his arms out. "Let's try this again. I cannot believe that someone so athletic can be so terrible a dancer."

"It's not the same thing," Edward grumbled. Mostly because he'd concentrated on athletics as a way to circumvent the cruel talk; he figured if he was stronger than any of his potential tormentors he could keep their comments at bay with the very real possibility of physical violence. And his strategy had worked; very few men dared to mention anything now, not after appraising Edward's physique.

"I do know," Bennett said as he adjusted Edward's hands, nudging his feet into the right place and heaving several exasperated sighs, "that you loathe dancing. I am well aware, nearly as much as you, of how much you hate all this rigmarole. But I also know you have to do it. You told me what your father said."

Edward felt his chest tighten at the mention of his father. Mr. Beechcroft. The man who, inexplicably, had loved and raised him as well as if he had been legitimately born. The man who wanted nothing more than to see his son take a position in society, a position that he himself could never take, thanks to his merchant upbringing. Edward wished it was enough that he had learned the business, and enjoyed doing it. His father wanted more for him though.

"Fine," he replied in a grouchy tone.

"And if you cannot bear it for another moment, there is usually an unused library or another type of room where you can go to escape for a bit."

Edward made a harrumphing noise indicating his thoughts on that idea. Running away from a problem was not his way; he usually did the opposite, running headlong toward it without considering the consequences.

Bennett, who was accustomed to Edward's grumpiness, ignored his friend, instead instructing him on how to count out the rhythm of the waltz.

If only Bennett could teach him how not to see mockery in everyone's faces when he attended his first society function.

But that would be even more difficult than his mastering the waltz. And he was currently smashing all ten of Bennett's toes.

"OH, HOW DELIGHTFUL!"

Olivia spoke to herself, since Pearl had disappeared in search of some refreshment, leaving Olivia to the side of the ballroom. Their mother was fanning herself in the chaperones' corner, talking nonstop as was her usual habit. Olivia and her sisters had gotten to the point where they were able to communicate with one another through hand gestures so they knew what topic their mother was discussing without having to listen.

Olivia's dance partner, a slight gentleman who had stepped on her feet at least six times, had made his bows and departed as soon as the music had stopped.

Was it, she wondered, because she had taken the opportunity to remind Lord Frederick of the essential steps of the dance they were engaged in? But surely he would welcome a gentle reminder of how he was supposed to move?

That settled, she glanced around the room, her gaze searching for Bennett.

The party was at the Estabrooks' house, and she knew—because of course she followed his career avidly—that Bennett was hoping that Lord Estabrook would lend his support to one of Bennett's ongoing projects.

She hadn't followed closely enough to know just what he was hoping to accomplish. When she was his wife, she would of course be conversant with the issues that occupied his time. But until then, she had to admit that reading all the arguments for and against a concern made her eyes wander.

But being Lady Carson would make her into the type of person who would be engaged and fascinated by the things that made her yawn now.

She wrinkled her nose as she spotted Bennett at the edge of the dance floor speaking with Lady Cecilia, a girl Olivia knew of but had never met.

Bennett looked bored, although her conscience

forced her to acknowledge that it was difficult to see his expression from this far away. But he had to be bored speaking with Lady Cecilia—Lady Cecilia was a debutante fresh from the school-room, and Bennett was a man, accustomed to matters of great importance, not where a gown was coming from or how many invitations one had received.

That type of flighty girl had been Olivia not so long ago, even though it felt like a lifetime. No wonder Bennett had always regarded her as though he were mildly amused by her. It was time for him to see her as she truly was.

Tonight.

Thus decided, she began the slow walk to where Bennett stood, skirting the edge of the room and smiling politely at the guests who nodded at her.

It wasn't entirely proper for her to approach him, but she knew that once he heard what she had to say he would forgive her. More than that, he would agree to what she asked him, and neither one of them would have to spend any more conversation with people who bored them. Who didn't share the same passionate interests in righting wrongs and justice and change that they did.

"Lord Carson?" she said as she joined Bennett and Lady Cecilia, the latter of whom raised her tiny, perfect nose at Olivia's intrusion. "Might I beg a private word with you?"

Bennett glanced from one lady to another, his brow furrowed, but after a moment he nodded. "Of course, my lady," he said. He bowed to Lady

Cecilia. "You'll forgive me? Lady Olivia is my sister-in-law's younger sister, nearly family."

Lady Cecilia shot a glare at Olivia, but her mouth curved into a sweet smile as she looked at Bennett. "Of course, my lord." A pause, then Lady Cecilia spoke again. "When you are finished with familial concerns, I would like to ask your opinion on a few things."

Olivia nearly emitted a noise that would have indicated what she thought, but that wouldn't be fitting for the adult young lady she was now.

So she just returned Lady Cecilia's smile and took Bennett's arm, allowing him to lead her into one of the rooms adjacent to the ballroom.

"Mr. . . . Wolcott?" the lady said, her pause between the "mister" and the "Wolcott" an indication she knew precisely who he was. Especially since one of Bennett's friends, a Lord Something-or-Other, had just introduced them.

Bennett's friend glanced from Edward to the Pausing Lady, his look one of confusion. Edward appreciated that Bennett didn't gossip about him, but giving this friend of his some word about why not everyone would want to meet Edward would not go amiss.

But that was Bennett. Seeing the good in everybody, and not recognizing that some people reveled in ignorance. Only one of the reasons Edward was grateful he was the one born a bastard, and not Eternally Optimistic Bennett.

"Yes." Edward accompanied his reply with a

bow. "I have just arrived in London, and my friend Lord Carson invited me to this function." He might as well get the explanation over with, given that she was likely about to question him about just how he happened to be here with the likes of her.

"Ah," she replied, visibly softening. Bennett had that effect on people.

Edward did not.

"And how do *you* happen to be here?" Edward asked, making Bennett's friend's face turn white and the lady gasp in outrage.

Damn. And he'd been doing so well. For at least fifteen seconds or so.

"If you'll excuse me," he continued without waiting for her to speak, bowing again and turning on his heel in search of one of those vaunted private rooms Bennett had promised. Anything but being open and exposed out here, like a frightened fox being stampeded by vicious dogs.

He had to admit to having far more sympathy for the animals he hunted right now. And also understood why they turned around and snarled rather than succumbing to the attack.

But he couldn't snarl. He had to escape.

"Is LADY ELEANOR all right? I know that Alexander was worried she was doing so much, what with the"—and then Bennett hesitated.

"Baby coming?" Olivia allowed herself the luxury of rolling her eyes at him. "Honestly, it is not as though we all don't know what is happening."

Bennett uttered a sort of strangled noise in his throat, then took a deep breath. "Yes, the baby."

"Everything is fine." She swept ahead of him and pushed a door open, one that was in one of the far corners of the ballroom. She glanced behind to see that Lady Cecilia had already found some other gentleman to converse with—so much for perseverance, she thought, wanting to toss her head in triumph, then gestured for him to precede her. "Go in. I want to speak to you."

Now that it was the moment she'd been thinking about for so long, she had to admit to feeling nervous. Not that he wouldn't agree, because of course he would, it was the right thing to do, plus she knew how he felt about her, even if he didn't. It was that this meant that her whole life was about to change; she would be Lady Carson. She would finally be able to do all the things she wanted, no needed, to do.

And she would spend the rest of her life with him.

Just thinking about it made her calmer.

She closed the door behind them, leaning against it with her arms behind her back.

He raised an eyebrow at her action, but didn't say anything. Wise man. Already knowing she had all the answers.

"What is it, Olivia?" he spoke brusquely. "It is not proper for us to be privately together, even if we are considered family." Perhaps he was so swept away with his feelings, feelings he hadn't acknowledged before, that he couldn't speak properly?

She didn't reply at first, just walked toward him and put her finger to his lips. "Shh," she said, when he appeared to be about to open his mouth. "The thing is, I have something to say, and I want to say it without interruption."

He looked as though he wanted to argue, but instead he gave a brief nod. She withdrew her finger from his mouth, and took a deep breath.

"You and I met when I was just—what, fifteen years old?" She walked past him and put her hand on the back of one of the chairs in the room. She took a moment to look around at where they were—some sort of sitting room, it appeared, since there were small tables and chairs scattered about, with one sofa facing a fireplace, though there was no fire blazing at the moment. A good thing, since she already felt quite warm. Likely due to Bennett's presence and what was about to happen.

"And I know at the time you saw me as someone still in the schoolroom," she continued, continuing to pace around the room, forcing herself not to look at him because she was concerned she would forget everything she wanted to say because of all the love she had oozing through every pore. Or something.

"But I am, if you have not noticed, a woman now." And she returned to stand in front of him, forcing herself to breathe naturally, looking him in the eyes.

His gaze appeared startled, and she wanted to reassure him that it would all be fine; they would sort things out and they could have their respective futures settled. Together.

But first she had to tell him how she felt.

"When I was younger, I said and did many things I am embarrassed about now," she began. "I didn't realize there was more to life than wondering what party you'd be able to attend next. When I first met you, I couldn't even attend any parties because Eleanor wasn't married yet." She cringed to recall how selfish she had been. But she wouldn't say all that to him—she wanted him to maintain his good opinion of her, after all. "And now that I have had the opportunity to be out in the world, I know that there are things I wish to change." And not just things like allowing ladies to waltz all the time, if they wanted to, although that would be lovely. She meant things like making sure all people had enough to eat, and that children be given an education, and that there should never be the possibility of an animal suffering because of human neglect or irresponsibility or even willful action.

"Those are excellent sentiments," Bennett said.

She beamed at him, glad they were in accord. "I know you feel the same way I do. I have followed your efforts in Parliament"—*albeit not that closely*—and then she paused, taking a deep breath before adding, ". . . Bennett."

His eyes widened at that, and he blinked a few times. Overcome by his emotions? She smiled reassuringly. "We feel the same way about so many things." She put her hand on his sleeve. His gaze went to where her hand lay, and she wished she was daring enough to run the fingers of her other hand through his hair. She wasn't, not yet. Perhaps later, after everything was settled. "And since we are of such the same mind, I know that it only makes sense for us to get married. So we can finally be together." She exhaled. "There. I've finally said it." And she tilted her face up so he could kiss her.

And edged forward, since it seemed that he wasn't going to. Perhaps he was unsure if a kiss would be welcome? She should let him know it would be perfectly welcome.

"You may kiss me, if you like. Since we are now betrothed."

He still did not kiss her, and she felt a pang of regret. Instead, he closed his eyes and leaned his head back so that even if she wished to initiate a kiss, she couldn't. He was too tall, and now his mouth was too far away from hers.

A slow uncomfortable feeling began to unravel inside her, and she felt her breath hitch.

"I am aware of the great honor you do me, Lady Olivia," he said, his eyes still closed. Then he opened them, and she wanted to leap back at what she saw in his gaze. Was it possible he did not love her? "But I do not regard you in that way, and I think it best if we forget this conversation ever happened."

Olivia froze for a moment as she absorbed the

words. And then felt her face blaze as fiercely as any fire she'd ever encountered. "You do not regard me in that way?" she repeated, hearing the words fall out of her mouth even though she didn't think she could speak. "You're saying you are not in love with me?" She snatched her hand off his sleeve and dropped it behind her back, her fingers wiggling in the air as though trying to find purchase. Because it felt as though she were falling off a very high cliff. "Not in love with me?" she said again, wishing he would step forward and take her in his arms and say it was all a mistake, he was testing her, but knowing that the likelihood of that happening was slim.

"Oh," she said in a soft voice, looking anywhere but at him. Something caught her eye and she walked forward, past him, to snatch it up from the small table. It was a dome encasing a small yellow flower, one of those ornamental things everybody had as part of their everyday clutter.

It would suit her purposes well.

She raised it over her head, all of her pent-up emotion channeling itself through her upraised arm, flinging it toward the opposite wall, not close enough to possibly hit him, but startling nonetheless.

The object shattered into pieces, the noise of the impact the only sound in the room. It wasn't loud enough to cause anyone to notice, not with the band continuing to play in the ballroom as though hearts weren't currently being broken.

"Olivia, you should consider," he began, but she shook her head before he could get more words out.

"Get out." She spoke in a low tone, because if she raised her voice she would scream, and she couldn't cause that kind of scene, not with being one of the duke's daughters already with a penchant for causing trouble. Not to mention it would be horribly embarrassing—*"Yes, Lady Olivia was proposing to me, and I was rejecting her, and then she threw a decorative object at my head."* If he said anything about it at all, which she knew, as a gentleman, he would not.

"Get out," she repeated in a stronger voice this time.

Something in her expression must have told him not to press the issue, because he shook his head and walked past her and back out into the ballroom, closing the door behind her.

Leaving her alone with her thoughts and her humiliation.

She took a deep breath and withdrew her handkerchief from her pocket, preparing herself for an epic cry.

"Pardon me," a deep voice said from the depths of the sofa opposite, "but I think it is probably best that I make my departure as well."

Olivia's mouth opened in shock as a man—a tall, perfectly dressed, and remarkably handsome man—emerged from behind the sofa, his hair disheveled as though he'd been lying down. He offered her a sly grin and she felt all of her ire direct itself onto this stranger who'd had the effrontery to listen to her make a fool of herself.

"And who are you?" she replied haughtily, taking refuge in her bred-to-the-bone aristocratic manner.

He spread his arms and made a low bow. "I am Mr. Edward Wolcott, at your service," he replied in an amused tone.

"Oh!" she said in recognition. "The bast—" she began, then put her hand to her open mouth.

His smile halted and the look in his eyes got fierce. "Yes, my lady. The bastard."

At Avon Books, we know your passion for romance—once you finish one of our novels, you find yourself wanting more.

May we tempt you with . . .

- **Excerpts** from our upcoming releases.
- Entertaining **extras**, including authors' personal photo albums and book lists.
- Behind-the-scenes **scoop** on your favorite characters and series.
- **Sweepstakes** for the chance to win free books, romantic getaways, and other fun prizes.
- Writing **tips** from our authors and editors.
- **Blog** with our authors and find out why they love to write romance.
- **Exclusive content** that's not contained within the pages of our novels.

Join us at
www.avonbooks.com